By Anne Doughty

The Woman from Kerry
The Hamiltons of Ballydown
The Hawthorns Bloom in May
A Girl Called Rosie
For Many a Long Day
Shadow on the Land
On a Clear Day
Beyond the Green Hills

Shadow on the Land

ANNE DOUGHTY

Allison & Busby Limited
12 Fitzroy Mews
London W1T 6DW
allisonandbusby.com

First published in Great Britain in 2010.
This paperback edition published by Allison & Busby in 2015.

A CIP catalogue record for this book is available from
the British Library.

10 9 8 7 6 5 4 3 2 1

ISBN 978-0-7490-1971-6

Typeset in 10/14.45 pt Sabon by
Allison & Busby Ltd.

The paper used for this Allison & Busby publication
has been produced from trees that have been legally sourced
from well-managed and credibly certified forests.

Printed and bound by
CPI Group (UK) Ltd, Croydon, CR0 4YY

For
Des Kenny of Galway
who finds me books I never knew existed
and sends my novels to Irish exiles

CHAPTER ONE

April 1942
Millbrook, County Down

Alex Hamilton closed the door of his office firmly behind him, strode along the short corridor to the main entrance of the tall building where he had spent most of the working day and stepped out into the freshness of the early evening. For a moment he paused, took a deep breath of the cool, rain-washed air, then ran his sharp, dark eyes around the wide expanse of tarmac stretched out between the brick cliff of the mill rising behind him and the curving access road that swept up the steep valley side to the main road beyond.

Even at this relatively late hour, there were two vehicles still loading. Bales and boxes stood piled high, as men in dungarees streaked with engine oil and lubricant lent a hand to the drivers and their helpers as they manhandled the bulky products. The spinning floors wère running double shifts, working through the night, the only pause in the constant roar of their rotating spindles twelve hours on a

Sunday to allow for essential maintenance.

Before he'd picked out Robert Anderson among the moving brown figures, Robert himself, the foreman of the evening shift, caught sight of him, raised a hand and moved briskly over to the elderly Austin which Alex was still permitted to use by virtue of the war work being carried out at all four mills.

'We're all set, Boss, if the worst happens,' he said soberly as he came up to him.

'Good man, Robert. I'll come straight over if I hear anything, but if you get the signal ring anyway, just to be sure. Emily will tell you if I'm already on my way.'

Robert nodded, turned towards the half-loaded vehicle behind him, thought better of it and added, with a small awkward smile, 'I hope ah *won't* see you till the morra.'

Alex nodded, his heavy and sombre-looking face transformed as he responded warmly to the brave attempt at humour.

'We live in hope, Robert, as they say in these parts,' he replied, the softness of his speech reminding his long-time colleague that although Alex Hamilton had come from Canada long years ago, he had never lost his accent, nor his pleasure in the particular phrases and expressions of the place he had always called home.

The Austin was elderly, but had responded to

Alex's gift with machinery and his love of driving. It sailed up the slope with the greatest of ease. He whistled softly as he always did when he was quite alone, turned right on the empty road leading to Banbridge and passed briskly through the almost deserted streets. On the outskirts of the town, he took the road heading east in the direction of Katesbridge and Castlewellan, the Austin the only vehicle moving under a clearing sky patched with great expanses of blue between piled up towers of dazzling white cloud.

The days had lengthened and with the clocks now moved back to create Daylight Saving Time, the sun was still high. Here and there, it cast fingers of brilliant light into fields and hedgerows fresh with new growth, illuminating the palest of greens and turning them into an even softer shade of gold.

With long hours of work and little enough time to spend with his family, his drives were the one chance he had to look around him and observe the changes in the countryside he knew so well. They also gave him time to turn over in his mind the strange thoughts that had come out of nowhere, thoughts that now returned to him at any quiet moment of the day and haunted his dreams at night.

At fifty-three years old, or thereabouts, a long-married man with even the youngest of his four children soon to be eighteen, a responsible job as Technical Director of Bann Valley Mills, he never ceased to be amazed, that after all these years, he should suddenly begin to puzzle himself about his background. Why should he be at all concerned about his unknown parents and the circumstances which had left him, a child of five or six, an orphan on a ship bound for America.

Why now, he would ask himself. Why was it suddenly important that around fifty years ago his only possessions were the clothes he had been given and a label, a creased parcel label, attached with string to his coat collar, just where it rubbed and scratched his ear however much he tried to push it away.

'Alex Hamilton,' it said. That and nothing else. It was his entry ticket to an upbringing in institutions in Canada and the USA. It had led to his being placed, first, as a child worker and then as a farm labourer. Had it not been for broad shoulders and a robust constitution he would not have survived either the rigours of the orphanage regime or the beatings handed out by some of the men with whom he'd been sent to work. But he *had* survived. Long enough for a chance meeting with a Trade Union worker in an out-of-the-way place called German Township.

That whole episode was ridiculous when you came to think of it. The man's name was McGinley, a friendly sort, well-educated, but not stand-offish. He had a shock of red hair, a soft Irish accent and his boots looked as if he'd recently been tramping across a piece of wet bottom land. After his address to the meeting on agricultural wages and conditions, he'd gone up to him to ask about membership of the union. When he'd given McGinley his name, he'd replied with a grin: 'That's a good Ulster name. I have a sister, Rose, married to a man called Hamilton. They live at a place called Annacramp, in County Armagh.'

Suddenly, he forgot the question he was going to put to him. It was as if he could think of nothing but this place in Ireland where there were Hamiltons. So he asked instead exactly whereabouts in County Armagh Annacramp was to be found. From that moment on, he had but one idea in his mind and that was how and when he was going to get there.

It was on a rough piece of road a short distance before he was due to turn up the steep slope of Rathdrum Hill that his eye caught sight of the waving needle on his dashboard. He stopped whistling abruptly, cursed quietly, and remembered the words of his old friend John Hamilton, the man who had once welcomed him as a member of his family purely on the set of his shoulders and his resemblance to his own father, Tom, who'd been a blacksmith.

'I've changed and modified and improved every working part of hundreds of motors, but I'm damned if I've ever been able to make a fuel gauge more

11

reliable,' he'd declared. 'The only safe way with fuel gauges, was to keep your tank topped up so that you never had to rely on the needle, unreliable even on the smoothest piece of road.'

Knowing John for the wise man he was, he'd always followed his advice, but things were very different now from how they were after the last war. Whatever petrol John needed for his continuous movement between the four mills, he'd simply to sign a chit at Bann Valley's own pumps, which he might well pass several times a day. Nothing was that simple now with petrol so strictly rationed. Even when he had the necessary coupons from his entitlement, their authorised supplier in Banbridge might have nothing in his tanks to give him.

There was nothing to be done about his fuel supply between here and home beyond slowing down even further and avoiding having to stop on the hill. There should be a gallon can for such emergencies up against the stone wall at the furthest end of the workshop, kept well away from a chance spark from the metal cutter or the acetylene welder.

But he was still annoyed with himself as he scanned the road ahead. There was so much to think about these days, so many extra problems with the machinery running at full stretch, but when it came to the bit, that was no excuse. First things had to come first. What would he do tonight if he was needed and he had no car to collect the three extra men from Ballievy and get them over to Millbrook to join the others?

He slowed down rapidly as he picked up a distant roar of engines and pulled in as far as he could to his own side of the road, grateful there was a rough, grassy verge when it might just as well have been a water-filled ditch. Moments later, a convoy of Army lorries accelerated towards him. It was a regular hazard these days to meet these large and powerful vehicles on the narrow country roads. Often driven by inexperienced drivers, they roared past without reducing speed. Tonight, they were so close he could have touched their dark canvas covers without stretching out the hand that rested lightly on his open window.

He waved to the young men in camouflage as they passed, helmeted and carrying rifles. Smiles began to crease pale faces as they returned his greeting. English boys mostly. *Yorks and Lancs* was the name of this particular regiment, but according to his own son, Johnny, the rank and file were from all over the north of England, mostly the old industrial cities. No wonder they looked so uneasy when he saw them swing on ropes across the swollen waters of the Bann or found them in the field behind Rathdrum trying to navigate cross country with a pocket compass and a badly copied map.

Judging by the hour, it looked as if they might be heading north to Slieve Croob for a night manoeuvre. Often enough on his way to work he'd seen a convoy return in the morning, faces blackened, eyes listless with fatigue. But, of course, this lot might just be moving on. Troops came and went without any preliminaries. They arrived as strangers and were made welcome. Dances and socials were organised for them. They became friends. Then they went away. Sometimes one heard where they had gone and how the regiment had fared, but, whether things went well or badly for them, they seldom came back.

He sounded his horn and waved at wee Daisy Cook, who sat on the wall of Jackson's farm, her arm round a sheepdog puppy. It had been Cook's farm for years now, but for him it would always be Jackson's, the farm at the foot of the hill where he'd boarded when he'd first arrived back from Canada, visited John and Rose Hamilton at Ballydown and been taken on by John as his assistant at the four mills. It was at Jackson's farm he'd met Emily, an orphan like himself, living with her aunt and uncle.

Tonight as he tooted and waved to Daisy, he thought of the April night he'd driven his good friend Sarah Sinton and her children back home from Dublin after the Easter Rising. He and Sam Hamilton, Sarah's brother, had gone down together in two motors when they'd heard the railway lines had been dug up north of Dublin and Sarah would have no means of returning. Emily had been so anxious about his going. She said she'd be waiting up till she heard the motor going past on the way up to Ballydown, no matter how late it was.

He pressed gently on the accelerator and built up his speed. With any luck, he could take a smooth line up the steepest part of the hill without meeting one of the heavy lorries from the newly-opened quarry beyond Rathdrum. They weren't supposed to come down this way because of the steepness of the road, but following the new quarry road north to the main road did make their journey longer if the crushed rock was hardcore for one of the many new airstrips being built in the south of the county.

The only sign of life on the long, steep hill was a bicycle parked against the garden wall of the farmhouse at Ballydown where Emily and Alex had made their first home after Rose and John moved up to Rathdrum House itself. Danny Ferguson, the new mill manager at Ballievy, would be down the hill in minutes if the signal went up.

He caught a glimpse of pink blossom as he moved steadily past. He wondered if it was Rose's camellia, the one she and John had cherished for all the years they had lived there, planting a garden from scraps and cuttings Rose had brought from her very first garden, back in Annacramp in County Armagh.

As he crested the hill and prepared to swing under the trees into the avenue leading to Rathdrum House, Alex was amazed to catch sight of a lorry parked closely against the hedge on the down slope some way beyond his own entrance, the tarpaulins that had covered its load neatly folded and roped down.

Even before he caught sight of the tailboard and read the familiar name, his face lit up. As he expected, it read: Fruitfield Jams and Preserves. He knew only one man who could park a lorry that close and that straight.

'Sam Hamilton. You're a stranger. How are you, man? It's great to see you,' he said, beaming, as he stopped the Austin in the cobbled yard at the back of his house and shook hands with the tall, broad-shouldered figure who'd hurried out into the yard to meet him when he'd caught the first throb of the vehicle on the road up the hill.

'Great to see you too, Alex,' replied Sam, grasping his hand firmly. 'Emily's been givin' me all your news, but she was afraid ye might not get back before I hafta to go.'

'Ach Sam, can ye not stay a while?' Alex asked, his face clouding.

'I can stay a wee bit longer,' Sam replied, reassuringly, 'but I hafta get back in daylight. This blackout is a desperit thing. No matter how careful ye wou'd be, ye can see so little with these masked headlamps. An' sure a lorry like mine cou'd kill half a dozen soldiers if they're on manoeuvres and had no white markers.'

Alex nodded sadly.

'You're right there,' he agreed. 'We've had so many accidents round here lately. And not just the blackout. With all these Army vehicles we've had some bad ones in daylight as well. There were four roadmen having their tea thrown into the hedge this time last year. None killed, thank goodness, but two of them left in a bad way for quite a while. People are just not used to this sort of fast traffic at all hours of the day and night. Their reactions are too slow.'

They moved together towards the back door where Emily stood watching them.

'Alex dear, there's some dinner in the oven, but I must go down to Cook's now you're home. Johnny was in for his tea earlier and we've no milk for the morning,' she explained with a wry laugh. 'I've just made you a pot of tea and left you some cake,' she added, as she picked up her shopping bag and set off.

'Has Emily given you your supper, Sam?' Alex asked, as he picked up the tray she'd left and led the way to the sitting room where a bright fire burnt on the hearth.

'No. Your good Emily offered me my supper the minute I set foot in the house, as Emily always does,' he replied warmly, 'but I was given a meal at Chinauley House when I delivered to them. Guest of the *King's Own Rifles*,' he added smiling. 'An' very good it was too. They said on their wee menu that it was chicken, but if I know anything it was rabbit. Aye and none the worse for that,' he added vigorously, as Alex handed him a mug of tea.

'There's a great warren just across the road from that big house,' he went on. 'The Nut Bank, it used to be called when I was a wee boy. They've a pontoon bridge across the river and it's a rifle range now. Bad luck on the rabbits,' he added sharply.

Alex laughed.

'Bad luck on us all, Sam. One man's wicked ambition that leaves poor people frightened out of their wits and half-starved and even kills the rabbits.'

'Aye, given how bad things are we've a lot to be grateful for and only the one loss so far in our family. I can't remember if I wrote to you about it,' he said cautiously. 'Sure it's well over a year since I got the chance to come over,' he said, breaking off, as he saw the anxious concern creep over Alex's face.

Alex shook his head slowly and waited.

'Ach dear. Well it was the Belfast Blitz. The big one on Easter Tuesday. A desperit business altogether. Young Sam's wife, wee Ellie, had her cousin Tommy Magowan killed. It seems he was fire-watching in place of a friend of his when his parents thought he was away in Bangor with his girlfriend. It was only when he didn't come home they began to worry. His father found him in St

George's Market the next morning, laid out with all the rest of the unidentified casualties. Not a mark on him. They said it was blast that killed him.'

Alex dropped his eyes from Sam's candid gaze, the images of that night now springing up as brightly as the flaming, onion-shaped incendiaries that had rained down on the city.

'Do you remember, Sam, when the last war came and the two of us sat in your workshop trying to decide what we'd do if there was conscription?' Alex asked, as the silence lengthened between them.

'Aye. I think we decided we could maybe get into an Ambulance Corps together, neither of us having any wish to kill our fellow men.'

Alex nodded slowly and stared into the red embers of the wood fire.

'Sam, I was in Belfast that night and I don't think I'll ever be able to forget it,' he confessed quietly.

'Man dear, how did that come about?' Sam asked, his eyes dilating with the shock of Alex's words. 'Were you there when it started, or what happened at all?'

For weeks after that night, Alex had thought of writing to tell Sam of his night in the burning city, but he'd not been able to face it. They'd been friends for so long and had always told each other the truth, even when it was not to their credit, but the thought of words on the page had been too much for him. So he'd said how busy he was and let Emily write the short notes they'd always used to keep in touch, two or three times a year and a longer one at Christmas. But now he'd have to make up for his evasion.

'Emily and I had just gone to bed when I heard a noise,' he began, easily enough. 'Couldn't place it at all. A vibration. Not thunder, but getting louder. I got up and went outside. It was full moonlight but I couldn't see anything to the south with the way our trees have grown up. What I *could* feel was the air moving. And there was a smell. I can't describe that smell, but suddenly I knew it was bombers and there must be hundreds of them to make the air move like that. So I went in and phoned the mill managers. By the time I·got down to Ballievy, Harry Creswell who lives on a hill beyond Seapatrick had seen the incendiaries falling. He said they were coming down so fast it was like one of those pictures of Hell you'd see in these evangelical tracts people put through doors.'

Alex paused for breath and finished his mug of tea.

'We're well organised for fire in the mills. We have to be, as you know,' he began again, his voice still steady, 'but the turn out that night was a credit, though I say it myself. The four engines, fully-manned were on their way in no time.'

He stopped, shook his head and dropped his face in his hands. When he looked up again his eyes were full of tears.

'Sam, you might as well have taken a child's bucket and spade as our four engines. The place was an inferno, the fires beyond anything any of us had ever seen, and when we did get into the city there was no water pressure. They'd bombed the reservoir and the water mains were gone. Even where there was a fire point still standing our hoses didn't fit.'

'Ach man dear, I'd no idea you were in Belfast,' Sam said, his face suddenly looking old and lined as he recalled that night himself. 'Sure we heard what was happening from the guard on the last train up. He told the Stationmaster at Richhill and he walked over to the farm and told us. Apparently the train was leaving Belfast just as it started. Our Jack went up to Cannon Hill to tell the Home Guard patrol up there, but he didn't have to tell them for you could see it from up there, the whole city on fire, the sky for miles around lit up with the flames. He said when he came back about all we could do was pray for the poor souls.'

Sam looked down at his hands. They were broad, thick-fingered hands, not the kind you would think best-suited to make the fine adjustments that were such a part of his everyday work.

'So what did you do when you couldn't fight the fires?'

'We got out the spades and the tackle and started digging people out of wrecked houses. And we brought a few out alive from under the stairs. But

21

most were dead. Some of those poor wee houses wouldn't give shelter to a mouse. Those people in the government up at Stormont have a lot to answer for,' he went on bitterly. 'I'd heard it said they spent more time in Cabinet discussing how to protect that statue of Carson they're so proud off than protecting the people of Belfast. I saw for myself that night. It was absolutely true.'

'Aye, I'm afeerd yer right about the government. I've seen m'brother James a few times recently. He's still in Economic Development, but he says there's no go in them at all, bar one or two labour or socialists like Tommy Henderson and Harry Midgley. Sure, they only meet now and again for a couple of hours when there's so much they could be doin' to help people. I think James would resign, but then he knows that wou'd only make it worse. At least in his Department he can do somethin'. . . Maybe, Alex, all we can ever do is *somethin'*. Who knows what value any action of any one of us, however small, might be. It could be far more important than we could ever imagine. We must live in hope, man, and with God's help we'll come through,' he said strongly.

Alex had never found any reason to expect God to help him or anyone else, even if He did exist, but then he had always recognised that Sam's God was a different matter. Now in his late fifties, Sam had become a Quaker many years earlier. He'd practised his religion quietly and firmly and now had a steadiness and assuredness about him that Alex found quite enviable.

'You're right, Sam. We can only do our best. I only hope that best will be good enough,' he said honestly, looking up at his friend as he watched him get to his feet.

The bright April evening was paling towards dusk and shadows were lengthening in the fire-lit sitting room. Although the journey was only some fifteen miles, Alex knew well the possibility of a delay if a convoy was moving somewhere between Banbridge and Richhill.

They walked down the avenue together, the fresh foliage above their heads now fluttering in a small, evening breeze, long fingers of light spilling across their path as the sun dropped to the horizon.

'I mind Sarah and Hugh planting these two trees here after a big storm,' Sam said suddenly, looking up into the interlacing branches as they tramped along together. 'That must have been a couple of years before Hugh died and you arrived back from Canada. And I mind too, you and young Hugh down there on the hill planting out wee oaks he grew from acorns,' he added, as they came through the gates and gazed down the hill at the mature trees which stood in the hedgerow opposite the single house on the right-hand side of the road, the well-loved home they had both known, Sam as a child, Alex as a young married man.

'*Great oaks from little acorns grow.* Isn't that one of the saying in these parts?' Alex asked.

'Aye, and your wee friend Hugh Sinton is doing great work down on Lough Erne I'm told. James had to go to Enniskillen on business and went to see him. He's moved there to test out some new plane he'd been working on at Shorts in Belfast. Sarah could only drop me hints in her last letter, but James told me it's to do with spotter planes. *Give the same man a while longer*, he said, *and we'll not be losing all this shipping to the U-boats.*'

They stopped by Sam's lorry and Alex asked the question that had been in his mind since the moment he'd seen it.

'Are you short-staffed at Fruitfield?'

'No, thank goodness, we're not. Most of us are too old to join up. It's mainly the girls from the office that have gone, so our Jack tells me. Why d'ye ask?'

'Well, I was wondering why the senior man who keeps the whole place running was out delivering jam.'

'Ach, now I see what yer gettin' at,' replied Sam, laughing. 'Sure I don't mind the odd wee run out. It's Security. If you deliver to the forces, you have to be cleared. They wouldn't let a couple of young fellas anywhere near Chinauley House or the Gough Barracks in Armagh or anywhere else where there's troops for that matter. It's the same with delivering war materials. Shell-Mex in Armagh have only the one man allowed to deliver petrol. They have to be certain they're trustworthy. Sure there's a black market in everything.'

'Well, they couldn't pick a straighter man than you, that's for sure,' said Alex, now laughing himself, as Sam swung himself up into the cab.

'Except perhaps yourself,' Sam came back at him promptly. 'Let me know how things go with the girls and young Johnny and I'll maybe get another chance to come over in another month or two when they've eaten what I brought today. God Bless,' he added, as he raised a hand in farewell.

Alex watched him move down the longer, gentler slope towards the main road, the noise of the batcher at the quarry now loud on the evening air. Breeze blocks for building. Crushed rock for hard standing. Gravel for mending overburdened roads. The quarry was working all the daylight hours, the dust from the crushers throwing a white mist over the nearby hedgerows until the next heavy shower came to rinse the foliage and leave it shining again.

He turned away as the lorry became a small moving object in the green landscape and walked back up towards his own gates, his stomach rumbling vigorously, reminding him of his supper in the oven.

The sun had gone now, down behind the low hill at Lisnaree, but there was still quite enough light to see two figures walking up towards him. One was clearly Emily. Beside her, carrying her shopping bag from which came the small chink of milk bottles, there was a man he did not recognise. From this distance, he could not even guess whether he was a friend or a stranger.

CHAPTER TWO

There was no doubt there was something familiar about the figure that moved easily up the hill, matching his pace to Emily's shorter stride. A man about his own height, but carrying more weight, comfortably dressed in a tweed overcoat and a soft cap. He was talking so animatedly that it was only when Emily interrupted him by the gates of Rathdrum he realised Alex was standing there waiting to greet him.

'Isn't it lovely to see Brendan again,' said Emily helpfully, assuming that Alex would never remember his name after so many years and so few previous meetings.

But Alex surprised her.

'Brendan Doherty, you're welcome,' he said with a broad smile. 'We haven't seen you for many a long day. I'm afraid it was your Aunt Rose's funeral when we last met and that must be seven years ago. What brings you up to the North?'

'Well I haven't come to spy, though there's those looked distinctly dubious when they heard my Southern accent,' he said with a wry smile. 'Believe it or not, there are still books to be bought and sold, especially where the owners are handing over their houses to the military. Though on this occasion it was maps. Sixteenth century, I hasten to add, as I was just explaining to Emily. I didn't dare mention the word "map" in the hotel in case I ended up in jail, so I told a lie and said "books" instead.'

'Is it as bad as that?' asked Alex as they rounded the house and came in through the kitchen door.

'Oh dear, yes. The North can't forgive de Valera for remaining neutral. Churchill goes on at length about the loss of the Treaty ports and some of the Northern papers are saying there's a thousand or more German spies in the South and they've brought dozens more into the Legation in Dublin.'

'And have they?' asked Emily solemnly, as she took her shopping bag from him and put the milk bottles in their bowls of water in the larder.

'At the last count, six staff, three typists and an old fellow to look after the boiler,' he replied, his dark eyes twinkling.

Alex laughed and led their guest through the kitchen and into the hall.

'Now Alex,' said Emily firmly, as she hung up her coat and reached out her hand for Brendan's, 'have you had your supper?'

'No, not yet,' he said quietly. 'But what about Brendan's supper?'

Brendan laughed.

'The hospitality of the Hamilton's is legendary, as I have no doubt told you on one of our rare meetings, but I have indeed been fed. Your local hostelry couldn't give me a bed, they being full of officers having a conference about gas, the poisonous sort, not the domestic variety. But good Ulster folk as they were, they wouldn't turn me away hungry. I had a rather good chicken casserole with plenty of vegetables and more milk to drink than I've seen in months. At least, I think it was chicken. It's a long time since I met chicken on my plate.'

Emily wondered why Alex smiled suddenly, but the moment passed as she led them into the sitting room, added another log to the fire and told Alex why Brendan had not been able to go straight back to Dublin as he usually did after one of his buying trips across the border.

'An Army lorry clipped his car,' she explained. 'Wasn't he lucky they didn't run him off the road?'

'They were pretty decent about it,' Brendan added quickly. 'At least they stopped and sent two squaddies to help me get the car to the garage. And by further good luck the garage was only down the road so I just watched the pair of them push. But I've lost a headlamp and the wing mirror and have a big dent in the offside. There's a leak too by the smell of it. Couldn't risk driving her till she's checked out.'

'I didn't fancy sleeping in a ditch,' he went on cheerfully, 'though I've done it in my time. So I set out for Ballydown. The Cooks were just telling me you'd moved up in the world when Emily herself appeared. I said a blanket on the sofa would have done but your good lady says I have a choice of rooms with all the girls gone,' Brendan continued, addressing himself to Alex, as he stretched out comfortably, his legs directed towards the leaping flames.

At that moment the telephone rang in the hall.

Alex was on his feet and out of the room before Emily or Brendan had registered the first strident ring.

'Oh dear,' said Emily, her face dropping. 'If that's what I think it is, it's bad news and Alex will have to go off right away.'

'Are ye expecting bad news?' Brendan asked soberly.

'It's nearly the full moon,' she said quickly. 'That's when we had the awful blitz in Belfast last year. There's been rumours going round that they'll have another go because the aircraft factory and the shipyard are more or less back to normal working. I don't know whether Lord Haw Haw said something on the wireless, for I refuse to listen to him, or where the idea came from, but Alex is responsible for the four fire engines and he was told to stand by.'

'Aye, that was a bad go ye had last year,' said Brendan, his lively, mobile face subsiding into a solemn mask. 'At least de Valera had the decency to send the fire engines up to help. We heard some grim stories in Dublin when they got back . . .'

He broke off as they heard the door open behind them. Alex moved quickly across to the fireplace, his face transformed, relief and joy bringing a sparkle to his dark eyes and softening a face that had always had a sombreness built in to it.

'It's all right,' he said quickly, a slight catch in his voice. 'We've been told to stand down. No details and we don't even know who sent the message, only that the code was right. If they'd been coming this far, they'd have taken off from France by now and been picked up on the south coast of England.'

'Maybe *now* you'll eat your supper,' Emily said, standing up. 'You'll drink a cup of tea, Brendan, won't you and we'll keep him company with a piece of cake.'

'That would be most welcome, Emily. I'm just sorry I'm not provided with the traditional bottle. I fear I've come with one hand as long as the other.'

Alex laughed delightedly. It was an expression he'd hadn't heard for ages, one he'd never forget. Emily had had to explain it to him, long years ago, when she was no more than a schoolgirl and he still the lodger, only recently returned from Canada.

'Sure we're all empty-handed these days,

Brendan,' she said, pausing by the door, 'as far as *bottles* go anyhow. We try to keep up a bit of hospitality for these young lads billeted all round the place, but I'm afraid tea and cake is the best we can do. You could count the raisins in my cakes these days. Few and far between, as they say.'

Alex was grateful for the covered plate Emily brought him from the oven. She was a good cook and he always enjoyed what she gave him, but tonight even bread and margarine would taste wonderful. However little meat in the pie, the rich gravy was appetising and he dug into the mound of creamy potato with vigour. Brendan watched him with pleasure and a certain twinkle of amusement.

'As I said earlier, Emily,' he began, as she handed him a cup of tea and a generous slice of cake, 'the Hamilton hospitality is legendary. Did Alex ever tell you about my visit to his friend Sarah Sinton when she was unavoidably detained in Dublin during The Rising.'

'No, I don't think I ever heard that one,' said Emily cautiously.

Alex grinned broadly as he finished his meal and wiped his plate clean with a fresh crust of bread.

'I'm afraid Brendan, Emily and I had a slight difficulty at that time over my relationship with Sarah.'

'Oh,' said their visitor, 'is that so?'

His eyes sparkled as they moved rapidly from husband to wife.

Alex grinned and glanced across at Emily who was now smiling too.

'You see, Brendan,' Alex began, 'when I first came to Ballydown, Sarah was a very handsome young widow. Not that I noticed what she looked like. The fact was, she was kind to me. She understood how I felt about not knowing who I was or where I'd come from. And she was sad and lonely herself. She said that without Hugh she didn't think she could go on running the mills. She couldn't stand the bitterness between Catholics and Protestants and the labour troubles and people never willing to listen to the other side of the story. So, *to cut a long story short*, as they say around here, Sarah and I made a pact to help each other and I made up my mind I'd not marry till Sarah herself married or went away.'

'And what happened?' said Brendan slowly.

'Well, you probably know that Sarah met Simon Hadleigh when she was over in Gloucestershire visiting Hannah and Teddy. She'd actually met him years earlier at their wedding when Hannah asked her to take the wedding pictures, but as she told me once, she was so busy photographing her sister and new brother-in-law that she'd not even noticed *him*. However, as soon as Sarah and Simon were engaged, I made up my mind about Emily. But I didn't say anything to her. Then, that Easter of 1916 when Sarah was in Dublin, Simon goes missing. He'd been in St Petersburg, in the diplomatic service,' he added quickly, when he saw Brendan looking puzzled.

'Anyhow, he was coming home from Russia on a Swedish packet and it hit a mine near the Dogger Bank. Luckily, he was picked up by a destroyer but because it *was* a destroyer he couldn't send her a message. There wasn't a word from him for weeks until finally the destroyer was able to land him in Scotland. Sarah was beside herself. I was with her when the telegram came to say he was safe. I knew then she'd go over and marry him as soon as she could, so I came and proposed to Emily.'

'And Emily was furious,' said the lady herself, laughing. 'I thought Sarah was the woman he wanted and now she was going away to marry Simon, I was second best. So I told him to go and jump in Corbet Lough.'

'Ah, women,' said Brendan raising his eyes to the delicate mouldings on the ceiling, 'Is it any wonder I never took the plunge.'

Working away at the sink next morning, her fingers already rippled with the continuous immersion and the scrubbing of Alex's dungarees, Emily thought what a splendid evening they'd had. It had been so lively and so completely unexpected. She hadn't seen Alex laugh as much for months. But then there was very little to laugh at these days. Just bad news and more bad news.

There was no doubt Brendan was a talker,

but if he was, everything he said was interesting, whether he was commenting sharply on the political situation in the North or in the South and the tensions between their respective populations, or simply recalling stories from family history. Emily could see from his detailed accounts that he missed nothing in his observation of people. She also felt she'd learnt a great deal more from him about what they called *The Emergency* in the South than she'd gained from her perusal of all the newspapers she could lay hands on here in the North.

Now the house was silent again, as it was so often these days. Alex had taken Brendan to the garage on his own way to work, Johnny had come in, eaten his breakfast and gone to bed, exhausted from his night's work, fire-watching at a local factory. Apart from the tick of the kitchen clock, the only sound she could hear was the song of a blackbird, perched on the roof of the workshop across the yard where he sang every morning regardless of weather or the affairs of men.

A pleasant-faced woman, now almost fifty, her dark curly hair already streaked with grey, Emily had worked hard all her life. Physically strong and always active, she had kept her figure and still dressed as well as she could. There was enough to depress everybody these days without her going round looking colourless and unkempt.

She had, 'hands for anything' as the Ulster saying

has it. She was never without an item of knitting, for Alex, or Johnny, or her Red Cross collection. There was usually sewing as well, a dress or a blouse for one of the girls, the pinned pattern, or the work in progress, laid out in pieces on the bed in one of the now silent bedrooms.

But beyond her family, her beloved garden and her considerable domestic skills, Emily's great passion was reading. Though Alex scolded her for not sitting down until her back actually ached, she did spend time every day with her library book. No print of any kind that entered the house escaped her eye, be it newspaper, magazine or church newsletter. In the days when her four children were at Banbridge Academy Emily would be been found reading not only the set books for English Literature but all their text books as well.

Given this passion, it was hardly surprising that a friendship should have developed between Emily and Brendan Doherty. It had begun on the lovely summer Sunday of Rose Hamilton's eightieth birthday party. Arriving early and walking round the garden of James Hamilton's house in Belfast, while Alex gave a hand with some extra seating, she'd found Brendan sitting in a quiet corner reading while waiting for the other guests to arrive. They had talked about books and bookselling, taken to each other immediately and made a point of finding each other again after lunch to sit in a corner of the huge marquee erected over the back garden and continue their conversation.

She had met Brendan briefly on previous occasions when he'd visited his Aunt Rose at Rathdrum, but she'd never talked to him at any length and certainly not about books. To tell the truth, she'd been rather shy of him. Not only was he rather handsome, but she knew quite a bit about his history from Rose. She wasn't sure what you could say to a young man who'd been a rebel, had fought against the British Army and spent years in English jails mixing with other rebels even better known than himself.

Rose had always been fond of the young man, the youngest son of her eldest sister Mary, who'd found a job with the Stewart family of Ards when the McGinley family had been evicted from their home in Donegal back in the 1860s. She'd married a local man and raised a large family on the outskirts of Creeslough where he had a flourishing drapery business, while her little sister Rose had been taken to Kerry with baby Sam when their father died and her mother found work there as a housekeeper with the Molyneux's of Currane Lodge.

Emily still missed Rose. For the years of Emily's girlhood, Mrs Hamilton, as she then called her, had been their neighbour and her friend. She'd seen her nearly every day, taking up eggs or milk, or making tea when she came down to visit the Jacksons at the bottom of the hill. Rose had always been good to her, lent her books and knitting patterns and was always willing to listen to her troubles. When she and Alex married, it was Rose who suggested they should move into her house at Ballydown now that she and John were going to live at Rathdrum.

No mother could have been kinder than Rose when she was first expecting and full of anxiety, nor when the babies were growing up and she worried continually as to whether she was doing the right thing by them. Rose had been with her when all the girls were born. She could hardly bear to think of the day Rose had not been there, the day young Johnny finally appeared after the longest and hardest labour she had ever had. That was the day Rose's beloved John had died, only a few hours after Alex had gone up the hill to tell him the longed-for boy had arrived at Ballydown and that his name would be John.

Emily wiped away her tears with a soapy hand and told herself not to be silly. It was all a very long time ago. Eighteen years ago, come August. She could not possibly forget the day, or the date, or the year, not only because it was her son's birthday, but because this year in August he'd be eighteen, old enough to do what he so wanted to do and join the Air Force, like his sister Elizabeth. Then she would be like mothers everywhere, living with the fear of his loss as every day went by.

As if to escape from her anxious thoughts, she

pounded the dungarees more vigorously, drained off the dirty water and began rinsing them. When she splashed herself thoroughly with the ice cold water from the tank on the roof, she knew she just wasn't paying proper attention to the task in hand, so she collected herself, dumped the wet, brown mass into a bucket and tramped out to the already laden clothesline.

She wondered why it was she was never as anxious about the girls as she was about Johnny. It was not that she loved them any the less, but they always seemed better able to take care of themselves than their brother. There was a casualness about him, an indifference to circumstances quite different from either of the two older girls, who had always been much more practical. More like herself perhaps. At present, however, the main reason she didn't worry about them was that all three of them were fairly well out of harm's way, for the moment at least.

Catherine, the eldest, had trained as a teacher, gone on a course in Manchester to learn more about children with writing difficulties and had met a young research chemist at a dance. She'd returned home, gone on teaching at a local primary school and they'd written to each other, enough pages to fill a book, in the following year. Being quite sure by then that war was coming, they'd decided to marry regardless.

Brian Heald had expected to be called up, but to his surprise when he applied himself, he was told he was to be reserved because of his qualifications as a chemist. He'd been sent to a laboratory recently relocated in the countryside south of Manchester. Catherine had found a job in a village school and a half-derelict farm cottage for them to live in.

Elizabeth was nearly two years younger than Catherine and probably even brighter. But Lizzie, as almost everyone called her, had no wish to train as nurse or teacher, the only two options her teachers appeared able and willing to approve. She wanted to travel, to see faraway places and meet new people. The recruiting poster for the WRAF could have been designed especially for her, even down to the blue eyes that looked so well with the uniform. She made up her mind to join. She'd applied, was accepted, and then tried to get a job with the Meteorological Service in Bedfordshire. With very good school results, particularly in geography, she might well have got what she wanted had it not been for a sudden prior need in Belfast.

To Emily's enormous relief, after a period of concentrated training, she was posted as a plotter to the Senate Chamber at Stormont, an impressive marble clad chamber which had been handed over to the War Ministry for use as an operational centre for the duration.

Not only was the formerly large and conspicuous

Stormont building well camouflaged, but as more than one person had put it, there was no need for Hitler to bomb it, for no one would ever notice the difference.

It was a bitter comment on an unpopular and inactive government, but it cheered Emily to know that her daughter's work kept her well away from any of the obvious enemy targets and that the girls' billets were right out on the edge of the city. There was also the wonderful bonus that occasionally, without any warning, Lizzie herself would appear at the back door, yawning from lack of sleep, grinning from ear to ear and saying, 'Hello, Ma, I'm home. Thirty-six hours. Can you stand it?'

Which left Jane.

Emily had never understood why Alex had wanted to call their third daughter, Jane. With both the other babies he'd discussed names with her and they had no difficulty coming to a decision together. Catherine was named for Emily's own, long-dead mother, Elizabeth for the aunt who had given her a home when her mother died. Any boy they ever had was going to be called John. But Emily could see neither rhyme nor reason behind Alex's wanting to call their third girl, Jane.

'They'll call her Plain Jane at school, Alex,' she had argued, when it was time to make the final decision.

'No,' he said firmly. 'Jane it has to be. Besides

that child will never be plain in any way.'

She had to admit he'd most likely be proved right, for little Jane had been a particularly lovely baby, full of smiles and blessed with great blue eyes that captivated everyone who saw her. Apart from being the prettiest of his daughters, Jane was the sweetest in nature. Soft-hearted to a fault, generous of spirit and possessed of a formidable patience, she seemed to sail through life oblivious to its dark side, protected by an unfailing sense of hope and possibility.

If ever Alex was downcast, overburdened by the job, or the endless labour problems that had dogged the industry between the wars, then it was Jane who was able to cheer him. It had taken Emily a long time to realise that having a son had been Alex's passionate desire, but it was his youngest daughter who understood him in a way that Johnny never would or could.

It was no surprise to anyone when Jane announced she wanted to be a nurse. She'd been looking after other children since she was old enough to go to school. She'd learnt to apply sticking plaster effectively long before her elder sisters. Nor was it simply cut fingers and grazed knees that Jane would wash and dress. Whatever hurt or damaged creature she laid eyes on, found in the garden or by the roadside, she couldn't rest till it had been cared for. Emily remembered well the times when she was afraid to move in her own kitchen, so cluttered was it with cardboard boxes holding small creatures parked in different places.

The Royal Victoria Hospital might not have been as safe as the Senate Chamber up at Stormont, but it *was* a hospital, and in the early days of the war it still seemed to Emily that it would not be bombed. At least the authorities had made provision for the protection of its staff when off duty.

Suddenly and unexpectedly, the April sun emerged from behind a cloud, throwing shadows on the grass path. It's sudden warmth caressed Emily across the shoulders which ached as always after the morning's washing. She stood for a few moments enjoying the comfort it brought.

'I'll just take another five minutes outside,' she said aloud, as she moved away from the vegetable garden where her clothesline was now full, the dungarees dripping vigorously.

She moved back towards the house and turned into the flower garden. Drifts of daffodils and crocuses splashed colour against a background of shrubs and trees and enlivened the still-bare earth of flowerbeds where perennials were just beginning to throw out rosettes of new growth.

She walked quickly to the end of the path to the one remaining space between the sheltering trees from where she could see the mountains. This had once been Rose's favourite place, the place Emily was sure to find her if she came to see her and found the kitchen empty.

As great spotlights of sunshine fell on the high, sombre peaks and spilt downwards to light up the patchwork of small fields and the occasional white-painted cottage on the lower slopes below, she saw why Rose loved this prospect so much, but for herself, the familiar prospect brought a kind of sadness. What Emily longed for was the sea. The Mountains of Mourne did indeed *sweep down to the sea*, as the song had it, but that vast, blue expanse which brought her both joy and longing, filled as it was with memories of childhood in one Coastguard Station after another, was *beyond* the mountains, completely hidden from this perspective.

She stood for much longer than five minutes, her eye travelling over the fields nearer at hand, following the traffic passing on the main road some distance away, her mind moving back and forth from the sights and sounds of childhood, the roar of the Atlantic from Malin Head to Galway Bay, the dark green water flecked with white when the light returned after a storm to the pleasure of the evening just gone. She thought again of the firelight and the conversation, the upsurge of joy and relief after Alex's phone call, the good news that had spared the people of Belfast from one more night of death and devastation.

After the call they'd spoken of so many things, moving from one topic to another so easily and so happily she simply couldn't remember how they'd come to talk about orphans in general and Alex in particular. She'd been surprised at how open Alex had been, she'd even heard him say the odd thing she'd not heard him put into words before.

However great a talker Brendan was, he was also a good listener. His questions, though gently put, were very acute.

'Would it make a difference to you if you knew who your father was?'

'Yes, I think it would, though I don't know why.'

'And what if you weren't a Hamilton at all? Would you cut them all off and turn your back on them?'

'No,' said Alex, laughing. 'Even if they are not my family, they have *become* my family,' he said confidently.

'Tell me, Alex, were you beaten?'

'Oh yes. Regularly,' he replied. 'It was standard procedure if you didn't understand what you were told to do.'

Brendan swore and shook his head.

'Is it *curiosity*, Alex?'

'No, Brendan, it isn't. I almost wish it was and then I could tell myself not to be silly and forget all about it. It's something else, but I don't know what.'

'Have you done anything yourself about finding out?' Brendan asked finally as the fire burnt low and they all knew it was time to go to bed.

'I didn't think there was anything one could do after all these years,' said Alex honestly. 'I started work in 1898 and I know the rule was that children had to be at least nine years old before they did, but I had no birth certificate, so we can't even be sure of when I was born. And the first orphanage I went to sent me somewhere else. I can't remember the name of the place, except it must have been Canada and not the US, because they spoke French.'

'And you didn't?'

'No, not a word.'

Brendan shook his head.

'So you were sent to work in a place where you didn't even know the language. It's a hard world my masters . . .'

He broke off and ran his fingers through his thick black hair and Emily noticed that, it was now well seeded with grey like her own.

'Did you have to pray to the Virgin, Alex?'

'No . . .'

'But you did have to pray?'

'Oh yes, morning and night.'

'Well, that's a start. It must have been Prod and not Catholic,' he said cheerfully. 'And if you came out from England, then the agency is more likely to be Anglican than Presbyterian. Some of these Children's Societies keep meticulous records. I've come across stuff of that sort sometimes when I've cleared a whole library and there are boxes of papers included. Amazing things you find in box files. Old parchment deeds. Copies of wills. Just occasionally, a pamphlet will turn up that would keep me in food for a month,' he said, raising his bushy eyebrows at them. 'I'll have a think, Alex, and see if anything comes to me. I might be able to help. It'll make up for coming unannounced and empty-handed,' he said with a wry grin.

She'd protested again at the idea of his coming empty-handed when he'd entertained them for a whole evening. Then she'd offered him cocoa, though she'd been more than a bit uneasy as to how much she'd find at the bottom of the tin. At least she knew they had plenty of milk. Cook's had doubled their herd of cows and the creamery had been enlarged. Thank goodness, milk was one thing you really could be sure of getting these days.

'Nice drop of cocoa, Emily. Don't know when I last had any,' Brendan said, as he clutched his mug comfortably in both hands. 'Which reminds me, of course, of the legendary Hamilton hospitality.'

'I was going to ask you about that, Brendan,' said Alex quickly. 'You mentioned it earlier and it sounds like a story I haven't heard.'

'I'm amazed, Alex. I'm sure I've told it to everyone I know and a brave few people I've drunk with back in the happy days of drinking,' he said, laughing.

'Well, this was the way of it,' he began settling comfortably. 'I was on a rooftop in Dawson Street in Dublin back in 1916. Down below the British Army had arrived and the city was burning. I'd been up there a couple of days doing good work for the cause, but I hadn't eaten for quite some time. And I'd run out of water, which is actually far more important for survival. Things were fairly quiet, if you discount the thud of artillery and the roar of flames, so I decided to visit my cousin Sarah. I knew where she was staying, because I'd actually caught a glimpse of her with Helen and Hugh in a nearby park some days earlier when we were redeploying.

'Needless to say, I was not in a position to knock on her front door,' he said lightly. 'I should have said she was staying with Lily Molyneux. She was the daughter of the Kerry family Rose and Sam once worked for. So I figured out which skylight it was and 'dropped in' as they say. And there a couple of yards away, in among all the junk in the attic, is Sarah.

'What are ye doing here,' says I.

'*I'm looking at the fires to see if we need to move out*,' says she. Cool as a cucumber, our Sarah. And at this point she didn't know it was me. I could have been any black-faced rebel with a gun.

'I told her she needn't worry about the fires for it had started to spit with rain and the worst of them were still a fair bit away anyhow. I could see

48

better from up behind the chimney pots than she could from inside. And she still didn't catch on who I was, till I told her it was a long time since she and I had played football in the field near the school in Creeslough.'

'Goodness, Brendan, what a way to meet,' Emily burst out, as Brendan paused for breath. 'What did she say when you told her?'

'To be honest, I don't remember, for at that moment I heard English voices on the roof and I thought we might have someone else dropping in to join us. They'd been after me all day. So I signalled to her to get down and I slid back into the darkest part of the attic. The pair of us were there for goodness knows how long. Poor Sarah told me later she was under a pile of old carpet and she'll never forget the smell of it. But we were saved by the rain. A great drumming storm of it sweeping across the roof. That got rid of whoever was wearing the boots we'd heard tripping over the skylight and we were able to go downstairs.'

'And have some supper?' asked Emily, with a smile.

Brendan laughed.

'There was one small difficulty about that. Food supplies had been completely disrupted. All Sarah had in the kitchen was half a small loaf and a pot of Aunt Rose's jam she'd brought as part of a present for Lily and enough milk for a cup of tea each for breakfast, for her and the children and Lily and Uncle Sam who was down visiting Lily as well.'

'So what did she do?' asked Emily anxiously.

'She filled an eggcup with milk for Lily's tea, cut a slice from the loaf for Lily and one for each of the children and gave me all the rest of the milk and all the bread made into jam sandwiches. I've never tasted anything so wonderful in my life,' he ended with a flourish.

'That's quite some story, Brendan,' said Alex quietly. 'I'd never heard that one before, but it fits the lady perfectly.'

'Yes, it does,' he agreed readily. 'I often think these days when I hear people talking about courage and bravery and people winning medals and so on, that some of the bravest things people do are never recognised. People like Sarah in Dublin with the children, just doing their best in circumstances entirely beyond their control,' he said thoughtfully. 'The way I've come to see it is that doing what she did was far braver than doing what I did. However dangerous it was up on that roof, at least I'd been warned and I'd had some training. Sarah just had to do her best without any warning or any help. Now that seems to me to take real courage.'

CHAPTER THREE

Emily was chopping shallots at the kitchen table when she heard the knock at the front door. For a moment, she was so surprised to hear such an unfamiliar sound, she didn't even begin to worry what it might mean. These days, every woman dreaded the knock at the door that might bring the telegram or the formal letter to say that a husband or a son was missing. Emily herself had thought often enough of such an event in the dark hours of the night when she woke and couldn't get back to sleep, but it never occurred to her as she pulled off her apron that the caller could be anyone other than someone who didn't know her well enough to come round to the kitchen door.

As she rinsed her hands hastily under the tap, she thought it might be a collector for the Red Cross or one of the other local groups raising funds to support the forces or the prisoners of war.

She hurried along the hall and opened the

heavy door. At that moment, her heart did leap to her mouth for there on the doorstep stood a tall, heavily-built man wearing the dark green uniform of the Royal Ulster Constabulary. She'd never laid eyes on him before and didn't much like the way he was studying the outside of the house.

Before she'd time to speak, he'd taken out his notebook, confirmed she was Missus Hamilton and said he wanted to ask her some questions.

Only as she led him into the sitting room and sat down herself on one side of the empty, well-swept hearth did she realise she should have asked for his identification. There wasn't much point now she'd let him in. If he wasn't who he appeared to be, she'd just have to keep her wits about her.

'Have there been any strangers about the place that you are aware of, ma'am?' he asked abruptly.

'Do you mean round the actual house here?' Emily responded, puzzled at his question

'Roun' the house or anywhere about this area up here.'

'No, I can't say I've seen anyone.'

'So you know nothing about a lorry parked on the hill last night over beyond your gates,' he came back sharply.

'Yes, of course I do,' said Emily, relieved that his business couldn't possibly be bad news about any member of her family.

'So what can you tell us about that?'

The tone was abrupt and instead of looking at her as he spoke his eyes moved round the room as if he were making an inventory of all the furniture and furnishings.

'The lorry was driven by my husband's cousin. He called to see us.'

'A social call, that would be?'

'Yes, it *was* a social call and no, he was not using petrol improperly. We were on his route home from a delivery.'

'And this delivery was to . . . ?'

'If you want to know I can give you the name of his employers.'

'So you are not willing to tell me where this person was before coming to park on the hill.'

'No, I'm not,' said Emily crossly. 'I've told you who it was and why he was here.'

Emily couldn't remember what she'd read about never giving the name of a military installations, but even if she could, she'd keep it to herself, for she'd taken an instant dislike to this man.

'He's employed by Fruitfield Jams, outside Richhill. He is one of their most senior men and entirely reliable.'

'His name?'

'Sam Hamilton.'

He wrote down the details laboriously, leaning on his knee, his shoulder half-turned from her like a child writing a message it didn't want anyone to see.

'And what about your other visitor?'

For a moment, Emily couldn't think what he was talking about. They had no *visitors* these days. Her older sister, living in Enniskilen, hadn't been to stay since before the war, Sarah and Hannah were over in England and James, who used to come to see them regularly, was probably as short of petrol as everyone else, even if he was in the government.

She sat looking at him, about to reply. He had the sort of red face that looked as if he suffered from high-blood pressure or was permanently angry, or both.

'You were seen, Mrs Hamilton, last night walking up hill with a stranger. We are reliably informed he had a southern accent. Perhaps the gentleman was another cousin of your husband's making a social visit,' he suggested, the sarcasm in his voice only thinly veiled.

Emily was so taken aback, she said nothing.

A part of her mind was trying to figure out her exact relationship to Brendan. If Sarah and Brendan were cousins and Alex and Sarah were cousins, did that mean Alex and Brendan were cousins? It was like one of those puzzles you got in the Brainteasers section of the women's magazines. And it didn't matter whether he was or not. It was still none of this wretched man's business.

'The gentleman you are referring to was not

actually a visitor. He is an old friend who needed a bed for the night after his car was damaged by an Army vehicle and the hotel was unable to put him up.'

'Which regiment?'

'I don't know.'

'And whereabouts did this so-called accident take place?' he went on without looking up from his notebook as he continued to write.

'Somewhere near Banbridge.'

'And what was this *friend's* business in the Banbridge area?' he persisted, scribbling furiously.

Suddenly and without warning, Emily lost her temper. Was it not bad enough that the war made life difficult day and daily, even apart from the continual anxiety and regular bad news, but now, because of it, this horrible man could come into her home, ask her questions and imply she wasn't telling him the truth. It was just too much.

She opened her mouth to speak and closed it again as she heard footsteps on the stairs. Her visitor heard them too.

'There is someone else in the house?' he asked accusingly.

'Yes. My son is here.'

'And why's he not at school or at work?'

'Why don't you ask him yourself?' she replied, standing up and striding across to the sitting room door, not trusting herself to say one word more.

Still in pyjamas, his fair hair tousled from sleep, looking much less than his almost eighteen years, Johnny glanced at his mother's face and sized up the situation in a moment.

'What seems to be the officer's line of enquiry, Mother?'

'He hasn't told me what he wants,' she began steadily, looking Johnny full in the face. 'He has merely asked a great many questions, some of which I consider quite unnecessary,' she added sharply.

'You don't decide what is necessary ma'am. I do that,' said the officer, standing up and drawing himself to his full height.

'May I see your identification, please?'

Emily couldn't believe her ears. Her son, given to communicating in short, rapid bursts in a mixture of the local dialect and the argot of gangster movies, had walked across the room and was now holding out his hand for the warrant card with a look on his face she had never seen before. Not exactly arrogant, but determined and certainly self-possessed.

The card was produced, whereupon Johnny walked over to the window and took his time to examine it closely in the bright light.

'Good,' he said briskly, thrusting it back at the waiting officer. 'That *seems* to be in order. Now, if you'll be so good as to tell us exactly *what* you are investigating and in what *particular* way we can help you, we will give you our full attention. Won't we, mother?'

'You really would have been proud of him, Alex,' Emily said, as she brought a tray of tea into the sitting room after their late supper.

'I keep telling you there's more to Johnny than he cares to let on,' said Alex slowly, sinking back wearily into his comfortable fireside chair and closing his eyes for a brief moment.

'Are you *very* tired tonight,' she asked quietly, knowing how much he hated her making what he called a fuss over him.

'No, no worse than usual,' he replied honestly. 'But I want to hear the end of your story.'

'Well, there's not a lot more to tell,' she said. 'Once Johnny appeared, your man sang a different tune, as the saying is. It seems some sticks of gelignite were stolen from the quarry and it *must* have been last night because the security man checks them last thing in the evening and then again in the morning. It was perfectly reasonable for him to be making enquiries. What was so annoying was the distrust. As if we'd be helping someone to come and do a thing like that,' she said angrily. 'Why on earth didn't they send a man from our local force who knows everyone round here?'

Alex shook his head slowly.

'I think it's policy not to use local men for something like this,' he said, leaning forward and taking his tea from the tray. 'Do you not remember Sam telling us about when his two eldest sons joined up? They were posted all over the place. Anywhere but Richhill. They're both sergeants now, but I think one is in charge of Moy and the other is down near Larne.'

'Johnny said to me afterwards that he thought your man would do well in the SS.'

Alex smiled ruefully.

'You get his sort everywhere, love. They're not very bright, but they've been in the job a long time and finally got promotion. A wee bit of authority and it goes to their head. Men like that will always boss women if they get the chance. There are plenty like him in the mills.'

'I didn't handle it well and I know it was because I had a bad moment when I saw the uniform. But I won't be so slow if it were ever to happen again,' she went on firmly. 'As Johnny pointed out, in this country one is supposed to be innocent until proved guilty, but your man was assuming guilt in everything he was asking. Until Johnny turned up, that was.'

Suddenly and unexpectedly, Emily laughed.

'What's the joke?' demanded Alex.

'I've just remembered, love. He called me

'Mother'. I didn't notice at the time, I was so busy watching your man's face when he saw he'd got a different customer to deal with.'

Alex grinned and took several large mouthfuls from his tea.

'What did you say about Brendan?' he enquired, as he emptied his cup.

'Not a lot. But we did *not* mention maps,' she said, as she picked up the teapot and came over to him. 'I never thought I'd see the day when I'd tell a lie to a policeman.'

'But then, Emily, you hadn't had the experience of policemen you've just had. There's good and bad in every group. You and young Jane tend to see the best in people. Women often do. But maybe we all have to be careful these days.'

He paused and shook his head, aware she was watching him closely.

'No, I don't just mean like the posters, 'Careless talk costs lives', and so on. That's only good sense, and I suppose we *do* all need to be reminded of it . . . what I mean . . . well, you can't *always* tell . . . even people you trust . . .'

'Alex, what's wrong?' she asked quickly, reading the look on his face. 'Was there trouble again at Millbrook with the engine men?'

'No, it wasn't Millbrook, it was Ballievy. There was a explosion sometime during the night. No fire, thank goodness, and the two watchmen safe enough

59

at the opposite ends of the building, but the main countershaft was badly damaged.'

'Oh Alex,' she said, knowing now why he'd looked so exhausted when he arrived home. 'Why didn't they send up for you? When did you find out?'

'There was a message waiting for me at Millbrook when I got there, but there was no point sending up here for me. I couldn't touch anything till the police had been. Anyway, the senior men knew there was nothing we could do ourselves, so there was no point pulling me back from Millbrook or Seapatrick when I'd be coming to Ballievy anyway.'

'So what'll happen now?'

'Well, I've spoken to Mackie's in Belfast. They're the only people that can help, but with their quotas for armaments, our machinery wouldn't be high priority with them these days.'

'But you're on war work too,' Emily protested. 'What about the tent duck? You can't have fighting men with no shelter in the desert or the jungle.'

'Priorities and paperwork, Emily,' he said wearily. 'Some Civil Servant somewhere who might not know a countershaft from a Bren gun carrier will decide whether we get a licence for the repair or not. Even when we get it, there'll be materials needed for the job and that'll be the same process all over again. We could be out of production for weeks and then the War Office will be on our backs for the tent material. I've called a Board Meeting for Monday. Maybe someone else can think of something I haven't thought of already.'

'Oh love, as if you didn't have enough on your hands. You don't think your explosion could possibly be connected with those sticks of gelignite from the quarry?'

'It had occurred to me,' Alex replied sharply, with a brief nod. 'Brendan said last night de Valera had given the IRA short shrift in the South and they were nearly a thing of the past down there. But its been going round that some of them might think us a softer option so they have moved up here. Rumours thrive, as you know, but someone's spreading bad feeling in the mills,' he went on. 'Security was doubled the last time we had an arson attempt, so whoever did the job at Ballievy must have had good inside information to be able to get in and out again without being seen by either of the two night watchmen. That's the hardest part for me to stomach. Which of the people I've worked with for years is putting lives and jobs at risk?'

'Ma, what in the name of goodness are you doing?' Johnny demanded, as he came into the kitchen next morning, a little before noon, his face still damp and gleaming from his weekly shave.

He stood looking down at his mother's bent head and the bizarre assortment of objects on the kitchen table.

'You're up early, love,' she said, glancing up at him over the piece of wire she was twisting. 'Are you sure you're getting enough sleep? Did you get any at all at the factory last night?'

'Oh yes. I had an hour or two. With three of us on, we can all have a couple of hours on the couch in the office, but sometimes I use part of my time off to work on the plane. Not everybody gets the chance to sit in a cockpit and go through specifications at their leisure,' he explained, as he sat down opposite her at the kitchen table.

'Can I help?' he asked, sizing up her struggle with a large pair of pliers rather too large for what she was doing.

'I'm not making a good job of this,' she replied, breathing heavily, 'but I'm not letting it beat me. This piece of wire has to go round this thimble, but the wretched little thimble keeps slipping out.'

'Have you got a bigger thimble?'

'Yes, I could thatch a house with thimbles, as the saying is. They were your grandmother's,' she explained, nodding towards the large, well-stocked sewing box in front of her. 'But it has to be *this* one to go into the milk bottle,' she said flatly.

'Right, this thimble it is then,' he said, trying to keep his face straight, as he took the thimble and wire from her.

She watched in amazement as he encircled the offending thimble in one deft movement and secured the wire firmly in place using only his finger and thumb.

'Anything to oblige,' he said, handing it solemnly back to her and then breaking into a huge grin.

'What is it, Ma?' he asked, bursting out laughing. 'Or is it's specification covered by the Official Secrets Act? Or is it something even the War Ministry don't know about, like the new plane they're working on down at Walkers?'

Emily waved the miniature ladle in the air and laughed at herself. Whatever manual skills she might have, and she did acknowledge some of them, she was no good at all with things mechanical. It was one thing being able to prick out hundreds of seedlings from one packet of seed, but she couldn't even get a new battery into a torch without a struggle.

'It's for Jane's birthday tomorrow,' she said triumphantly. 'If she can get home as planned, we'll be having a special dessert with whipped cream garnished with jewels of raspberry jelly. This is for skimming the cream out of the top of the bottles.'

'Couldn't you just pour it off?'

'No. That's the secret. If you pour the cream off it gets diluted with the milk and then you can't whip it. If you use this device you get the cream and nothing but the cream . . .'

'So help me, Mother,' he added, laughing. 'And what about the jewels?'

Emily stood up, went to the larder and brought back a large white plate covered with a thin layer of bright-red, well-set jelly.

She set it down in front of him and watched as he inspected it at eye level to see how thick the jelly was. One of the most endearing features of her son was that unlike many of his contemporaries who talked at length and in great detail about what interested them, he was interested in what *she* was doing and would listen to her as patiently as she listened to him.

'When I have made the dessert, piled it up suitably in the best trifle dishes and put the whipped cream on top, I shall take a very sharp knife and cut this into tiny, tiny squares and scatter them over the cream in a kind of cascade.'

'That will look lovely,' he said, nodding slowly. 'Clever Ma.'

'Can't take the credit, Johnny. It was Cathy read it in a magazine and wrote to me about it. Just hope it'll taste as good as it looks.'

'Of course it will. It always does. Ritchie says he doesn't know how you do it. He thinks your food is great. He says his Ma is always complaining she can't get this and can't get that. That's why he never asks me to go there. You don't mind, do you?' he added, suddenly looking anxious.

'Mind what?' she asked, puzzled.

'Ritchie coming here and me never going

64

there. It's not really fair on you with rationing.'

'Of course, I don't mind. He's your friend, so he's welcome, even if I didn't like him as much as I do. Are the pair of you doing one last night tonight?'

He nodded vigorously.

'It's been great going down to the mill every night these holidays. We've both learnt such a lot. It's one thing building model planes, Ma, and it was a good start, but seeing the actual things they're making down there, like the torpedo airtails, is just so different. And the really big thing is that a few of them are working on a real plane, a plane I mustn't mention, even to you, because its not official in the first place. But they're working on a prototype. They're hoping to have something to test by the end of the summer.'

'A plane? In Walkers? But surely there's not enough room with all those pillars. I think I've only been in it once, long before it closed as a mill, but I can't imagine how you'd get a plane in there.'

'Depends on the plane, Ma. STOLs are small to begin with and you can easily work on the wings and the tailplane on their own and then put it together later. It's all wood and very light, Canadian silver birch . . .'

He broke off as she raised her hand.

'Please, sir, what's a stall?'

He shook his head, his bright blue eyes shining with merriment.

'S. T. O. L.' he spelt out. 'It means Short Take Off and Landing planes and they are very good at *not* stalling, that's why they're used as spotter planes. They're designed to cope with small fields enclosed by trees, places where there's no space for a runway, however small.'

Emily listened, following as well as she could the technical language that now came to him so easily. He'd always been good about explaining what she didn't know. Putting up her hand was one of their jokes, but she didn't like interrupting all the time. Often, she'd just memorise the unfamiliar words and look them up in the dictionary afterwards. But there were two problems with doing that. How did you spell a word you'd never seen or heard before? And what did she do if it was one of the many new technical developments the war had brought about and the word for it wasn't in any dictionary?'

'Did I tell you, Ma,' he said suddenly, 'that Ritchie's father says he's giving us both some extra money for all the cleaning up we've done while we we've been fire-watching? Job specification didn't say we had to clear up any pockets of sawdust we found, but we thought it was a hazard, so we did. That'll be a bit extra and I'm going to save it for my kit,' he said, looking pleased with himself. 'The stuff the RAF don't provide,' he added, when he saw her doubtful glance.

Emily nodded and tried hard not to let herself

react to that word 'kit'. Such a simple word, but look what it meant. Johnny going away. Johnny not tramping into the kitchen full of sleep in the mornings before school. Johnny not spreading his books and papers across the dining room table to work for his exams.

She pulled herself up short and focused on the expense ahead. She should be pleased about what he'd said.

Money wasn't a big difficulty with Alex's salary as a director and all the girls working away from home, but that wasn't the point. The point was, she'd tried to make all her children aware that money was important, especially if you didn't have any.

When she'd first come to her aunt and uncle after her mother died, she hadn't had a penny to her name. The Jackson's farm was small and wasn't doing well. Things did improve, but she'd never forgotten what it was like to have nothing to call upon however great their need might be.

'Must go, Ma. Lots to do.' he said, jumping to his feet.

'Where to?' she asked, as she glanced up at the clock, knowing it must be almost lunch time.

'Dining room,' he said, briskly. 'Revision. Unless we are dining.'

'That's tomorrow,' she said, laughing suddenly. 'You can have a bowl of soup when your father comes in, or when you get hungry, whichever comes soonest. But it will be served right here,' she said, pointing down at the well-scrubbed surface of the kitchen table. 'You could have a couple of biscuits to keep you going.'

'Thanks, Ma. That would be great,' he said, giving her a quick hug and reaching for the biscuit tin.

CHAPTER FOUR

Alex had long ago given up trying to keep either Saturday or Sunday clear to spend with his family. There were engine men he knew, good, solid Presbyterians, who had not darkened the door of their respective churches for months, so why should he be any different? In fact, the war meant people couldn't expect to work regular or predictable hours any more. Time off was random, to be cherished when it came.

Fairly, there were those in the mills who were happy to do extra shifts and claim the overtime and his own friend and neighbour, Michael Cook, told him happily he'd never in his life been able to save money until now. With the larger herd, he admitted the hours were long, but he was his own boss, the price of milk was guaranteed and there was a nice cheque from the creamery every month.

The war had brought badly needed jobs to Ulster and life was better for many, especially small farmers like Michael. But it was still hard work, paid or unpaid, and people got tired. Not everyone worked with the sky and the fields for company as Michael did. Indeed, he was only too well aware how much sickness there'd been in the mills over this last year, not just in winter, but in summer as well, as the demands went up and energy began to flag.

On this last Sunday in April, a little before noon, the sun high on a perfect spring day, Alex cleaned the oil off his hands in the washroom at Millbrook and prepared to put all such thoughts out of mind. He'd told the four mill managers the previous day that short of disaster, he would not be available on Sunday after his usual morning visit to see what problems maintenance might have revealed. They'd all assured him they'd do their very best to make sure he'd be left undisturbed.

The Austin was hot from sitting in the sun. Amazed to find its interior almost as stuffy as it would be in summer, he opened wide the doors and stood looking round him, waiting for a few moments to let the light breeze blow away the heavy smell of hot leather.

'Away home man and forget all about us,' Robert Anderson said, as he rounded the corner of the mill and caught sight of him. 'Sure isn't it great wee Jane is able to get home,' he went on, a broad grin breaking on his sweat-streaked face. 'Say

Happy Birthday from me. What age is she, if it's not rude to ask a lady's age?'

'She's nineteen today and very nearly finished her training,' Alex replied, delighted by the enquiry. 'And what's more, Robert, Lizzie is coming too, though just for a couple of hours. She found someone only last night willing to change shifts with her.'

'Ach, that's just great, man, just great. Your whole family, bar Cathy. I'm sure your Emily is in the kitchen making some wee treat.'

'I'm sure she is,' began Alex laughing. 'I was warned to keep well out of the way last night.'

'*What the eye doesn't see, the heart doesn't grieve*, as the saying is. Some of the things these women manage you couldn't be up to,' Robert said, shaking his head and pausing to lean against the roof of the car beside him. 'One of my wee lassies went to a birthday party a couple of weeks ago and came home and told us she had banana sandwiches.'

'Shure when did we last see a banana?' he asked, laughing. 'The Missus and I though maybe she was imaginin' things the way wee ones do, but at the heels of the hunt we found out that you can mash up cooked turnip with banana essence, if you have any left from before the war, and you wouldn't know the difference. Especially if you've never met the real thing,' he added, dropping his voice to a whisper.

They laughed together before Alex climbed into the driving seat and Robert walked away to finish his extra day shift in the silent mill. Before Robert left he'd have made sure every moving part of the hard-pressed machinery was inspected, adjusted, cleaned, greased or oiled.

There was neither car nor Army lorry on the road as Alex sailed along, all the windows open, the hot leather smell now replaced by the first hints of perfume from the dazzling, white blossoms on the hawthorn, the May blossom, arriving early in the south-facing hedgerows.

'What the eye doesn't see, the heart doesn't grieve.'

Unexpectedly, Robert's words came back into his mind and he smiled to himself. The expression he knew well, but as he drove, he began to wonder why he'd always taken such a delight in the expressions and sayings that were such a part of Ulster life.

'Here's one for you, Da.'

He could hear Jane's voice as she came into the room, a piece of paper in her hand. Someone in the hospital, a porter or a patient, had used a word or a saying that caught her ear and her first thought was always to share it with him.

'Sure you could pass for a native, Da.'

That would be Johnny's comment should he himself try one of the phrases now familiar enough for him to risk using it.

So why was he so fascinated and delighted by what he picked up? As suddenly and unexpectedly as if he'd just received a message written on a piece of paper the answer came to him. There were no expressions or colourful phrases in the orphanages, nor on the farms where he worked. Bare instructions. Do this. Do that. Bald questions. What age are you? Where was your last place?

No one had talked to him, except one lovely lady he would never forget. And no one expected him to talk to them, a lesson he had learnt very early on. *Talking back* was a crime and even the simplest reply to a question was regularly construed as *talking back*. Silence was much safer. Even in the barn with the other workers, as lonely and neglected as he was himself, it was often safer to say nothing.

All that had changed after he'd met Sam McGinley and made up his mind to come home and look for his lost family. He'd needed to earn more money, for it would take him years to save his fare from the pittance he was paid as a farm labourer.

He had managed to find a better place where he was allowed to work with the machines, but the pay itself was little better. What had actually earned his passage money was writing letters. Late in the evening after his work on the farm, when it was too dark to see any more, or when he was finally let go, he would make his way to the houses where the emigrants gathered. There he was made welcome, because for a very small fee he would write letters for them.

Most of them were illiterate, but even those who could handle a pen often found themselves defeated when faced with a sheet of notepaper. He had encouraged them, got them to talk about their homes, the people and places they once knew. Then he asked them about what they did now, how they felt about the new country and what they planned for the future.

For the first time in his life, here were people who talked to him and trusted him with their fear of not being able to express themselves for they had been glad when he suggested the subjects they might write about that might be useful to them. They found it hard to tell the folks at home how well they were doing, especially when they weren't. They wanted to know how their families and friends were getting on and hoped they were remembered. Most of all, they wanted to feel they still had a place in that old life, even though they'd set out to make a new life in a country so far away and so very different.

To his own surprise, Alex discovered he always seemed able to find the right words and he had no difficulty remembering their stories. He was always ready to remind them of what they'd said in their previous letters, even without looking at the copies he kept for them. What they welcomed most of all were suggestions as to what they might say this time that was different from the last, when their lives were so full of hard work there was little to relieve the monotony of one day following the next.

Now he had his own stories. From the very first day he'd arrived in Ballydown and was welcomed by Rose and then by John, he had been told their family stories. By sharing their stories, they had woven him into the fabric of their life. As he looked back on the way he'd collected up the sayings and expressions used by the people around him, he saw that he had used sharing their speech and their humour to weave himself into the life of this new place.

The greatest unhappiness he could think of was to be a child with no story. Or a young man with no story, as he had once been.

He tooted his horn as he passed Cook's farm, knowing that Michael in the yard, or Mary in her kitchen, or one of the children helping her would say: 'There's Alex going home early. It's Jane's birthday today.'

He smiled through the mist of his tears as he soared up the hill.

'Go on then, Ma, tell us how you did it?' demanded Lizzie, as Johnny stood up to clear away the dinner plates.

'Not a lot for Fido,' he commented dryly as he stacked them up.

The best dinner service with its pretty borders of flowers and its elegant serving dishes bore not the slightest trace of the succulent roast beef and its accompaniments, roast potatoes, carrots stored from last autumn's bumper crop and tender, early cabbage from Emily's cold frame in the sunniest part of the garden.

'It's a good thing you can feed a phantom dog on phantom scraps,' he added, as he headed for the kitchen.

'That was lovely, Ma,' said Jane, when she stopped laughing at his comment. 'I didn't know roast beef still existed. How *did* you manage it?'

'Maybe you shouldn't ask, Jane,' said Alex. 'Your mother has ways and means that are not available to most of us,' he added, his eyes twinkling.

'Did you chat up the butcher, Ma,' asked Lizzie matter-of-factly.

'Bit old for that, Lizzie dear,' Emily came back at her. 'And so's he for that matter.'

'No, you're not,' Jane insisted. 'You'd make a lovely spy.'

'Thank you, Jane, I'll remember that on my bad mornings,' Emily replied laughing.

If anyone would make a good spy it would be Jane herself, Emily thought, as she looked from one daughter to the other. Jane was wearing a pink jumper she'd knitted for her a couple of years ago over a white blouse, clearly a survival from schooldays, and a navy skirt that had most certainly seen better days, but she still looked lovely.

But then, Jane always did, for she had beautiful

skin, huge blue eyes, soft, blonde curls and a smile that lit up her face and made you feel the world was a much nicer place than you'd thought it was.

'I'd still like to know,' said Lizzie firmly.

'Well,' said Emily, looking at her directly and knowing full well that Lizzie would not be satisfied until she had her explanation. 'The secret lies in advance planning,' she said, attempting a suitable solemnity.

'She means she went out and killed a cow three weeks ago,' Johnny declared as he returned for the empty vegetable dishes.

Jane giggled and Lizzie smiled patiently. She was not much given to smiles, though her face was lively and alert enough

'If you were to ask your father and brother what they had for Sunday lunch for the last three Sundays, you could probably work it out from that,' Emily said with a sudden smile.

To her great delight, Johnny was tramping back and forth to the kitchen carrying the larger items of her precious dinner service one at a time. She'd never wanted to discourage him when he'd offered to help clear the table once Lizzie and Jane had both gone away, but for years now she'd sat, her heart in her mouth, watching him pile up their wedding present from Rose and John into a perilous tower even before he attempted to lift them and carry them out of the room.

'Shepherd's pie, last Sunday,' said Johnny, leaning over for the large oval dish which had been piled high with roast potatoes.

'Toad in the hole, the previous one, wasn't it?' added Alex helpfully.

'And three weeks ago?' prompted Lizzie.

'Can't remember that far back,' Johnny replied, as he came into the dining room once again, carrying a tray to collect up the cutlery and the remaining small items.

'Beef casserole,' Emily provided, smiling across at Lizzie, now deep in thought.

Lizzie nodded and looked pleased while Jane and Emily exchanged glances.

'I still can't see how you magicked up such a wonderful dinner, Ma. You'll have to explain,' said Jane, shaking her head and appealing to her sister.

'Saved up her meat coupons,' Lizzie said promptly. 'Knowing Ma, she did a deal with the butcher. Mince, sausage and stewing meat for three weeks and a piece of beef for your birthday,' she went on smiling at her younger sister.

'Now, ladies and gentlemen, I crave your full attention,' said Johnny, as he whisked a few crumbs from the double damask table cloth and returned to the centre of the table the small arrangement of spring flowers, exiled to the sideboard due to lack of space during the main course. 'I go to fetch the dessert, or the desert as my dear sister Jane used to spell it,' he announced, throwing the last remark over his shoulder.

'Oh my goodness, Ma, pudding as well!' Jane exclaimed.

Emily took a deep breath. Johnny was carrying the tray at shoulder level, like French waiters in American movies. She need not have worried. He lowered the tray slowly and safely to the table in front of his mother, and waited, open-mouthed for their response.

'Ma, how lovely!' said Lizzie peering at the tall well-filled dishes. 'Surely that's not real cream.'

'How pretty,' said Jane. 'What are all those lovely little bits?'

Alex looked across at Emily and gave her a great beaming smile. Even Johnny didn't know he'd had to help Emily rearrange the four beautifully-prepared dessert glasses to make a fifth when Lizzie had phoned to say she could come.

'I hope it tastes all right,' said Emily, who had never got used to the fact that the food she produced was never less than edible and often very good indeed.

The ensuing silence reassured her. A fitting end, she thought, for the remains of the Christmas bottle of sherry and a sponge cake she'd baked, anointed with her own strawberry jam and allowed to dry out in a sealed cake tin.

As the spoons were scraping the last delicious

vestiges of trifle and cream from the pointed bottoms of the tall glasses, they heard the phone ring in the hall.

'Oh bother,' protested Lizzie. 'That's probably for me. I had to give them my number in case there was a flap,' she explained, taking time to lick her spoon and put it down carefully on her side plate before she went out into the hall.

'Elizabeth Hamilton,' she said, as she picked up the receiver.

The dining room door was open and one by one they put their spoons down and listened.

'Yes, yes, of course. No, I think you're quite right. It's not easy at all. Hold on and I'll get him, Robert.'

At the mention of Robert, Alex was on his feet and half way across the room. Of all the reliable people he knew at the four mills, Robert was one of the best. He took the receiver from Lizzie and asked what was wrong.

They all listened intently, but for many minutes Alex said nothing. Only Emily, sitting at the head of the dining table opposite the door into the hall, could see him nodding his head vigorously.

He strode back into the room.

'I'm sorry everyone,' he said quickly. 'A plane has crashed on the edge of the Millbrook reservoir. They've rescued the pilot, but he's injured and none of the men who got him out could get any sense out of him.'

'But why should *you* do any better, Da? Why don't they just take him to hospital and let them cope?' asked Johnny crossly.

'It's not as simple as that,' said Lizzie coolly.

'No, it's not,' agreed Alex, looking down at Jane who was watching him carefully. 'Robert knew you were here and thought you might be willing to come with me.'

She nodded vigorously and got to her feet.

'Robert also remembered that I speak German as well as French.'

The young man was stretched out on the couch below the window in Alex's office, the books and papers that usually rested there now stacked hastily on the floor by the filing cabinet. Robert had bandaged his head, but blood was already making a vivid stain on the white dressing. Where it was not obscured with dried blood and some dark residue released by the impact of the crash, his face was deathly pale. His blonde hair fell unkempt over his closed eyes.

Alex took a deep breath and swallowed hard. The young German pilot who lay before him looked even younger than Johnny.

'He's passed out again,' said Robert quietly. 'He tried to run away when we got him out of the plane, but I think he may have broken his leg. Certainly it wouldn't hold him, or we mightn't have caught him.'

81

'Da, where do you keep the proper medical kit?'

'It's in the storeroom, Jane. I'll get it for you,' Robert said quickly. 'D'you want anything else? Hot water?'

Alex turned to his daughter to find she'd already peeled off her pink sweater, parked it on his desk and was now rolling up her sleeves.

Robert returned moments later with a large wooden box. Perched on top, a bowl of hot water steamed gently. He set the bowl of water down next to her, opened the box and stood beside Alex watching as she removed the dressing, inspected the wound and went to work cleaning the young man's face.

'D'you think it was reconnaissance?' asked Alex soberly. 'He's a bit young for a spy, isn't he?'

'He thought we were going to shoot him when we pulled him out of the water. He said something like 'Nicht schlossen,' but I only know German from war films,' Robert replied.

'He's not a spy,' retorted Jane sharply, as she dropped bloodstained surgical wipes into the wastepaper basket.

'How d'you know, Jane? Robert asked.

'Just look at his face,' she replied, as she wiped his brow and pushed his hair back.

'Appearances can be deceptive,' said Alex. 'But we need to know. I don't want to see him shot any more than you do, Robert. Do our people shoot spies?'

'Oh yes. But they do get a trial as far as I know.'

At that moment, the young man stirred, moving agitatedly even before he opened his eyes.

'Please don't move,' said Jane quietly, 'not till I've finished.'

His eyes flicked open, wide with amazement and stared at her. Both Alex and Robert saw the look he gave her as his blue eyes met hers, but only Alex understood what he said before he passed out again.

'I must be dead for you are an Angel.'

'Oh the poor boy,' said Emily, her face creased with distress, as she listened to Alex's account of the afternoon. 'Are you sure it was safe to take him to hospital?'

'As safe as we could make it,' Alex said firmly 'We did manage to get assurances from the Chief Constable that he would be guarded until he was fit to be moved. Thank goodness we had a Justice of the Peace on the Board.'

'I expect he and the Chief Constable went to school together,' she said briskly.

'More than likely. He was certainly sympathetic when I told him what I'd been able to find out.'

'Oh Alex, what would have happened if you hadn't spoken German?'

'He had a little English, but not much use for explaining himself. I'll tell you something though,' he added with a little laugh, 'he seemed to understand every word Jane spoke.'

Alex paused, unsure how much more he should say about Jane's part in the afternoon. He could certainly tell her just how capable she'd shown herself, but Emily would know that already. She'd seen Jane in action many a time, whether it was splinting a bird's wing or bandaging Johnny's knee.

He thought back to the afternoon and tried to remember the exact sequence of events after Jane had brought him round by bathing his face and hands.

'I need to ask you some questions,' he had begun somewhat hesitantly in German.

He was amazed that a language he'd spoken so seldom since he was a labourer in German Township should come back to him so easily after all these years.

The blue eyes regarded him anxiously.

'This is my father,' said Jane quietly. 'He wants to help you.'

The young man had turned to look at her. Just one brief glance, then suddenly there were huge tears running down his face. Jane took his hand and held it, smiled at him and said, 'You'll feel better soon. Drink some more water.'

He'd wiped his tears with the back of his hand, drunk the water as obediently as a child and begun to speak, his voice husky. He'd told them he'd had to join either the Army or the Luftwaffe because it would be bad for his socialist father who had been sent to a labour camp if the family did not support the Fuhrer. Both his brothers were already dead, one shot down over England and one killed in a raid on the French airfield where he was based.

As for himself, he did not want to fight or to kill anyone. He was trying to fly to Ireland. It was a neutral country and they would not shoot him, but he had no maps and there had been cloud over the sea when he set out from the north of France. So he had got lost.

When he came out of the cloud and saw the coast to the west he was so happy. But when he came lower he saw airfields below him. He could see the markings on the planes. They were British and he had no more petrol. The plane was stalling and he had to bring her down quickly. He saw the lake and headed for it.

'Have you a headache?' asked Jane, before Alex could make any comment.

He nodded.

'Yes, it is very sore.'

As she gave him some Anadin and encouraged him to drink another glass of water, Alex realised that she made tiny gestures with her hands whenever she spoke to him. She might have no German, but he was beginning to wonder just how much of the young man's story she already understood simply from looking at him.

'So what will happen next?' Emily asked anxiously.

Alex realised he'd fallen silent, his mind moving back over the afternoon's events.

'X-rays tomorrow. They might transfer him to a military hospital if the leg *is* broken. Then a POW. camp. He'll be no worse off in the North than in the South.'

'Can one visit prisoners?' Emily asked, folding up her knitting and putting back in its cretonne bag.

'I don't know. But I know someone who'll be trying to find out.'

'Would that be our Jane?'

'Yes.'

Emily looked at him and waited, and waited. Finally he gathered himself and looked into the embers of the dying fire.

'I've never seen two people read each other like open books the way Johann Hillmann and our Jane did this afternoon. Not a dozen words between them, but his blue eyes near as big as hers,' he said, taking a great deep breath, as he stood up and switched off the table lamp on his side of the fire.

CHAPTER FIVE

As Emily finished the second sleeve of Alex's best shirt and turned round to pick up a clothes hanger from the kitchen table, she saw a glint of sunlight strike the wet panes of the wide window beyond the kitchen sink. She moved across the kitchen, glanced out into the cobbled yard, noted the wind rippling the shallow puddles and sighed. It would take an hour or more with a good drying wind before she could pick peas and much longer if she wanted flowers for drying.

Today was the first Monday in September and it was days since she'd been able to do anything in the garden, even weeding. As sure as she set foot in the yard, she'd feel the first spits of rain in the wind. One look up at the dark base of the cloud above warned her it was about to pour at any moment.

She picked up another shirt, noticed how worn the collar had become and wondered if she should turn it before it got any worse. She sighed again. It wasn't that she minded sewing in itself, but she did mind sitting indoors when she needed to be out in the garden.

The high summer months had been so disappointing. After a most lovely May, full of sunshine and sudden showers that kept the garden watered, but never lasted long enough to damage the growing plants, June had been almost completely dry. She'd had to get the hose out when her back ached from carrying buckets and watering cans, but June was also endlessly sunny and warm. Whenever she wanted to do a job, she had only to change her shoes and walk outside. She'd gardened morning, noon and night, glad to have so much she could do when Alex was away for long hours and Johnny was at school or shut up in the dining room with his final revision for his all important final exams.

She'd been so pleased with her early vegetables. Some she'd given to the hospital in Banbridge. The rest she'd sold at the Women's Institute market to raise funds for the Red Cross. She'd made so much money that Alex had teased her and said if she would only go into business he'd be able to retire.

But July was a different matter. There was rain nearly every day, less sun, and humidity as bad as on a spinning floor. But unlike working on a spinning floor, there was no relief at the end of the day. The humidity persisted, making the nights clammy and sleep difficult. She'd gazed at the rotting blooms on her geraniums and viewed the well-nibbled leaves of vegetables beaten down by the rain and hoped that August would be better.

August was even worse. There was just as much rain, but even less sunshine. Fairly, it was less humid, but she'd felt she had no energy for anything. When she did get a dry afternoon, she found herself wandering up and down the rows of peas and beans not able to decide whether to tackle the rampant weeds or to pick the swollen pods before they burst and the birds got them.

Then Johnny went. And she was quite alone.

She paused, took a deep breath and decided she'd done enough ironing. There were only two of them now and Alex had enough everyday shirts and clean handkerchiefs to see him through a week, never mind till tomorrow, or the next day.

She'd done her best, she really had, but she'd not been able to hide from Alex the fact that she was so very low in spirits now there was no Johnny to help her keep them up. She refused to say 'depressed'. Although the women's magazines said it was nothing to be ashamed off and told you how to deal with it, she couldn't bring herself to admit that she just didn't know how she could keep going if the war went on much longer. It had been bad enough at times these last three years with shortages and the endless problems at the mills, but now there was one more worry, Johnny was out there too, with his sisters, learning to fly, which could only lead to certain danger, wherever it might happen to be.

Three long years since that morning when they'd stayed at home from church knowing there was going to be a broadcast on the wireless at eleven o'clock. They'd listened in silence and then, as soon as Mr Chamberlain finished, Alex said he thought she should phone Cathy. So she had. Cathy had cried, because she knew Brian would be called up.

But, of course, in the end, Brian had been reserved, the last thing either he or Cathy had expected.

Perhaps she should try to remember that so far none of her worst nightmares had come true. Worrying about any of her family wasn't going to get her anywhere. It might even make her ill and how would Alex cope then, with all he had on his plate.

She filled the kettle and made herself a cup of tea. She'd sit in the conservatory with the flowers that weren't rain-battered and rotten and read her book for an hour. Then, this afternoon, wet or dry, she'd go out and pick some peas for Mary Cook and take them down to her when she went for the milk.

She'd done exactly what the Dig for Victory pamphlet said she should and planted her peas and beans every three or four weeks instead of all at once. The residues of the first rows had long since shrivelled on the compost heap, but the later plantings were now heavy with fresh green pods. To her surprise, the rain had held off and now a few gleams of sun came to dry the still damp foliage and to create little pools of quicksilver where tiny drops of water lay in the broad leaves of cabbage and rhubarb.

She gathered what she needed for Mary Cook and their own supper, and then decided to pick some more for her old friend, Dolly Love, in Dromore. Dolly might be feeling just as low as she had felt, for her Tom had gone last week. What a pity it was that Tom, and Johnny's best friend Ritchie, only a couple of weeks younger than Johnny himself, had all been sent to different training camps though they had applied at the same time and hoped to be together.

Emily might well have gone on pulling out weeds and thinking her own thoughts long after the peas were picked had it not been for the sound of a car on the hill. At the sudden vibration on the now warm air, she straightened up, stretched her back and listened.

It *did* sound like Alex all right, but she couldn't remember when he'd last arrived home at four o'clock in the afternoon. Moments later, she heard his car swing into the avenue, out of sight behind the flourishing hedge.

She arrived back in the yard just as he slowed round the corner of the house and stopped.

'We have a visitor,' he said, grinning as he caught

sight of her Wellington boots. 'Do you want me to head him off and bring him in by the front door?' he asked, as she caught the sound of another vehicle on the hill.

But before she'd had time to consider this possibility a jeep with the big white star of the US Army on its bonnet swooped down the avenue and pulled up sharply behind Alex's Austin, a flutter of fallen leaves caught up on the wheels settling gently to the ground.

'Major Hicks, how lovely to see you,' said Emily with a great beaming smile.

'And you too, ma'am,' he said, dropping down from the driver's seat and holding out a large hand. 'I don't know when I last saw a lady in muddy boots. Makes me homesick for Vermont.'

'Major Hicks has come to consult you, Emily,' said Alex, a twinkle in his eyes.

'Now, Alex, this won't do,' the tall American protested. 'I may be on official business, but I will not be called Major Hicks standing in your backyard. The name is Christopher, but no one except my Ma calls me that. So Chris it is. And you ma'am are Emily, if that's all right.'

'Of course, it is. Now let's go in and see if I can find a piece of cake for tea.'

'Well, don't worry if you can't, Emily. I've brought some cookies and coffee. Just a few things might come in handy,' he said casually, reaching into the back seat and producing a large, over-filled cardboard box.

Emily stared at it and then laughed.

'Chris, I haven't seen coffee since 1940. And I *love* coffee.'

'That's just great. I could sure use a cup of coffee, cake or no cake,' he said laughing. 'If you're going to make it for us, can I look around your backyard?' he went on as he carried the box over to the house and set it down on the doorstep.

It was Alex who laughed at the startled look on Emily's face, but it was Christopher Hicks who apologised.

'That's one down to me, Emily,' he said shaking his head and smiling wryly. 'The correct word is 'garden.' I forgot *again*. We have a book, official issue, telling us the obvious mistakes we can make because we all think we speak the same language. That one is on about Page two.'

'I'd like to see your book, Chris,' said Emily smiling. 'It would help *me* when I meet your young men navigating cross-country. It ought to work both ways, you know.'

Chris Hicks nodded vigorously.

'That's exactly why I've come to you, Emily. I need your help. If your good man can spare you, that is,' he added cautiously.

He looked sideways at Alex, found him grinning broadly, and turned again to Emily.

'We'll see about that,' she said promptly, as she waved towards the flower garden. 'We've a good view of the Mournes, Chris, if you're not fed up crawling round them already. Alex, dear, try to keep him away from all the neglected bits. It's even worse than I thought it was,' she added, as she bent to take off her boots.

She put the kettle on, pulled a kitchen chair over to the tall cupboards on the wall adjoining the conservatory, climbed up and opened the double doors of the over-cupboard. There, among the stored items, like the pretty, hand-painted water carafe for the guest room, the collection of jam pots for January's marmalade and the spare mantles for the emergency oil lamps, sat the coffee-pot. Beside it, an empty ceramic jar said COFFEE. They were both perfectly clean but for a thin layer of dust on their lids.

She brought them down carefully, one at a time, the kitchen chair wobbling slightly on the worn tiles and fetched a pack of coffee from the doorstep.

'Oh wonderful,' she said aloud, laughing to herself as she took a great deep breath of the rich aroma, remembering how she'd once said to Alex that if she ever passed out he could forget the smelling salts and just wave an open jar of coffee under her nose.

There was more cake in the tin than she'd remembered, but as she cut it up and waited for the coffee to filter, she thought how kind it was of Chris Hicks to bring his own cookies. But then, he was a kind man, and she'd already had good cause to be grateful to him.

They'd met on one of the sun-filled May evenings when the town council of Banbridge had given a reception for representatives of all the regiments who had taken up quarters locally. The idea was that they could meet local people. The entire Board of Bann Valley Mills were there with their wives, the local clergy, doctors, solicitors and businessmen. *The Who's Who of Banbridge*, Alex had whispered, as they gathered in the Recreation Hall at Millbrook, the largest space immediately available with so many halls and public rooms being used for other purposes.

Somewhere in the course of the evening Emily had found herself on the edge of a large group and had slipped aside to look out through the tall plate-glass windows which framed the small reservoir outside. Created many years earlier after a bad fire which could have been dealt with had it not been for lack of water, it had been planted with willows and other water-loving shrubs. With its irregular shape, carefully planned by Sarah and Hugh Sinton, it had become an entirely natural part of the landscape. All the more so because there was always at least one pair of swans to be seen moving silently across the still water. This year there had been five cygnets as well.

The water was mirror calm, the trees a perfect reflection in the gently paling light.

'Looks so peaceful, doesn't it, ma'am? That's the thing I find hardest in this lovely countryside of yours.'

She turned and smiled at the broad-shouldered figure looking down at her, his uniform immaculate, a variety of markings suggesting he was a fairly senior officer.

She nodded vigorously.

'Sometimes when I put out washing or pick some flowers for the table, I think how incredible it is that armies are fighting through towns and villages, destroying everything around them as well as each other and here I am . . .'

'Holding the world together for someone, no doubt,' he said thoughtfully, 'as my wife does for me.'

'And she's so far away,' she replied, hoping he wouldn't notice the tears that had sprung to her eyes.

'Vermont.'

'I've read about Vermont,' she said, recovering herself. 'I'm afraid autumn here won't be nearly so dramatic.'

'If we're here.'

She nodded.

'That's the other hard thing, isn't it?' she said quietly. 'Never knowing what's going to happen next.'

She asked about his wife, found he had a young family, the eldest boy eight, the youngest, a little girl, only just two. Then, he asked about her family and she told him of Cathy, Lizzie, Jane and Johnny, how old they were, what they were doing, and where they were, as far as she knew where. Just recently, both Jane and Lizzie had written to say they were being moved. Obviously, in a letter, they didn't say where. She would have to wait as patiently as she could for a visit home to find out about the new posting.

'That's Alex, my husband, over there,' she said nodding to where Alex stood deep in conversation with a fellow director. 'I'm afraid he's being naughty and not doing his social duty,' she said with a smile. 'With that look on his face and talking to James Willoughby I'd say he was talking about a damaged countershaft at one of the mills.'

'That's his line, is it?'

'Yes, he's Technical Director for the four mills that make up Bann Valley Mills. Trying to repair machines is a nightmare in war time. I'm amazed that he manages to stay sane,' she added honestly.

There was something so solid and reassuring about this man, the way he listened so carefully to everything she said, took it all in and asked sensible questions that she found herself setting out the whole problem for him.

'The textile machinery specialists are all on

war work,' she explained, 'aircraft or munitions. Anyway, materials are almost unobtainable.'

She paused, lowered her voice and went on. 'What makes it so bad for Alex is that there has been some deliberate damage.'

He nodded slowly, his lips pressed together.

'You know I'm an engineer, don't you?'

'No, I'm sorry,' she apologised, 'I know I should be able to tell from your insignia.'

'Not important, ma'am,' he said, shaking his head, 'but I think I might be able to help out. I've got materials and my boys need real work, real problems to solve, not just exercises. Why not textile machinery? It's all part of the war effort, isn't it?'

Alex left them after a lively half hour over coffee and cake.

'Board Meeting at six,' he explained, as he stood up.

'Can't appear in dungarees,' he added, looking down at Chris. 'War or no war, it has to be a suit. Most of my fellow directors are accountants or solicitors and they come straight from work.'

'I sometimes have that problem too, Alex, but there's not many top brass around here at the moment. I can still wear fatigues.'

'Emily, I need advice and perhaps help,' Chris began, as Alex closed the sitting room door quietly behind him.

'These boys of mine are homesick. And how can I blame them when I'm homesick myself?' he went on, with the open smile she found so endearing. 'I don't need to tell someone like you about morale. It's critical. We don't know how long it will be before we see action, but if morale is low we get illness, a poor response to training and high casualties when we do go into a frontline situation.'

Emily nodded.

'I read about the Midwest Giants and the Kentucky Wildcats playing baseball up in Belfast in July. I loved the names,' she said, laughing. 'But I guessed that was to try to keep up spirits,' she went on more soberly.

'Yes, it was and I hear baseball at battalion level has been a great success too. Sport is always good. And so are the dances up at the camp, or in the town, or even in that lovely hall where we met at Millbrook. People have been great helping us to find places for the boys to meet girls. The trouble is, Emily, my engineering boys are younger than many of our fighting troops. Some of them were only in first year at college. I think what they're really missing are their kid brothers and sisters.'

'Ah . . . yes. I hadn't thought of that.'

'I didn't catch on till I saw some of our boys making paper aeroplanes for some of the canteen ladies' little lads that have to come up to the camp after school. That little group were just in a world of their own.'

'So, the problem is how to get your boys together with families with younger children,' she said thoughtfully.

'That's it, Emily. I can provide transport and any food you need . . .'

He broke off as he saw a great smile light up her face.

'Brownies,' she said. 'Aren't they a favourite form of cookie with Americans?'

'Yes, they are. But proper brownies are home-baked. I'm afraid they wouldn't travel.'

'They wouldn't have to,' she said smiling happily. 'There'll be no problem finding children. The primary teachers and the churches can help, but your boys need some home-cooking. They need little presents to give to the children they meet. Do you think your wife could provide me with a cookery book? And have you got a copying machine on the base? I can think of at least four other women who'd bake each week if they could get the ingredients.'

'Emily, you are wonderful!'

'Don't say that Chris, till you see if I can deliver. But I do have some ideas.'

'That is *very* obvious,' he said, shaking his head and looking relieved. 'I'll contact home right away and get a requisition in for the sort of stuff you'll need. That'll be no problem at all.'

There were two more attempts to blow up machinery in the course of September, both at Ballievy, where the damaged countershaft had been repaired within days of Alex's meeting Chris at Millbrook. The devices used had not been very effective, no one had been hurt and repairs were done speedily by a party of Chris's young lads. Nevertheless, anxiety over who was causing the damage affected everyone, from Alex and the Directors and the whole staff at Ballievy to the managers and senior men at the other three mills who could easily find themselves the next target for sabotage.

'What did the police report say, Alex?' Emily asked, as they walked out into the flower garden after supper one pleasant evening at the beginning of October.

'Not a lot,' he replied, reluctantly, looking around him at the fallen leaves splashing colour on the grass path.

Leaves from the huge chestnut that dominated the vegetable garden had blown over the hedge and now lay pink and gold among those carried down from the avenue, the still-perfect golden globes from the limes.

'Do you want to try and forget all about it, love?'
'Wish I could.'

Even after all these years, there were times when Emily didn't know what to say to him, and couldn't guess what he was thinking. His face gave her no clue, though the set of his shoulders told her how low he was feeling.

They moved slowly down to the end of the garden and stood looking out at the mountains, the air fresh and full of the smells of autumn but not yet edged with chill.

'How did the picnic go?' he asked abruptly.

'Great. It was an enormous success,' she said turning towards him. 'Chris was delighted. He said he hadn't had as much fun in years. Rounders on the beach. Rides in jeeps. Three-legged races. His boys made up take-away presents with sweets and biscuits . . . and chewing gum. Not sure how popular I'll be with the mothers over that, but never mind. Kids love it.'

She looked at him closely as he turned his gaze back from the far mountains.

'Alex, are you missing Johnny? Are you worried about our children?'

'Guilty as charged, ma'am, as our friend Chris would say,' he replied, with a ghost of a smile.

'Good. That's splendid,' she said, slipping her arm round his waist.

'What's good about it?' he asked, looking startled.

'Only that now I know. What about that saying

you learnt long ago: *A trouble shared is a trouble halved*. Why do you think I work so hard, Alex, baking and cooking and arranging the Sunday visits and so on? I miss Johnny and the girls and Ritchie too. I'd go mad if I hadn't something useful I could do, people I needed to phone or write to. Mary Cook to talk to when I go for the milk. Do you give yourself time to go and talk to anyone these days, even Robert, or any of the managers?'

Alex dropped his eyes and looked sheepish.

'Maybe, love, we're homesick too. Homesick for the life we made for our family and the life we all had before the war. But if we accept that we are, perhaps we could do something about it. Why don't we ask Chris to come for a meal one evening?'

Alex said nothing. He just nodded.

But Emily saw the way he looked when they walked back to the house and she offered him a cup of coffee. Loneliness had been such a part of Alex's life for such a long time, he still didn't know when that was what he was feeling. Nor did he remember there was any comfort to be had.

CHAPTER SIX

With the eyes of the world on a Russian city on the Volga no one in the Banbridge area had ever heard of before, November unrolled its chill and fog over the low green hills and mountains of County Down. Young men in uniform crawled though ditches and slithered over stone walls as if these impediments were of as little moment as the cushions and pillows which Emily and her friends spread out on the floor of the Recreation Hall at Millbrook, to provide an obstacle race for lonely college boys, the temporary steeds of excited children already looking forward to the tea and cookies which would follow their games and races.

These were not the same young men who had played rounders and given jeep rides along the beach at Newcastle when Major Chris Hicks first enlisted Emily's help. Those young men, now trained to bridge gorges, mend tanks, throw up defensive works and support the fighting men had been despatched to North Africa with the Winnipeg Rifles, one more of the many groups to be seen tramping the roads round Banbridge developing stamina between bouts of practice on the rifle ranges and assault courses.

Their departure one chill, misty afternoon had brought Banbridge to a standstill and struck a blow to Emily's good spirits in a month she had always dreaded, the month in which her own mother had died after a long illness, the chill and misty weeks when, year after year, all her bright plans seemed to fade with the dankness of the weather and her energy to ebb away in sympathy with the shrivelling of the daylight hours.

'I'm afraid it's champ again tonight, Alex,' she began apologetically as he came into the kitchen, wisps of cold moisture clinging to his dungarees. 'There was a big tailback when I was in town this afternoon and I couldn't get across the road to go to Quails.'

'And when have I ever objected to your champ?' he replied. 'You can save the coupons like you did for Jane's birthday and we'll have another roast when one of them comes home.'

'It was Chris's regiment, Alex,' she continued. 'Some of the lads spotted me and waved. I didn't see him, but he'd have been up front wouldn't he? So it looks as if he's gone. He always did say he'd not get much warning. He'd be off one day and *Goodbye* would only be a note in the post,' she ended sadly.

'Well, I have *good* news for you.'

'You have?'

'Yes. Chris phoned me this morning. He hasn't gone. He's staying. Top brass think *his contacts on the ground* are so valuable they want him to go on training here,' he explained, raising his eyebrows. 'So his boys have gone, but there'll be a new lot arriving at the end of the week. He's got a few days breather till they land, so he phoned to ask us to come up and dine at the camp tomorrow evening. His new officers are flying in ahead of the boys. Full regalia,' he said, teasing her, as he saw relief and pleasure spread across her face. 'And don't tell me you've nothing to wear.'

'I wouldn't dream of it,' she replied, pretending to be cross. 'If Scarlet O'Hara can make a dress out of the curtains, why can't I?'

'Which curtains had you in mind?'

'Oh Alex, I'm only joking,' she responded with a little laugh. 'I've a perfectly nice dress. I just haven't worn it since . . . oh goodness . . . I can't even think when the last time was. Perhaps it was Cathy's twenty-first. Something like that'

'It *is* good news, Emily,' he said, dropping down wearily on a kitchen chair, as she lifted the lid of the saucepan and gave the champ another stir to keep it from sticking. 'I'd have been as sad as you if he'd gone. He's a good-hearted man and great company and he's taken a weight off *my* shoulders with the repairs he's done for us. I'd have been waiting still for that work on the countershaft if I'd had to *go through official channels*, as the saying is.'

Emily smiled, glad to hear him admit his own feelings for their friend and delighted by the unexpected prospect of a night out.

'Will we take our supper to the fire, Alex?' she asked, seeing the lines of tiredness in his face. 'I lit it a wee while ago and it'll be blazing up nicely by now.'

'Why not?' he replied, standing up and struggling out of his dungarees. 'If we're dining in style tomorrow night, we can have it in a bowl tonight, can't we? Easier than a plate on your knee.'

'What a good idea. I'll heat a couple of bowls. I never thought of that.'

The phone rang just as she was pouring hot water into what Jane always called the 'Daddy Bear' bowls, the biggest ones they had.

'I'll answer that,' he said quickly. 'You serve up,' he added, as he disappeared into the dark hallway.

The champ smelt good as she spooned it into the warm bowls. She had to admit to herself it always did. They had their own scallions from the garden and there was always butter to put in the well at the centre, for Mary Cook had bought a device with a rotary beater which was proving most successful at producing small quantities without the use of a churn.

She laid the tray on the kitchen table, went into the larder to pour glasses of milk and came out just as Alex returned.

'I'm sorry, love. It *is* bad news this time.'

He waited till she put the two glasses of milk safely down on the table with a shaking hand and then went on.

'Ritchie was killed this morning. It was his second solo flight and his plane crashed and went on fire . . .'

It was Alex who put small logs on the dying fire and insisted that she sit there while he reheated their abandoned supper.

'We're entitled to cry, Emily,' he said, his own face pale, his eyes red. 'But we've got to keep going. Both of us. Whatever happens. Now be a good girl and say you will for I can't do it by myself.'

She nodded, knowing that if she spoke, the softness in his voice would bring the tears pouring down again.

She wiped her eyes again after he'd gone, shutting the door behind him because of the cold air gathered in the unheated hall and stairwell. It felt as if she was living in a small, safe space, warm and comfortable, while all around her there was death and darkness and cold and destruction.

One woman weeping by a bright fire and hundreds of thousands of young men lying dead in Stalingrad, Russian and German locked in a desperate struggle for a city. A crucially important strategic point on the Volga to the German generals, yet a place where people once lived and loved and had a life and were now caught up in a devastating battle. How many millions of women would weep in the cold, chill winter days ahead? How many hearts would break for young men like Ritchie, so full of life and energy.

'Stop it, Emily,' she said to herself quickly, as she became aware of small sounds from the kitchen and heard the electric kettle being switched on. 'You must not let yourself think of them. You must not disable yourself with grief.'

Suddenly and totally unexpectedly, she thought of a May evening. Beyond the window, the water of Millbrook's reservoir paper calm, two swans and five fluffy cygnets moving across its perfect surface, marking it with smooth grey lines like a pencil marks on a sheet of paper. Chris Hicks was looking down at her, as if he understood something about her she hardly understood herself.

'Holding the world together for someone, no doubt, as my wife does for me.'

He was right. However good, or clever, or wise, there were things a man had difficulty in doing for himself. But if he had someone to help, someone to hold the world together for him, then his own courage and wisdom would flow and he would return the gift in his own way. Through action, like Chris and Alex, or in other ways she had not thought about. But before they could act, they needed to be given that gift of being held.

She heard the kitchen door close, wiped her eyes again, blew her nose and ran her fingers through her hair. She even managed a small smile as the sitting room door opened and he came back in with a tray.

He had his back to her as he put it down on the low table between them, but when he picked up the coffee pot and moved to set it down on the hearth to keep warm, she saw his face had lost its look of bleak desolation.

'If you eat up your nice supper, I'll pour you a cup of Chris's coffee,' he said, as he sat down opposite her, a Daddy Bear bowl in one hand, a fork in the other.

'Thank you for my supper,' she said, picking up the other bowl which now steamed gently. 'And especially for coffee,' she added. 'And for being honest. You *are* right. We have to keep going. We just have to. But we don't have to pretend it's easy.'

Emily woke early next morning, her eyes flicking open in the completely dark room. She'd hated the darkness when the blackout first went up, for they'd always slept with the curtains drawn back. Even when there was no moon there was usually starlight and however bad the weather, there was always the outline of the window and some pale light reflecting from the mirror of her dressing table, or the pictures on the walls.

In the darkness, she had felt trapped, suffocated. She'd struggled to adjust, but finally, when she could bear it no longer, she'd plugged in a smiling green gnome with a red hat and bright sparks of light for eyes that had once been used for Johnny. After a few weeks, she found she was forgetting to switch on, but she never moved the green gnome from the floor on her side of the bed.

'Ritchie,' she whispered, as she turned on her side and stretched cautiously, unwilling to wake Alex a moment earlier than necessary.

No more Ritchie. No more tramping feet on the stairs as he and Johnny went up to Johnny's bedroom to work on a model aircraft kit they'd bought by saving up their pocket money or their holiday earnings. No more Ritchie eating as if he were half-starved, leaping to his feet with a *thank you* and an offer to wash up, or to carry the laundry baskets to the clothes line. Never again. Gone. Flown away. Beyond the bright blue sky.

At the thought of Heaven, she shivered. There would be a funeral, a service, a eulogy from the local minister. Yards and yards of pious reassurances that the parting was temporary and it was all part of God's plan. Would he tell her Stalingrad was part of God's plan if she asked? No wonder Alex didn't believe any of it. She wasn't sure she'd got much belief left either though she noticed that she'd never stopped praying. Not that she ever got down on her knees by her bed like her mother had taught her to, but often enough over the kitchen sink or the ironing board, she caught herself asking for strength, remembering all her family and naming her friends. Even if it was only to say silently to herself, 'God keep them safe,' she probably prayed most days.

'God help his poor parents and all like them,' she thought, as the strident ring of the alarm clock shattered the silence.

She would have to phone Ritchie's mother, of course, and perhaps visit her. But it would be proper to phone first to see what the arrangements were. And Johnny would have to be told before anyone else in the family.

She offered Alex the one remaining slice of bacon in the larder with a fried egg and soda bread, but to her surprise he said 'no, just tea and toast as usual.' They ate their breakfast in silence, exchanged a few words over ringing Johnny's Training Camp and the timing of their evening engagement. They parted with a brief hug that had something of desperation about it.

It was only half past seven and still pitch dark as she peered out of the kitchen window to pick up the tiny glow of hooded headlights as he drove out of the garage and headed down the avenue. Tuesday, the 10th of November, 1942, it said on the calendar when she turned away from the window and stared at the pattern of squares outlined in black, the numbers blocked solidly in red.

When she finally gathered herself to make the call to Ritchie's home, she found herself speaking to a most unfriendly woman who said shortly that her sister couldn't possibly talk to anyone, the funeral would be private, and besides, she didn't know when it would be. Emily offered the usual condolences, got off the line as quickly as possible and found her hands shaking as she put the phone down.

After that, she was even more uneasy about ringing the Training Camp at Greencastle. Their number had been supplied to parents with strict instructions that it was only to be used in emergencies. It was certainly not available for contacting any of their trainees.

'Greencastle Camp. Please state your business.'

Emily nearly dropped the receiver. The voice, so cold and so distant, sounded positively ethereal. She listened in a kind of trance as the voice, female it seemed, repeated the message exactly as before.

She'd have to do better than this.

'I'd like to speak to my son's Commanding Officer,' she said with a confidence she most certainly did not feel.

'About what, madam?'

'About the death of my son's closest friend in a similar training unit to yours.'

There was a click and silence.

Emily stared into the black mouthpiece and noted the tiny beads of moisture where her warm breath had condensed on the stone-cold plastic. There were radiators in the hall. Hugh Sinton had installed them before the turn of the century when Rathdrum House had been one the first in the district to have central heating. But Hugh had run the radiators from his own gas plant, which burnt coke. There was no coke available for domestic use any more.

She shivered and was about to put the phone down when a voice startled her.

'Good morning, ma'am. Maybridge here. Can I help you?'

'Yes . . . yes, that would be very good of you. My name is Hamilton, my son John is with you.'

'Yes, ma'am.'

'I'm afraid I have bad news for him. His closest friend, Ritchie Johnston, was killed yesterday. His plane crashed on his second solo flight.'

'I take it *you* knew this young man, ma'am?'

'Oh yes. The two were inseparable. He was in and out of our house all the time.'

'Then may I offer you *my* sympathy. This is very hard on you, as much as it may be on John.'

Tears sprang to her eyes once again. The accent

114

was upper class and English, yet shot through with a gentle warmth which she found it hard to believe. Johnny and Ritchie would have made fun of it, of course.

'*What ho, Caruthers. I say this is a bad show, old boy.*'

'*Damned natives. Can't trust one of 'em. Must have got into the Clubroom again. Taken the glue, by Jove. Can't fix the jolly old fuselage if there's no glue.*'

She could hear them and see them. She'd laughed at them and got on with her work. And now an unknown man with a Caruthers accent was saying he was sorry for her distress and meaning it.

'I wondered about telling my son the news,' she continued. 'And there is the question of the funeral.'

'Yes, I understand and I'm glad you've rung me. I shall tell John myself and I will arrange for him to phone you this afternoon between 4pm and 5pm,' he went on briskly. 'I'm afraid for practical reasons he will only be allowed six minutes. Sadly, we cannot give him leave to attend a funeral other than one involving his immediate family. We are not unsympathetic, but there are questions of morale involved. I'm sure you understand.'

'Yes, I do. We all have to keep spirits up. Low moral costs lives just as much as careless talk,' she said quickly, without considering at all what she had said.

The response was immediate and heartfelt.

'You are so right, Mrs Hamilton. I wish more parents could understand that.'

There was a sort pause and Emily was wondering if she should say 'Thank you' and ring off, when he cleared his throat and spoke again.

'Mrs Hamilton, I can give you no word of comfort for the death of John's friend, but I *can* say to you that your son is one of the best potential pilots we have here. That doesn't mean he will come home safe at the end of this show, but it does mean his chances are higher. I've seldom seen a young man so at home in a plane.'

As Emily and Alex walked up a broad, carpeted stairway and into the Officer's Mess of Chris's small training regiment, Emily was sure the room must have been the original dining room.

They both knew the handsome, linen merchant's house requisitioned at the beginning of the war, but although neither of them had ever been inside it before, it seemed to them both as if it had remained much as it had always been despite its new inhabitants.

A huge marble fireplace with a most welcoming wood fire was overhung by an enormous portrait of a fierce-looking man with a hooked nose. The furniture was heavy, but much of the light provided came from old oil lamps, carefully converted to electricity. Through misted glass mantles and delicately engraved globes it spread softly on mahogany and rosewood, drawing out its warmth and colour.

'Now then, Emily and Alex, I want you to meet my new team,' Chris said, as five young men waiting by the fireplace came to attention, saluted and then, at a single glance from Chris, relaxed and shook hands. 'They flew in yesterday and we have till the end of the week to prepare for our boys arriving by sea. We've been busy,' he added wryly, with a warm smile.

There was some laughter and Emily guessed that getting the hang of the camp and how it functioned, visiting the assault course and the workshops would have made a pretty busy day for young men just arrived after such a long flight.

'So this is a Welcome Dinner for them and a Thank You for you two, for all you do to help us, and a chance for you all to meet each other.'

'Now Lieutenants, a word in your ear,' he said easily. 'Your little grey book with instructions for 'dealing with the natives' may not prove helpful with our guests tonight. They are *rather* special. To begin with, they've been educating *me* for some months. I no longer put my foot in it by asking for the washroom when I do not desperately need to wash my hands, but I do have a desperate need. Neither do I ask, as I once did, to see their 'backyard' when what I meant was Mrs Hamilton's garden.'

The young men laughed and Emily observed how easily Chris had made them all feel at home. No wonder top brass, whoever they were, had decided to keep him here at Castlewellan Road Camp and move new parties of engineers through, rather than sending him off with the young men he had already prepared for the front.

Behind them, the dining table was laid for eight, a beautiful candelabra at its centre, but before they made any move towards it, a waiter appeared with a tray of drinks.

Chris beamed as they were handed round.

'Lady and gentlemen,' he began, with a little bow to Emily, 'I have some good news for you. It is no longer classified. A certain gentleman by the name of Eisenhower has landed in North Africa and has taken the surrender of French troops in Casablanca, Oran and Algiers. Operation Torch has got off to a very good start.'

Emily and Alex exchanged glances as they touched their glasses and they drank to the continuing success of the campaign in North Africa.

It was then that Chris made the introductions, beginning with Emily herself.

'This good lady is Mrs Emily Hamilton,' he said easily. 'She is one lady I will take orders from and you will *all* do the same,' he added softly. 'She may not wear stripes, but I assure you she always knows exactly what she is doing.'

Before Emily even had time to blush, he had moved on.

'My good friend, Alex Hamilton, appears to know everyone in this area, not just the hundreds of people who work in the Bann Valley Mills where he is Technical Director. Thanks to Alex, you may well be given work for your team in one of the mills, but whatever chance you get, in any project outside the camp, *ask for his advice*. He came here as a stranger, just like you have, but as a result he knows people here better than they know themselves.'

Watching Alex's face, as he registered what Chris had said, it was all Emily could do to concentrate on the names of the young men who had listened with such close attention. She wasn't sure she'd be able to remember all five first time, but what she would not forget was where they came from. Could she ever have imagined that one day she might stand in the same room with dinner guests from Vermont, California, Kansas, Michigan, New York State and Boston.

The meal was superb, the conversation both interesting and relaxed. Emily was intrigued to see that, although Chris was the senior officer and was addressed by them all as Sir, there was no deference. They were completely at ease with him and with each other as they each declared for the benefit of the others what they thought of their own state, or city, or town, or village. Their stories were a delight, both shrewd and humorous. They answered her questions with a directness that surprised her.

She was amused to be called ma'am and eventually asked if that wasn't what one had called Queen Victoria.

'Slightly before my time,' said Chris. 'Though in the eyes of these youngsters, I probably predate Christopher Columbus.'

'Perhaps Lewis and Clarke, sir,' suggested the one from Boston, who struck Emily as having a Canadian accent.

'Thaaaa-nk you, Hank,' said Chris, turning to Emily. 'He's just paid me a compliment,' he explained. 'Lewis and Clarke are a couple of centuries later than Columbus, but still a helluva long time ago,' he said amid the general laughter.

'I should also explain, Emily, that this character sitting opposite you may have been named Alexander Lachlan Ross, as I've told you, but it appears he answers to Hank the Tank. No doubt there are other such names here present, yet to be declared, but that one got as far as the official record on my desk. Has to be a compliment, Hank,' said Chris, nodding to him. 'Pity you have stenters and not tank tracks, Alex,' Chris added.

Hank blushed slightly and looked pleased. Emily smiled across at him and caught an answering smile in his bright blue eyes. A lightly built man, his blonde hair cropped in a regulation cut, he was the one from Boston, the one who seemed somehow familiar though she couldn't think why. Maybe it was just the Canadian accent. At least, she thought it was Canadian. It might well be. One thing she had found out this evening about North Americans was that no one ever stayed where they didn't want to be. They just moved on.

CHAPTER SEVEN

In the weeks that followed Emily and Alex's evening visit to Chris and his lieutenants, suddenly it did seem as if hope had been rekindled. Spirits lifted as each news broadcast reported the German army in North Africa being driven back yet further as Operation Torch proceeded. Then came the news of General Montgomery's resounding defeat of the Afrika Corps at El Alamein and the Eighth Army's hot pursuit of the enemy, now in full retreat.

In all this heart-lifting activity, local regiments had played their part, along with the Americans and Canadians everyone in Banbridge had befriended.

December proceeded, wet and sunless, but the many thanksgiving services that followed the victories were well attended and the feelings of both relief and hope were very obvious. Alex reported a better atmosphere in the mills. He said Christmas decorations had suddenly appeared in unexpected places, draped from rafters and wound round pillars. He had asked the managers to make sure they were firmly attached if they were suspended anywhere near moving parts of machinery, but he told them on no account to have them taken down.

Try as they might, Emily and Alex found it hard to share in the general rejoicing. In the middle of November, Cathy had written to say she could now tell them that Brian had been moved to London, to the School of Tropical Medicine. She had told them the previous year that he was working on a new preparation for the treatment of serious infection, but neither of them had any idea then that the work would suddenly be moved forward with such urgency.

He'd been given a bare week's notice to move to London. With a class of forty in a one-teacher village school, there was no possibility of Cathy's going with him, though she said she'd be able to join him in his lodgings for the Christmas holidays.

Emily was torn between wishing Cathy could stay in the relative safety of Cheshire and hoping that Brian would be able to find them somewhere to live as that was clearly what Cathy wanted. Uneasy about the feel of Cathy's letters, Emily arranged to ring her on the school telephone in the lunch hour or if she wasn't free then, after school.

Calls to Cheshire were often unavailable, even more liable to be cut off than those to the capital itself, but Emily persisted. When she did manage to get through, she was quite sure that something was badly wrong. There was a tone of anxiety in her daughter's voice that had not been there before, not even when she and Brian had lived for a time in Manchester itself and had been driven regularly to the air-raid shelters.

Cathy had never been one to share her troubles, however, even though her mother had always encouraged her to talk about what made her anxious, so Emily was left to wonder whether it was a problem between her and Brian, the burden of coping with so many children and only an untrained, part-timer to help her, or some fear she couldn't speak about, because she herself couldn't even recognise it.

When a quick scribbled note from Lizzie arrived saying she had a 48 hour pass for the first weekend in December, Emily breathed a sigh of relief. With only eighteen months between them, Cathy and Lizzie had always been close to each other. Their closeness had increased after Jane was born, for though Jane was the most good-natured of children she never asked her older sisters to play with her.

She was always perfectly happy to be by herself, talking to an imaginary friend, or singing to herself as she moved objects around. Toys, or clothes pegs, or scraps of left-over dough which she made into small figures, it was all the same to Jane, as she created stories for them and acted them out. She loved flowers, arranged daisies, dandelions and leaves in jam pots and lined them up on whatever windowsills she could reach. And as soon as Johnny could walk he attached himself to her. He'd seek her out, watch what she was doing, then sit down smiling and simply wait for her to amuse him.

Jane had always loved looking after him, and didn't mind a bit when, in due course, he went off to play with other little boys. Even when he went to Banbridge Academy and made lots of friends, Ritchie especially, he still came looking for her the very moment he came home, to tell her what he'd been doing or who he'd been with.

To Emily's surprise Lizzie arrived the following Saturday morning, on foot and in uniform. She looked exhausted.

'Oh love, you do look tired. Did no one give you a lift?'

'No cars, Ma,' she responded, as she parked her small suitcase on the floor, dropped down on a kitchen chair and took out a packet of cigarettes. 'But I wanted to walk anyway,' she went on quickly. 'I haven't seen the light of day for weeks. D'you mind me smoking in your kitchen?' she asked abruptly, as she was about to strike a match.

'No, no,' replied Emily, flustered.

She didn't know Lizzie had started to smoke, but she supposed it was the stress of the long hours on duty. As she watched the practised way she lit up and inhaled deeply, she also noticed the tone of her skin and hair. Though not as perfect as Jane, both the elder girls had good skin, the tone warmer as with anyone dark-haired. Cathy and Lizzie had both had masses of dark curls as children but Lizzie now wore her hair so short few curls survived. Although it *was* so short, normally it still shone and had a spring in it, but today it was dull and lifeless. As she looked down at her through the haze of cigarette smoke, all Emily could think of was the Before and After pictures in those shampoo advertisements one saw in the newspaper.

'Extra duty?' Emily asked casually, as she made tea and reached for the cake tin.

'Training course. Endurance was part of it. If you've got a complex situation, you can't just hand over. You may have to keep going regardless,' she said, turning her head to blow smoke away from her mother. 'Got a stripe though,' she added. 'Thought I might ask you to sew it on. Always lousy at sewing.'

Emily smiled and offered congratulations as enthusiastically as she could manage, but she felt little joy. However successful Lizzie had been, there was something different in her whole manner and in the abruptness of her comments and replies, that worried her.

She did indeed seem pleased by whatever it was she'd done that had gained her a stripe, but there was a withdrawnness about her that was quite

126

new and made Emily feel she had put up a fence round herself. One might approach and look over to see what one might see, but entry was forbidden, even to her. Like Chris's camp, unless you had your authorised pass, there was no possibility whatever of getting beyond the guards.

'Heard from Cathy lately, Ma?' she asked, as Emily put mugs of tea on the kitchen table and offered cake.

'Yes. I finally managed to get a call through on the school phone on Wednesday. She can't answer it unless her helper is there. They only have it in case of an emergency with a child and they need to ring out. Mostly it just rings and rings when there's no one but Cathy to answer it.'

'But you persisted?'

Emily nodded and drank thirstily. She noticed that Lizzie had ignored the cake, so she put it back in the tin.

'How was she?'

'I was going to ask you that,' Emily replied. 'I wasn't very happy about the way she sounded. I hoped maybe you'd know more.'

'She thinks she's pregnant,' she replied, drawing vigorously on her cigarette. ' It was an accident, but she blames herself and Brian is worried silly about having to leave her behind in Cheshire.'

Emily took a deep breath and told herself it could be worse. At least it wasn't another

127

marriage breaking up under the strain of war.

'But surely if she's pregnant she can't go on teaching, so she can go with him,' she said, thinking of the local country schools she knew. 'I know teachers are short, but surely no one is allowed to go on teaching once it becomes the slightest bit obvious.'

'Might be different in England, Ma. Pregnancy is a form of sinfulness in this province,' Lizzie replied, as she stepped over to the sink and stubbed out her cigarette butt fiercely on a metal soap dish.

Emily watched in silence as she ran the dish under the tap and followed the course of the butt disintegrating under the flood of water which swirled the fragments down the drain.

'No use worrying, Ma,' she said with a brief smile. 'She'll end up in London with Brian sooner or later and then I'll be able to go and see her.'

For one happy moment, Emily simply thought how good it would be for the sisters to be together again. Then the implications of what Lizzie had just said dawned upon her.

'How come, Lizzie?'

'Posting. Probably south coast to begin with, but Air Ministry later. Official Secrets and all that. But it's even better than what I'd wanted when they kept me here in Belfast.'

'When are you going?'

Emily heard herself ask the question as if it

were a polite enquiry about a perfectly normal arrangement, as if Lizzie were off to see a friend or merely taking a day in town to do some shopping.

'Sometime on Monday afternoon. As soon as I get back to base, depending on flights.'

Emily was almost grateful when Lizzie explained that she was very short of sleep and needed to catch up. Even apart from the Official Secrets Act, which meant she couldn't talk about her work, it seemed to Emily in the hour they'd spent together that she was very reluctant to talk about anything very much at all.

Emily had tried to share her own activities, organising Sunday visits to families for Chris's boys and indoor picnics, when they could meet and play games with local primary school children. She spoke of their friends and their neighbours who'd once been such a part of Lizzie's life and told her about some recent local events. To all of this, Lizzie listened politely, but made no response.

Late on Saturday afternoon, Lizzie was still in bed when Alex arrived home to find Emily puzzled and concerned. She told him what she'd observed and suggested he might do better at conversation than she had. She went as far as to remind him of the story Jamie Macpherson had told him about his own daughter, an old school friend of Lizzie's.

'Oh yes, Olive,' said Lizzie indifferently, as they

settled by the fire on Saturday evening after supper, a pot of coffee in the hearth. 'She joined the Land Army, didn't she? Wanted to get away from that awful mother of hers, I expect. Where did she end up?'

Emily saw Alex's eyes widen as the cigarettes came out, but he had promised not to say a word.

'Well, I knew it was Gloucestershire somewhere,' Alex began, ' but when I met Olive's father shortly after she went, he told me it was one of those stately homes the Ministry of Defence took over as a centre for injured Airmen. It seems they specialised in treating burns and doing plastic surgery.'

He took his coffee from Emily and settled back in his chair.

'Well, you probably won't remember your Aunt Sarah, Lizzie. She used to come and visit us before she and her husband were posted to Germany with a trade mission. Sarah had an older sister, Hannah, who married the son of Lord Harrington who'd inherited this huge mansion in Gloucestershire called Ashley Park . . .'

Emily watched Lizzie as she inhaled and then flicked her ash into the saucer she'd provided for herself.

'Apparently Olive and her colleagues were drafted in to grow vegetables in the parterres of this place. When the old gardener who'd stayed on to help run things heard Olive speak, he spotted the accent right away and said his Lady Hannah was from Ireland too, just like she was.'

'Well, of course, the mansion was Ashley Park. Lady Hannah was brought up at Ballydown as you know, only half a mile away from your friend Olive at Lisnaree.'

Lizzie made no response at all. For a moment, she just looked into the fire, then she took a long pull at her cigarette and looked from one to the other.

'The war does throw up some strange coincidences,' said Lizzie slowly. 'Sometimes it's hard to believe just how differently people behave. I must say I never thought a sister of mine would apply for a transfer to a military hospital to be able to look after a German spy.'

Emily sat stunned, her coffee going cold as she heard Alex ask Lizzie quietly what she meant. She registered the replies and the interchange which followed but what she was seeing was Jane's face, Jane smiling at her as she arrived for her first weekend break almost six weeks after her interrupted birthday lunch.

She'd written quite openly about what had happened between her and Johann. Now she sat down at the kitchen table, curled her hands round a large mug of tea and told her the whole story.

'Ma, Johann has asked me to marry him,' she said, her eyes shining, her face radiant.

Emily opened her mouth to speak, but Jane jumped in and began to reassure her.

'Oh, Ma, we know it will be ages and we know it's going to be difficult, but as long as we know we're going to be together we can manage. Lots of couples are parted in wartime and most of them are in danger, far more danger than we are.'

Emily laughed.

'That wasn't what I was going to say,' she said, shaking her head.

'Sorry, Ma,' she apologised. 'I should have known you wouldn't say I was too young, or he was German, or any of the things other people might say. What *were* you going to say?'

'I was just going to ask how Johann managed to propose, given how little English he has.'

Jane clapped her hand to her mouth and laughed happily.

'Ma, I couldn't believe it either,' she began. 'You remember he wasn't on my ward at Musgrave, don't you? Well, it took about a week before I was able to visit him after work, though I had been able to send him some little messages with one of the male nurses I knew from the Royal . . .'

She paused, took a large mouthful of tea and broke a small corner from her cake before she went on.

'I walked into the ward and found him sitting in the bedside chair, the leg sticking straight out in front of him and the bed covered with books and pieces of paper. And, do you know what he said?'

Emily waited patiently.

'*I am so pleased to see you, Jane. I have been employed. But I have some operational difficulties. I hope you will assist me.*'

Emily laughed, as much at Jane's face as at Johann's English, but she felt her heart lift as she recognised that Jane had found the man she wanted and whatever the difficulties, she would master them. The language problem might well be one of the easiest.

Indeed, after that unexpected gift of four weeks under the same roof, it had not been easy. Johann was moved to a camp at Dungannon, some fifty miles away, a slow bus journey up through County Armagh and into Tyrone with a long walk to the camp at the other end. It had taken weeks of negotiation between the Red Cross and the Camp Commandant to get permission for a monthly visit. Their letters were limited to one a week and had to pass through the censor.

What had been a delight to Emily was to see how happy her daughter was and how the obvious difficulties of the situation seemed to melt before her. Jane's letters were often brief and hasty, but she told her how she was contacting anyone she thought might be able to help Johann. It was no surprise to her at all when late in the summer Jane reported that an elderly solicitor had taken on the task of considering a plea of 'political asylum' for Johann and had said he would be pleased to explore the situation for his own interest and would therefore not be requiring the customary fee.

Johann had played his part. His command of English had proceeded by leaps and bounds and he was now able to help other prisoners as well as the staff with whom he got on very well. As his leg healed and he was able to join the work parties, he made friends with local people and discovered great pleasure in the work of creating a new park, planting trees and shrubs, which one day in the future would be complemented by herbaceous borders. The spaces for flower beds had been laid out, their curving shapes a part of the whole plan, though for the present they were filled with vegetables.

'Well that's a matter of opinion, isn't it? As far as I'm concerned, the enemy is the enemy, and that's that. There's no such thing as a good German.'

Emily heard the sharp edge to her tone, which Lizzie made no attempt to conceal. Her heart sank, for she knew that tone of old and it always meant the same thing, that Lizzie had made up her mind and would not be persuaded to change it.

It was the bitterness that upset Emily most. She just couldn't understand what had changed in Lizzie, so that the facts of the case had no bearing at all upon her response, when she had been the one who was always so coolly logical. Lizzie wasn't listening to a word of what her father was telling her about Johann. Or perhaps she *was*, but refusing to give them any weight.

Alex pointed out that Jane's transfer to Musgrave Park had been mentioned on the day of her birthday, though possibly she'd had not been able to tell them till after Lizzie left. Jane hadn't known then whether it would happen or not.

Besides, no one that day had any idea what would happen to the young airman. If he hadn't had a broken leg, he would almost certainly have been sent straight to a Prisoner-of-War camp, so there was no question of Jane planning a move to Musgrave to be with him. As for his being a spy, common sense suggested he'd hardly have been picked for the job if he couldn't do better than run out of petrol and risk killing himself in a crash landing.

If that wasn't enough evidence for her, what about the grillings he'd had from Army Intelligence? Surely, if they were satisfied after their rigorous interrogations that should be enough for her.

But there was no talking to her. She had found out from a friend at Musgrave that Jane and Johann had spent every possible moment together while he was there and that she was still running up and down to Dungannon to see him. He had her on a string and God knows what information he was getting out of her.

Tears of weary frustration rolled down Emily's cheeks as she and Alex got ready for bed.

'I'm sorry, love, I'm not making much of a job of this,' she said, as she threw back the bed clothes on her own side and lay down, exhausted.

He put his arm round her and drew her close.

'We've done our best for *all* of them,' he said patiently. 'If something goes wrong in *their* life and they don't face up to it and don't want to share it with us, there is *nothing we can do*. At least she's still alive. Not like Ritchie. She may come back to us when she sorts it out, whatever it is. We can only live in hope, as the saying is.'

Lizzie left with Alex on Monday morning so she could have a lift to the station and Emily began baking as soon as she'd gone. It wasn't that she was behind with her schedule for the visits and picnics, she just badly needed to keep busy.

When she was agitated, she couldn't possibly settle to read, or sew and ironing or housework gave her too much time to think. Only the more vigorous or more demanding activity of gardening or baking, would serve.

The thought of the garden, bleak and chill under a grey sky was too much for her, though there were still pea rows to clear out and compost that needed turning, so she took out the baking tins and worked her way steadily through her now practised routine.

Together with her four friends, they turned out large quantities of fruit bread, cake and a variety of small cakes, including brownies, each week. All the ingredients were supplied by deliveries from the camp and at Chris's insistence, each woman kept at least one item for her own family's Sunday tea.

When no reward had been expected or asked for, they had all appreciated the kind thought. What they certainly had not expected, but received most gratefully when they suddenly arrived, were the food parcels delivered to each woman in turn. Packed by American supporters in Vermont, even Chris didn't know what might turn up in a box, or what women in Vermont might think most useful to their counterparts in wartime Britain.

Mary Cook had received a bottle of perfume in among the more obvious offerings of cigarettes, coffee and chocolate. Dolly Love and Freda Wilson had found silk stockings, now almost unobtainable, in one of theirs. Emily had been surprised by a box of paper tissues, something she'd never seen before. She'd smiled at the perky little cartoon figure on the cardboard box and wondered if they were intended for use as handkerchiefs. If they were, how did you carry them round with you?

Her most recent parcel had contained knitting wool and crystallised fruit. Apples and pears and greengages packed in pink tissue and silver paper. She'd never seen a greengage before and she and

Alex shared one by the fire one wet, cold evening out of pure curiosity. It didn't taste of much except sugar, but they thought of ripening fruit and some kind person far away and agreed she'd put the rest away for the young people at Christmas.

The wool was a delight. 'Delphinium Blue' it said on the label. Perfect for blue-eyed Jane, or Johnny. Alex helped her to wind it into balls, so she could work out how much wool there was in the huge American skeins. She didn't think it would stretch to a jumper each but she might manage two of these new v-necked sleeveless pullovers that were so popular.

By four o'clock the house was full of the comforting, warm smell of the morning's baking and the kitchen had been returned to its clean and well-ordered state. When the phone rang in the hall, the short winter day had already ended, though she hadn't yet taken time to go round and draw the curtains and check the blackout.

Reluctant to switch on a light, she groped her way in darkness to the invisible source of sound, felt its cold shape and picked up the receiver.

'Hi, Ma, it's John.'

'Hello love. How lovely to hear you. We got your letter. When are you arriving?'

'That's why I'm ringing, Ma. I'm afraid leave's cancelled. We've all got three minutes to phone home, but I won't be able to write for a while.'

'You mean you've been posted?'

'Oh yes.'

'But when? Where?'

'This morning, Ma. We had our shots?'

'What shots?' she asked, totally bewildered.

'Inoculations,' he said, lowering his voice, as noise in the background made it even harder to hear.

'Ma, I must go before the pips or I'll get cut off,' he said urgently. 'Give my love to Da and the girls. And lots for you. Don't worry, it may never happen, as the saying . . . .'

She heard the pips and the phone went dead.

That, at least, she could understand. If the whole squadron had to phone their parents, of course it had to be brief. She thought of the six minutes they'd had when Ritchie died and found she was shivering with cold and shock.

She went back into the kitchen, the only warm place in the house, pressed her icy hands against the oven door and found that it was already stone cold.

She knew she was going to cry, there was no point pretending she wasn't, so she pulled out a chair from under the kitchen table, put her head in her hands and let the tears come.

'Middle East, I'd say,' Alex commented crisply, when she'd told him about the phone call.

'What makes you think that?' she asked, startled.

Alex smiled wryly.

'He said 'inoculations'. He was trying to tell you

139

they were going overseas. Could be Egypt. Certainly, North Africa. With the Germans in retreat, the Eighth Army will need all the air support they can get to keep them on the run.'

'It never occurred to me we wouldn't see him before he went.'

'It's something we have to get used to. Remember the day you thought Chris had gone.'

She smiled, remembering how upset she had been and how grateful she was when Alex told her he was staying. Then she remembered the call that same evening to tell them about Ritchie.

'What's wrong, love?' he said looking at her closely.

'Sorry. My mind moved on. I thought about Ritchie.'

'And why wouldn't you? I'd be telling you a lie if I pretended I didn't think about Ritchie at some time, most days. Usually when I'm thinking about Johnny.'

She put her arms round him, hugged him briefly, and laughed.

'Don't take it personally, but something smells awful,' she said stepping backwards.

To her great delight, he laughed. A small laugh, but a real one.

'Clean ones tomorrow?' he asked, looking down at the smears of oil.

'Definitely.'

* * *

'Poor old, Jane,' Emily said, as she decorated the small tree they dug up from the garden every year.

'Why so?' he asked, looking up from *The Leader*.

'Well, she'll be all on her own. Just you and me. Not even any of her friends from school we could ask over for tea.'

'It won't bother Jane,' he replied easily. 'Not many families will be able to get together this year. Even if they're free to meet, there's no petrol,' he went on. 'I can barely manage the job on what I'm allowed even adding in my so-called "personal" allowance.'

'I wonder what it'll be like in Egypt.'

'Warmer, I would think,' he replied absently, folding up the paper. 'Do you want me to put up the fairy on the top?'

'Yes, please.'

As she unwrapped the tissue and took out the blonde doll, its satin dress trimmed with tinsel, its hair crowned with glass jewels, she heard the phone in the hall.

'I'm nearly afraid to answer that,' she said honestly.

'I'll go.'

She sat down, smoothed out the blonde hair and straightened the wand that got bent every year, no matter how carefully she packed it.

She seemed to be waiting for a long time, though Alex's distant voice sounded perfectly steady and there were no horribly long pauses.

'Jane,' he said, striding into the room. 'She's fine,' he said quickly even before she could ask. 'She's been given an extra pass for Christmas week to see Johann, but her own leave is cancelled. They've opened two new wards and are bringing over seriously wounded from the south of England. She'll get an afternoon to go and see Johann but that's the height of it. I told her you wouldn't mind at all. Was that all right?'

Emily laughed.

'Yes. You were *quite* right. I'm so glad about the pass.'

'There'll be other Christmases,' said Alex reassuringly.

'Yes, there will. But we mustn't waste this one.'

'No, we'll not do that. There's maybe someone on their own that we don't know about. You could ask Mary Cook. She'd know,' he added wryly, for Mary Cook knew everything.

'Good idea. That's just what we'll do,' she said nodding, as she handed him the Christmas fairy, newly smoothed and straightened.

CHAPTER EIGHT

If there was any sun at all, as there was this bright February morning, the lawn still white with frosted spikes, but the sky a perfect blue, then the warmest place in the whole house was the conservatory, the glass-roofed extension to the kitchen, the joy of every woman Emily had ever known live in Rathdrum.

Even without lighting the tiny oil burning bowl-fire which Alex had made to keep the temperature just above freezing point on very cold nights, it was often warm enough on a sunny winter morning to sit with a rug round one's knees and write letters, provided you got up and kept busy in between.

This morning, the last Monday of the short month, Emily collected up her materials from the bureau in the dim, shadowy sitting room, walked back through the bright, cold kitchen and stepped gratefully into the scent of geranium leaves lying on the sun-warmed air.

All around her, their vibrant blooms stretched up and above the canopy of their rich green leaves. She smiled as she wound the rug round her knees, sat down, and immediately thought of the day, years and years ago, when Rose Hamilton had brought her in from the kitchen, presented her with a sharp knife and shown her how to take cuttings, so that a favourite plant would never grow old and die.

Looking round, she was sure some of these plants were descendants of those very cuttings. The bright red and the purple most certainly were, for it was those colours she herself had first carried away to tend on a windowsill in the kitchen of her uncle's farm at the foot of the hill.

Rose would be pleased to see how prolific these plants were and delighted by the new shades and varieties she herself had added over the years. There was now a tradition that Rathdrum had to have its collection maintained and developed. Alex had no skill whatever as a gardener, but even he had once brought a carefully-wrapped addition back from a machine-buying visit to Manchester. He'd seen it in a flower shop, noted its variegated leaf, and bought it because he was sure there wasn't one like it at Rathdrum.

Sarah Hadleigh had come to gardening late and always insisted she had no talent for it, till she was left alone in the house after Hugh died and discovered the comfort growing things could bring. Whenever she'd visited before the war, she'd always brought a cutting or two. Not many conservatories could boast blooms whose originals came from Paris, Berlin or Leningrad.

Emily sighed and looked around again, reluctant to begin. At least there *was* some good news. The Germans had finally surrendered at Stalingrad and Chris Hicks had told them there had been big American victories at sea in the South Pacific. Of course, it mattered terribly. Without battles on land and sea and bombing raids to knock out German industry, the war could not be won, but sitting here on a quiet Monday morning faced with the letters she needed to write, she found no help in any of these world-changing events.

'Come on, Emily. There's no use putting it off,' she said aloud.

She inscribed the address, added the date, 22nd, February, 1943 and began.

My dear Cathy,
I'm so sorry you and Brian have been having such a worrying and unhappy time. A miscarriage, however well handled by midwife or doctors, is still a very upsetting event.

Yes, I did miscarry twice before you were born, but I had the great advantage of having your Granny Rose to help me at the time and afterwards. She herself had miscarried twice, the second time at quite an advanced stage. It meant that the third time she was expecting both she and Granda Hamilton were very anxious indeed.

What she told me and what I've now found out from many other women that I've met or read about is that an initial miscarriage is very common. Doctors don't tell women that because they think it would upset them, but I think they are quite wrong. Richard Stewart has always insisted that an initial miscarriage is nature's way of correcting a mistake, and most women who have miscarried, once, twice, or even three times, will go on and have a perfectly normal birth subsequently.

I think you would be very wise to wait as you had planned till the war is over, but please don't be anxious that this upset is other than an upset. Do try to put it behind you.

It must be very trying indeed living in digs with so little privacy. There is nothing worse than not being able to get a proper night's sleep. Bad enough if there is a raid or even a false alarm, but to be kept awake by other people's inconsiderate noise-making is just dreadful.

That may well be why you are feeling so low. I know I am a real cross patch if I can't get my sleep. Quiet is never a problem here as you well know, but I often find myself unable to get to sleep at times and I certainly suffer for it the next day.

I'm so glad you've joined the WVS. You will meet all sorts of very different women in that organisation, so I'm told. Hopefully you will make some friends. It is hard for you as you say to keep up friendships with everyone moving around all the time but at least the WVS don't get posted.

Yes, I have had a letter from Johnny, very lively and happy, but I've not had anything from Lizzie since Christmas except a short note saying how busy she has been. The postmark had been obliterated by the censor, but I take it she is nearer to you than to us.

I'd be very grateful to have news of her if you can tell us anything without breaking confidence. As I've already told you, she seems quite incensed by Jane's newfound happiness. I can't give you details in a letter, but your father and I are quite satisfied that Jane knows what she is doing and there is no objection to her choice in the longer term.

What can be upsetting Lizzie so much?

Now, my dear, my legs are getting cold despite the rug. I am in the conservatory and the sun is bright, but I've been sitting too long.

Do take care of yourself and Brian and write when you can.

Your father is well, if overworked, and sends his love with mine.

She re-read the letter, added her signature with hugs and kisses and thought of her daughter in a gloomy bed-sitter backing on to the railway line out of Euston.

No wonder she was feeling depressed and lonely. But there wasn't much one could do to help. The trouble was that the more down you were and the less you felt like making an effort, the more that was precisely what you needed to do.

Cathy was not lazy, but she did expect things to go right for her, while in the same situation Lizzie would be busy working out exactly what she was going to do and Jane would already be setting off, following her intuitions, which almost always led her in the right direction.

She wondered what she would say about Johnny if she were adding him to that perspective on his sisters. Over the last months, he had surprised her so many times. Even over Ritchie's death he had not reacted as she might have expected.

It wasn't that he was unmoved. On his one brief visit home mid-way through training, he'd said he never expected to have a friend again that would be so close and so utterly reliable. But he had also said that Ritchie 'knew the score'. They had both known that the accident rate in pilot training was very high and that neither of them might actually make it to the frontline. But that was just the way it was.

Emily tried to think how she'd felt about death when she was eighteen, but nothing of any value came to her. Even though her mother had been in her thirties when she'd died and her father not much older when he was drowned, their deaths had still seemed to her utterly remote, something she could make no real relationship to at eighteen.

The most vigorous job she could think off was brushing the stair carpet with a stiff brush to raise the pile, clearing up the mess with a dustpan and a soft brush as she descended and wiping the parts of the treads not covered by the carpet with a damp duster. The vacuum cleaner Alex had bought for them just before the war did a good job lifting crumbs and fluff on the sitting room and bedroom carpets and the rugs on the woodblock floor in the hall, but it was useless on stairs and it did nothing for trampled pile. Sometimes the old-fashioned methods did work rather better however uncomfortable they might be.

She was half-way down the stairs and was just beginning to cough because of the dust and fluff, when she heard the Austin sweep down the avenue and round to the back door.

'Any chance of a pot of tea?' Alex enquired brightly.

Rather too brightly, she thought, as she reached for the electric kettle, her pleasure at seeing him off-set by her immediate feeling that all was not well.

'Have you had your sandwiches?'

'No, not yet,' he replied, producing his lunch box from under his arm, 'I thought you might be having one yourself.'

'Hadn't got to it yet, but I can make mine while the kettle boils.'

She broke off.

'Alex, what's wrong?' she asked abruptly. 'I can see you're all right and that helps, but *something* is wrong.'

He nodded. Tight-lipped.

'Could be worse,' he admitted, as he watched her add slivers of cheese to buttered bread, press the slices together and cut the result into neat triangles.

He stepped into the conservatory, sniffed the air, and lit the paraffin stove kept there for heating the hall when the house began to feel damp as well as chill.

'You haven't been down for the milk, have you?' he asked quietly, as they sat down together.

'No, but I've got plenty of milk from yesterday if you'd like some.'

'Tea's fine. I just wanted to be sure you hadn't been talking to Mary Cook.'

She put down the sandwich she'd just picked up and looked at him sharply.

'Alex, will you just *tell me* what's wrong before we go any further.'

'There were a series of bombs at Millbrook,' he began. 'One went off in the engine house and caused a fire. Two were placed in the main work areas. Two more were placed under the main staircases and timed to go off five minutes after the others when people were trying to get out. No amateur job like Ballievy.'

'Alex,' she exclaimed. 'What happened? Were many hurt? Don't tell me anyone was killed.'

'We were lucky,' he said reassuringly. 'We could have lost quite a few, including Robert Anderson, if he hadn't been so sharp. He went into the engine house on a routine check and saw something on the floor. It was only a tiny, wee scrap of paper, but it shouldn't have been there. He was sure that floor was spotless at the end of maintenance last evening and none of the night watchmen would have dropped anything on their inspections. When he listened he could hear something too. He ran over to my office and we phoned the police and the army bomb disposal. But the engine-house went up while we were phoning.

'Oh Alex,' she gasped, catching a hand to her mouth. 'What did you do then?'

'Got everybody out of the mill. That went very well. Broke our own best record,' he added with a little smile. 'Everybody thought it was the usual fire-drill till they got outside and smelt the smoke and heard our fire-engine coming round from the back. Then the police and army arrived and went all over the building.'

'But they could have been killed too,' she protested.

'They could, but that's their job and they did seem to know what they were looking for and where to look. They found all four *devices*, as they call them, and made them safe. In fact, there is some good news. They think they know who's behind it. But that is absolutely confidential,' he warned, raising his eyebrows. 'Apparently, if you're an expert in this sort of thing you can tell by the way a device is made who actually made it. They even questioned Robert in detail about that wee bit of paper and said he'd been a great help.'

'Is Robert all right?'

'Right as rain, as the saying is.'

'Maybe it hasn't hit him yet,' she said thoughtfully. 'If he'd gone in there a bit later he'd have been killed and you might not have know it was a bomb, so you wouldn't have cleared the mill . . .'

'Now, Emily, don't think what *might* have happened,' he said, pausing to demolish a sandwich. 'Just be grateful for good people like Robert,' he went on, reaching for his mug of tea. 'He deserves a medal and I'll certainly be putting it to the other Directors that he's saved more than a few lives and weeks of production.'

'But what about the engine house?'

'That's not as big a problem as structural damage to the mill would have been, given our American friends up the road. Don't forget we have the auxiliaries we've been using when we run three shifts in twenty-four hours, but we might be able to use electricity from the grid instead of generating our own for the time being. I'll be asking Chris what he thinks when I see him,' he continued as he mopped up the last sandwich. 'I've spoken to him on the phone, but we can do nothing till the police and the army finish their work. I'm heartily glad security is not my job, for there'll have to be changes at all the mills after this. We just have to find out why, when the mill was working and there were two night watchmen with dogs outside, it wasn't enough.'

'Have to go, love,' he said finishing his tea in a long swallow and standing up, the familiar lines of concentration now marked upon his face after the brief respite. 'Let me know tonight what version you get from Mary Cook when you go down for the milk.'

'Thanks for coming up, Alex,' she said, walking out to the car with him. 'I try not to worry, but you know I do. Do you think all women are the same?'

'Can't say. Never paid any attention to any of them bar you and the girls,' he replied, his face breaking into a great, beaming smile.

* * *

There was another cup of tea in the pot and she was glad to sit down again and drink it as she went over again all Alex had told her. She thought of Robert Anderson's wife and their three young children and of all the wives and mothers working on the spinning floors.

Given there was so much to give thanks for, why did the grim possibilities come to her so easily? Why did she always see the potential for loss and despair?

She wondered what Rose Hamilton would have said if she'd put the question to her. As a girl and young woman it was to her she'd always turned when troubled or confused. Her aunt was a kind and good-natured woman who had given her a home without question, but she was not a thoughtful person and was always uneasy if she should ask a question that didn't have a known and practical answer.

As she sat, the quiet and warmth soothing her, she remembered some of the things Rose said most often. She had come to the conclusion that some of our earliest experiences left us vulnerable to what happened to us later in life. After what had happened when her own family were evicted, she confessed she'd always feared being homeless, though in fact on the one occasion when it did happen, she'd coped quite well.

Maybe, if Rose were here, she would remind her that she'd lost both her father and her mother and with them the homes and life of her childhood. Her father had been a sudden loss, hitting his head as he was swept overboard from the lifeboat during a rescue, so that he was unconscious as he struck the water. With a heavy sea running the attempts to save him didn't stand a chance.

Though a delicate woman herself, her mother had coped for a time, then she'd lost heart and became ill. Emily and her sister had looked after her for months, knowing all the while she'd given up and had no real wish to live.

'That's one answer for you, Emily', she said aloud, as she finished the last tepid mouthful of tea.

Rose would certainly tell her she'd got to keep up the will to live, whatever the circumstances. Hope was necessary, not just for her own sake, but for her family. She needed to think what her loss might mean to her children. She'd been fortunate in the new home her aunt gave her, but that *might* not have been so. The loss of her mother could have brought loneliness and misfortune when she was still too young to have the experience or maturity to cope with it.

She sat for a little longer watching the sun begin its descent on the short winter day, and then, thinking it a pity not to make use of the warmth from the stove, she decided against finishing the work on the stairs and turned back to the small sheaf of letters she'd hoped to reply to in the course of the day. She sorted them out into a new pile and picked out a large, heavy envelope postmarked Dublin. It contained a letter and a manuscript. The letter she'd read back in January, but the wedge of flimsy sheets of a carbon copy with its somewhat erratic blue print she had yet to read.

The letter itself was from Brendan, a vigorous scrawl on invoice paper, all he'd had to hand on a cold, January day when no one appeared to be interested in buying books.

She began to re-read it, remembering with pleasure his reference back to their meeting of last April. Of the rest of the letter, she had only the vaguest idea, for it had arrived along with the news of Cathy's sudden collapse and Brian's desperate attempts to get back to Cheshire to see her. She had set it aside to re-read later. Only now did she realise how much later.

> *My dear Emily,*
> *Sometimes the well rubbed phrases of common exchange do serve our purposes precisely. I have had good cause to thank the ill-wind, or more precisely, the Army lorry that did me a mischief last April and was the means of bringing me to your hospitable fireside. Not only do I reflect with pleasure on that happy evening spent under your roof,*

*but your letters through out the year have
cheered many a dull hour.*

*I am seldom guilty of such foresight as
when I asked you if you'd be so kind as to
keep in touch with me re the activities of
the Hamiltons, especially those of the next
generation with whom I am only slightly
acquainted, but I am now exceedingly glad
that I did. An entirely selfish demand on
someone who has so many demands upon
her time, let me at least say how much it is
appreciated.*

*By way of some recompense for your
efforts, though I know your generous nature
requires none, I have been continuing my
researches into the mysterious origins of my
cousin Alex. Whatever they may prove to
be, I assure you I will insist on retaining the
rights of cousinhood on grounds similar to
those put forward by a sitting tenant.*

Emily put the letter down, smiled and realised
that she really must not read in the fading light
without her spectacles. She fetched them from
the sitting room, and sat down again, reluctant
to switch on the electric light till the last possible
moment.

The sky was a pale yellow on the horizon, shading
into blue if she looked up into the arch overhead

and was completely cloudless. There would most certainly be frost tonight. When she moved the paraffin stove into the hall at dusk she'd have to leave the little bowl-fire lit for the geraniums.

'They'd get a shock if I didn't,' she thought to herself, as she settled back to Brendan's letter again.

Now, you will remember that only weeks after our meeting, I came across a box containing a correspondence with a gentleman named Andrew Doyle who it seems was commissioned in 1875 to investigate the whole question of child emigration to Canada.

It is, of course, a rather curious thing to have only one side of an on-going correspondence, but it certainly stimulated my interest in a subject of which I knew nothing. A strange thing to say, from one whose own country has poured streams of people across all the oceans of the world to populate some of the remotest corners of the globe.

Naturally, 1875 is some twenty years before our good Alex was despatched, but it seems that the general situation of emigrant children was established by this time and despite 'the highly critical report' which my correspondent refers to when commenting on Andrew Doyle's activity, later letters show that, while some changes were made in an attempt to improve the situation of the children, the abuses which Andrew Doyle outlined were only partly addressed and only in some areas.

None of this, my dear Emily, would appear to tell us anything about Alex that we didn't already know, but by an even stranger coincidence than acquiring the box of letters, when I mentioned the subject to my much older friend and partner, Sean Henessey, I found I had started a deluge.

To begin with, a relative of his was active in the founding of the Fairbridge Child Emigration Society of 1909. He overwhelmed me with facts and figures, though the only one I can at present remember is 100,000. That was the number of children sent to Canada alone between 1869 and 1935. When you add on America, Australia and New Zealand, the exodus of the Irish Famine seems to shrink before one's very eyes.

However, I digress. Sean is delighted by your interest in his subject and has copied out the most relevant parts of a book he is currently researching on the subject of child emigrants and the people who were responsible for despatching them. It may well be that your sharp eyes will pick out something in the text that I have missed, a hint that might lead us forward in discovering Alex's past.

What Sean assures me is that copious records do exist. After 1865, it was obligatory for ships to have manifests that recorded all passengers, including escorted groups of children. He himself has obtained copies of some passenger lists as illustrations for the points he is making, so, with patience and time, we might well be able to find one Alexander Hamilton. If we did, Sean assures me, we would also find his age, destination, place of future residence or employment, together with his place of origin and his sponsoring organisation.

I am quite overwhelmed by this impressive bureaucracy which I myself would have thought entirely an innovation of the twentieth century.

Good luck with your researches. I shall continue my random pursuits here in the brightly-lit capital where some Northerners at least come to find food, drink and solace from the woes of war. I do hope you and yours fare well. At least it looks as if we 'neutrals' are not now to be invaded by our current enemy or our traditional one, apart, of course, from local excursions back and forth across the border where the smuggling of everything from milk cattle

to packets of Rinso at least provides some
entertainment amid the gloomy realities of
the time.

My loving good wishes to both you and
Alex and my greetings to all the members of
my extended family.
Brendan.

Hungry, dirty and ill-treated children were
nothing new to Emily. She was old enough to
remember the crowded cabins in Galway, followed
by those of Ballyshannon, Derry and Donaghadee,
the ports where her father had served, and she knew
that she and her sister were fortunate to have beds
to sleep in, food to eat, and parents who neither
drank nor abused them. But reading about the
gangs of street children in London and the big cities
of England who survived by stealing, the children
beaten to death by harsh masters or left to die when
they became ill, deeply shocked her. She had known
it was bad, but had never imagined it was quite as
bad as this.

Sean Hennessy had begun his work with an
account of two women, Maria Rye and Annie
McPherson, each driven by a fierce commitment to
remove children from the destitution in which they
were found, but even more from the moral corruption
which they perceived. Following the stories of both
women, Emily found herself admiring the zeal with

which they pursued their objectives, but wondered if they looked at the children themselves.

It came as an even greater shock to discover that many of the children sent to 'grow in moral strength in the unpolluted air of Canada' were not orphans at all, but children of poor parents who could not afford to feed them and had been forced in despair to bring them to the workhouse.

As Sean Hennessy pointed out, it was easy to show how unfortunate the circumstances of these children were, but what was not pointed out was what the 'bright, new open-air life' might actually mean for a child adjusted to the city streets, to poverty and to the company of its own people.

The more Emily read of the true situation of many of the emigrants, the more she agreed with Brendan's Andrew Doyle. After 11,000 miles travelling round Canada to see what had happened to at least some of those sent out, no wonder his criticisms were so severe. Children as young as one year old carried off from the ship at Quebec by unknown people, boys and girls from the same family separated by the width of Canada, girls abused and then returned pregnant and in disgrace to the orphanage for punishment . . .

Emily had to stop. She could not bear to think of what the reality had been behind all the pious words, the fund-raising, the support by members of the government and the aristocracy. Children raised to be slaves, badly fed, badly housed, but expected to be grateful for this new life an ocean away from any familiar face or well known place.

No wonder Alex had never talked about what had happened to him. Apart from the story about him going in a ship across a grey sea with a label on his coat collar that irritated him, in all their years together she had gleaned from him only the merest fragments.

He'd spoken of a woman who was kind to him, a young woman with an old husband. He used to bring her flowers from the meadow or the riverbank, but he had to be careful not to get caught in the little garden where she used to sit. If he was, he'd be beaten and sent back to his work, or kept working half the night when his companions were let go to their beds in the straw.

The light had gone now and Emily could read no more without putting on the light. But still she didn't move. He must have been five or six when he went to Canada, but by the time he was eight he was speaking French and had 'forgotten' his English. And then he had learnt German. And where exactly was this place called German Township where he had met Sam McGinley?

She gathered up the letters, the blue carbon copy of Sean's manuscript and Brendan's letter, stepped back into the kitchen and laid them on the table. She drew the blind, pulled across the blackout and switched on the light. As it spilt down on the bare, scrubbed table, she saw that Brendan had added a PS to his letter on a separate sheet which she hadn't seen.

She took it up and read it twice through in quick succession, not able to grasp it the first time.

PS: Talking about Alex the other day, Sean made a suggestion I hadn't thought of. But then, that's hardly surprising as he is much more familiar with the location of all the orphanages in Canada.

He said that it was possible the label Alex wore was not actually his name, but his Christian name and his destination i.e. Alex to Hamilton. (Hamilton, Ontario).

She paused, put the paper down and thought about it. Given all she'd read about the collecting and the despatching, it was a real possibility.

My poor love, to have nothing of your own but the one short word, Alex. To have done what you've done. Perhaps you deserve a medal as much as Robert Anderson.

CHAPTER NINE

The wild March wind caught Emily in the face as she came round the gable of Cook's farm, crossed the cobbled yard and stepped out onto the empty road leading back up to Rathdrum. The wind was boisterous, but not cold, the glints of sun had real warmth in them and the hawthorn hedges were already sprayed with new green leaves. She took a deep breath of the fresh air and smiled as she saw little swirls of dust run across the tarmac in front of her and disappear into the dry grass of the rough roadside verges.

She was heartily glad to be on her way home, the milk, butter and eggs for the next few days safely packed in her shopping bag, her returned copies of *Woman* and *Woman's Own* carefully wedged to stop the bottles from rattling. The last thing she wanted on her way up the hill was to listen to the chink of bottles when in all the hedges the birds were active, singing their hearts out to mark their territory or fluttering and scuffling amid the branches as they began to build their nests.

She had looked forward to her regular twice-weekly visit to the Cooks, always a source of news and lively stories, but today the time she had spent there had been both wearing and agitating. Normally the most outgoing of women, seldom without a fund of conversation or even of monologue, Mary wasn't herself at all. Though a much less talkative person, Michael too was surprisingly quiet. His widowed father had arrived for a visit and, from the moment she'd been introduced he'd taken over the conversation and more than made up for both.

Emily had said, 'Good afternoon,' and commented how nice it was to have such a pleasant spell of dry, sunny weather. Immediately, the older man had protested. It was all very well for women spring-cleaning and getting the Monday washing dry and suchlike, but if this dryness went on then the milk yields would be down and forby Michael would have to feed hay to make up for the shortage of new grass and sure look at the price of hay, even if it were available in the first place.

Emily would have been more than happy to pick up her supplies and leave, but courtesy required she stay at least fifteen minutes and exchange news. Not that there was any news from Rathdrum, certainly none she wanted to share, but to begin with she did her best by enquiring about a setting of eggs Mary wanted for a broody hen and confirming the plans for the next children's outing.

'You'd think those American boys out the road had better things to do than run around with a lot of children,' Mr Cook announced, finally dropping down into a fireside chair, just as Emily thought his hovering awkwardly meant that he might be about to leave. 'We're hardly goin' to beat the Jerries with all that lot are doin'. Why aren't they out with them convoys that are gettin' sunk left, right and centre? If these U-boats have it all their own way shure they'll starve us out. Isn't that exactly what Hitler wants to do?'

'Now Da, be reasonable,' said Michael coolly. 'These young lads are still trainin' to be engineers. One soldier is not the same as another. Different men do different jobs.'

'All right, I give you that,' he said abruptly. 'They'd be no use out there in the Atlantic. So what are they doing marchin' roun' the place here with their faces black, if they're engineers?' he went on, grinning and showing his small, brown teeth, as he took his pipe out of his pocket.

'An' I'll tell ye somethin' else,' he said, fixing them all with his eye, 'some of these dances and socials and what have ye, *for the troops*, as they say, are open to all comers. And who d'ye think comes? Girls from over the border. As nice as ye please, *their* clothes aren't on coupons, are they? And then they go back with all the details of which regiment is here and which regiment is there and what every one of them's doin'. Shure we might as well ring up Mr de Valera or the German embassy in Dublin and tell them all our business in the first place,' he said, applying a match to his pipe and breaking off while he sucked furiously to get it going.

'An I'll tell ye more forby, for ye don't seem to have one bit of a notion here what's going on. If ye go down to Dublin and into one of these posh hotels you'll see it full of people from the North and there sitting beside them as large as life these Nazis with their swastikas, eating and drinking and chatting away as if they were at home in Berlin.'

Emily had said nothing. Many well off Northerners went down to Dublin for weekends to escape the black out and the general weariness of wartime. Her own friend Dolly Love, from Dromore had gone down with her husband to visit her sister on her birthday. They'd no sooner sat down in the restaurant where they'd booked a special meal than some men in German uniform sat down at the next table. Arthur Love fought in the first war and was so incensed, he'd marched them straight out. Poor Dolly had been so looking forward to her dinner. Back home, all her sister could produce for them was scrambled egg.

'Da, if the South is neutral, then anyone has the right to be there. There's Americans and British in

Dublin as well, in uniform and out of it,' Michael said coolly.

'Neutral, ma foot. Yer man is hand in glove with Hitler. And Hitler's just biding his time to invade. Sure, isn't it the best way to get at England?'

Emily was beginning to wonder just whose side Cook senior was on. His reference to England was just as hostile as his reference to the Germans in Dublin.

'Well, maybe, Da, we might be grateful yet for the wee American lads with their guns to give us a han' when the Jerries come up the road from the South,' said Michael quietly. 'Right now I have cows to milk.'

'And I have washing to bring in and a meal to cook,' said Emily, as she stood up quickly and moved across the room to where Mary was standing by the entrance to the dairy, waiting for her, her eyes cast up in a heavenward glance as Cook senior clumped out through the back door without a backward glance or a word of farewell.

'Emily, what am ah goin' to do? He's here for three more weeks, an' he never stops. It's the Germans and the South and de Valera. Mornin' noon and night. An' he thinks our postman is spyin' for them, because he asked me how my brother was. Sure the two of them were at school together till Jimmy joined up. But you can't tell him anythin'. What am ah goin' to do?'

Mary turned a tearful glance towards Emily as she refilled her clean milk bottles and put their tops on, wrapped her eggs to fit the small cardboard box that had been going up and down the hill for years now and then opened her larder for butter.

'Oh Mary, I *am* sorry,' said Emily. 'I don't know *what* I would do,' she added honestly. 'I'd like to tell him to shut up, but then, if he were Alex's father, I'd probably not feel I could do that any more than you can. Why does he come here?'

'He gets lonely, Michael says, since Ma died. Sure he has no friends.'

'I'm not surprised,' said Emily, watching Mary as she deftly wrapped her butter in a sheet of greaseproof paper and then in the clean tea towel Emily had brought with her.

'An' we'll have none left by the time he goes,' Mary added crossly.

Emily laughed.

'Oh Mary dear, don't worry about that,' she said, handing over her money in a battered envelope. 'They'll all be back as soon as he goes. It might even be good for us all to have no news and no good stories for a while. Then we'd appreciate them all the more,' she added smiling. 'I'll maybe send Alex down on Tuesday and see if he does any better than I did. I don't think your father-in-law has much time for women, has he?'

170

'No, he never had,' Mary agreed, shaking her head. 'I don't know how Michael's Ma put up with him. But now he's lost without her.'

'Don't let him get you down, Mary,' Emily said encouragingly, as she picked up her loaded bag. 'Three weeks does seems a long time, but if we can stick three years of war, we can stick three weeks of your man, can't we?'

Mary managed a weak smile.

'Aye, we can and I'll be lookin' forward to seein' you and our friends at the Church Hall on Friday next. At least the wee ones will have a smile for us. I think yer man's face would crack if he tried it.'

Emily enjoyed her walk. Though the bag began to feel heavy by the time she'd passed the steepest part of the hill she was still glad to be outdoors and grateful for the same dry weather that had so irritated Michael's father. Thanks to it, she was well ahead in the garden, the soil now easy to turn after three years of crops and digging in compost. It had been a real triumph for her to do something she'd never done before and know what she was doing was worth all the effort.

She wasn't the only one who must feel pleased at her success. So far, producing food had been Ulster's best response to the war. While the farmers in England, Scotland and Wales had reached the targets for opening up new land by ploughing fallow

171

and meadow and even digging up the London parks and gardens, in Ulster they had excelled themselves, far exceeded the targets they'd been set.

Their efforts helped to make up for the half-hearted start to war production she'd read about in all the papers for the first couple of years of the war. She still wondered how the Stormont government could have managed to do so little in the face the huge demands the war created that unemployment had actually *gone up*. Worse still, there'd been even more labour troubles than during the severe depression of the thirties.

Perhaps, she thought, catching some hair out of her eyes, there was now a wind of change blowing. If they got the new government as most people thought was about to happen, then they would be active in stepping up production. If farmers and gardeners could do so well producing food, surely factory workers could make more planes and munitions, but people needed to be encouraged to do their best.

She remembered how, right at the beginning of the war, the farmers had each had a personal letter from Basil Brooke, the Minister of Agriculture. Michael Cook had showed her his letter which he still kept, for he said doubling the herd was the best thing that had ever happened to his farm. There must have been many more encouraged by that same letter, written as one farmer to another, though Brook's estates at Coalbrook were enormous compared to the handful of acres of people like Michael.

If there was one thing in particular she had learnt from Chris Hicks and his boys, it was that individuals really need to feel what they are doing is worthwhile. They also need to feel they themselves are valued.

Thank goodness there weren't many like Michael Cook's father around, she thought to herself, as she passed through the always open gates of Rathdrum. Hitler ought to recruit more like him. Perhaps he already had. Perhaps Cook senior was a secret weapon for undermining morale. Undermining someone as irrepressible as Mary took some doing.

Emily laughed as she tramped down the drive. Wasn't it strange the silly things came into your mind when you were free to walk at your own pace with no one expecting you and no particular need to hurry, not even to save yourself from getting wet.

She was completely taken aback when she came round the corner of the house and saw a jeep parked by the back door. To her surprise, there was no one in it.

She looked around the yard and peered down what was visible of the garden path as she opened the back door and lowered her bag gratefully onto the table. At that instant, the door to the hall opened and a tall, blonde young man in uniform appeared.

'Oh thank goodness, ma'am, I was afraid something was wrong,' he said hastily. 'The door was open, but you weren't in the garden. I was sure you wouldn't leave the door unlocked, so I went looking for you. I'm so sorry, I hope you don't think . . .'

He broke off looking flustered and awkward.

'That I thought you might be going to steal the family silver or were inspecting to see if I'd dusted under the beds,' she offered, laughing.

To her relief, the stricken look on his face disappeared and he smiled.

'Well, it's not funny to come into your own house and find a stranger looking round,' he said apologetically.

'But, you're *not* a stranger. You're Hank the Tank and you are also Alexander Lachlan Ross. I can't imagine any harm coming from a man with a name like that. Besides, you were concerned about me. That was very kind of you. I must confess, I never lock the door when I'm just going down the hill for the milk. Maybe, I should in future.'

'Well, perhaps . . .'

'You're perfectly right. Now, sit down while I put the kettle on. Whatever it is you've come for, as Major Hicks might say: *'I could sure use a cup of coffee.'* How about you?'

'Yes, ma'am, I could indeed.'

Emily put a tray together so that they could sit

in the conservatory with the last of the afternoon sunshine.

'Now, do have some cake,' she said, cutting him a generous slice. 'Without you, there wouldn't be much fruit in it and without you I wouldn't have any coffee either. Do you mind being called Hank or shall I use your other names?'

'Call me what you like, ma'am, if you give me cake like this,' he said appreciatively as he swallowed the first mouthful. 'There's a saying we have at home, *Call me anything you like except too early in the morning.*'

Emily laughed and decided his accent was definitely Canadian, not American.

'Yes, we have that one here too. But then, it's hardly surprising you know the saying when your name is a good Scots name like Ross and Ulster is full of Rosses. Do you know where your family came from?'

'Well, my father's family actually came into Ontario from Nova Scotia. My great-grandfather started writing the whole story in the front of the family Bible from the time they left Scotland on a ship called *Polly* in 1810,' he began, smiling gently. 'We don't actually know about my mother's family. She was adopted by Lachlan and Fiona Ross in Quebec, in 1895, and then they moved west to farm in Saskatchewan. She married my father, George Ross, out there and I was born in Saskatoon, but he was a lawyer and his uncle had a practice in Boston, so he moved back into the States to take over from him when he retired. I'd have been joining the firm as soon as I'd done with College if I hadn't joined up.'

'How very interesting, Hank,' said Emily, looking into the candid blue eyes. 'I'm fascinated by the way people move around on that great continent of yours. So many people here in Ireland live for generations in the same place,' she went on, 'that is, *if they stay.*'

'But of course, thousands of them go and you yourself have got the names to prove it. Alexander, Lachlan and Ross are all Ulster or Ulster-Scots names. Usually here, families call children after relatives. There's a tradition that you call the first boy after his father's father and the first girl after her mother's mother and so on down the family. It can create dreadful confusion. My friends John and Rose Hamilton used to have two Uncle Sam's and a son Sam and later a grandson, Sam as well,' she ended laughing.

'I didn't know that tradition about naming,' he said nodding thoughtfully. 'My grandfather *was* Lachlan and my father was Lachlan but you know, I never knew anyone called Alexander till I met your husband.'

'That is strange, isn't it?' Emily responded, suddenly curious to hear more. 'Why do you think your mother called you that?'

'Well, it's a bit of a family story,' he said smiling. 'Ma always insisted she had a brother, but even when she was first adopted my grandparents thought she might be romancing. She had several "brothers" she played with when she was five or six. They never knew what age she was. They just collected her from the ship with her little suitcase.'

'She still has the suitcase,' he added looking at her directly. 'She kept it because her brother had written her name on it, so no one could take it from her. She said *his* name was Alexander.'

'How remarkable,' said Emily, suddenly seeing the lines of blue text on the carbon copy Brendan had sent her back in January.

Another child sent out across the ocean. Clearly Hank's mother didn't have a label on her coat, so there was even less chance of finding out where *she* had come from.

'Any idea what year that would have been, Hank?'

'Oh yes, Grandpa Ross recorded it in the family Bible. I used to look at it often when I was a kid. He wrote; *26th May 1895. Today, we drove to Quebec and there by the grace of God did receive into our care a girl orphan from Liverpool, England, a longed for daughter.*'

'My goodness, what a happy landing for that child,' she said, aware of tears suddenly springing to her eyes. 'I've been reading about the boatloads of orphans sent to Canada. A hundred thousand between 1865 and 1935. Did you know that?'

'No, ma'am.'

He looked shocked, his eyes wide and troubled.

'Neither did I till last January,' she said honestly. 'We'd been talking about Canadian orphans to our bookseller cousin from Dublin and he discovered his colleague knew a great deal more than he did. He sent me some of the material from the book his friend is working on. You know, of course, that my Alex was an orphan, don't you?'

'No, ma'am,' he said, looking quite taken aback. 'I knew your husband *came back* from Canada to find his family, but I didn't know he'd gone out as an orphan. I thought his family had emigrated and then when he lost his parents he came back to find his aunts and uncles.'

'No, Alex was sent off, just like your mother,' Emily said, shaking her head, 'only he had a label on his coat that said Alex Hamilton. Perhaps boys didn't have suitcases . . .'

She broke off, once again overwhelmed by the enormity of what had happened to these two children such a long time ago.

'Don't look so sad, ma'am,' he said quietly. 'They haven't done so bad. My mother is a lovely lady, I know you'd like her and Mr Hamilton is a very successful man. All the boys are pleased when there's work to do at the mills. He never hassles

178

them, but he keeps them right. He's good to them.'

Whenever he spoke, he always looked straight at her and in those wide, blue eyes she could see exactly what he was thinking. She was touched at his trying to encourage her, because he saw she was sad. Just what her youngest daughter would have done.

'You're right, Hank, it's all a long time ago. Isn't it strange that we can be so sad about what happened to your mother and my husband nearly fifty years ago when all around us thousands are dying every day?'

'No ma'am,' he said firmly. 'It's not comparable. Being sad is part of being human. If we didn't feel such feelings, then we wouldn't be fighting Hitler. If we want to win, we need to know what we think is wrong, like sending those children away.'

She nodded, startled by the strength of his tone and his clear conviction.

'Ma'am, I do so enjoy talking to you, even apart from the coffee and the cake . . .'

'Hank, I'm sorry, it's my fault entirely. Of course you must get back. Did you have a message for me?'

He nodded and said rather reluctantly: 'Major Hicks presents his compliments and thought it might help if he warned you Friday next might be cancelled at short or no notice.'

'Oh dear, that means posting?'

He nodded.

'All of you?'

'Could be. I guess he'd tell *you* if he knew. But we've only got a hint at when, nothing on who, apart from the boys, that is.'

'So we might not meet again?'

'That's about it, ma'am.'

Emily suddenly found herself overwhelmed with grief and anxiety. This young man with whom she had felt such a bond, such an unexplained familiarity from that first meeting at dinner the night after Ritchie died, would walk out of her kitchen and into a world of tanks and bridges, of men killing and being killed.

It never got any easier. Her fear of loss. Another young man, full of life, kind and unexpectedly sensitive, going into battle, blonde and blue-eyed, as totally committed to what he had chosen as her own Johnny.

They stood up together and she gave him a message for Chris Hicks. 'Tell him I really appreciated the warning. The food will certainly not go to waste. Wish him luck if he goes. Ask him to keep in touch if he can. Alex and I won't forget him, or you.'

She walked out with him to his jeep, held out her hand, then as he shook it warmly, she leant forward and kissed him.

'That's from your mother, for luck,' she said, smiling. 'You didn't tell me what her name was.'

'Jane,' he replied, beaming at her, as he climbed up into his seat. 'But she wasn't a *plain Jane*. Da always declared she was the prettiest girl he'd ever met,' he said, laughing, as he reversed the jeep neatly and drove off one-handed, waving to her all the way down the avenue.

CHAPTER TEN

Alex Hamilton closed the door of his office firmly behind him, removed the jacket of his suit, hung it over the back of his chair and rolled up the sleeves of his well-ironed shirt. He thought, as he always did on such occasions, that he'd rather strip down an engine any day than sit on a platform in what his friend Sam Hamilton always called his Sunday-go-to-Meeting. But if one was a member of the obligatory platform party lending their presence to support the Chairman of the Directors addressing the entire workforce, it would hardly do to turn up in dungarees.

Not that the Chairman, Sir John, was a very formal person. He was, in fact, a very likeable man with an easy manner, just what was needed in the present situation. Nevertheless, as a former military man he always expected a correct turn-out. When she'd heard what was planned, Emily had insisted he come home at lunchtime to change his clothes, so that she herself could make sure he looked *immaculate*.

The desk was piled with paperwork and just looking at it, Alex felt intimidated. The requisitioning systems had been put in place at the beginning of the war when things in the Atlantic were much worse than they were now. It was hardly surprising they were so detailed when they were designed at a time when the U-boats were sinking supply ships faster than they could be replaced and every rivet and screw was costing lives. Thankfully, the situation was a good deal better now. Convoys remained at risk of attack, but they were better armed and better protected. Even more heartening was the fact that U-boats were being spotted more regularly and hunted more successfully. If the work going on behind closed doors paid off, there would be an end to the losses of both men and materials, one of these days. He thought longingly of that time and the mountain of paper that could be salvaged if only the process of accessing materials could be made simpler.

He had worked his way down one of the neatly stacked piles when the door opened after a perfunctory knock.

'It did the trick, Boss. We're in business,' the tall, broad-shouldered man said as he hovered over the visitor's chair.

'Sit down, Robert, sit down,' Alex said, waving

to him impatiently. 'Are you going to go all polite on me because I'm wearing my suit?' he demanded.

'Ach, no. But you look kinda different behind that desk the day.'

'So I should hope after all the brushing Emily put in. I told her she was adding years of wear to the fabric and at that rate it might not last me till the war was over.'

Robert grinned and stretched his legs out more comfortably on the worn strip of carpet that lay under desk and visitor's chair, but failed to reach any further across the bare boards of what had once been a storeroom.

'An' what did she say to that?'

'She said, 'Here and now, Alex. No use thinking too far ahead.'

'Aye, that sounds like Emily,' he said warmly.

There was a moment's comfortable silence between them, a point of rest and reconnection after the effort of the day.

'How d'ye think it went?' asked Robert, who had been able to use the brief shut-down to tackle an intermittent fault with one of the auxiliary engines.

'I think it went well,' Alex replied. 'But I can't make up my mind whether we did right or not,' he added more soberly.

'Sir John was good,' he went on, 'he always is, you could've heard a pin drop when he explained what the problem was. He laid it on the line all right, and he paid *you* quite a compliment. He described exactly what would have happened if Mahoney's plan *had* gone as he'd intended. But then he said the problem remained that there were more Mahoney's about. He was very tactful. He said he didn't care whether they were local or foreign, right wing or left wing, political or anarchist. If they were bombers, they were murderers in his book. They were willing to kill innocent people and kill their jobs along with them, which meant depriving hardworking families trying to do their best at a difficult time.'

'Aye, that puts it nicely. *Killing jobs as well as people*,' repeated Robert, nodding and pressing his lips together as he waited for the older man to go on.

'I was wondering how he'd manage to put the next bit. I have to admit he surprised me,' Alex went on, a small smile on his face. 'He said that sometimes we don't notice the small things. When there's danger around, we look for a big thing, a machine gun nest, or a tank, or an enemy aircraft. We don't think of someone walking round the mill in their lunch hour, or asking their friend if they're on the late shift, or taking a ride on their bicycle on a wet night.'

Robert narrowed his eyes full of attention.

'He had them all listening to every word and then he just said very simply . . . *Mahoney received information from someone who knows this mill inside out*. Then he said it was possible this person, or these people, didn't realise what they were doing. They could hardly see such questions as they were asked having anything to do with something as threatening as *Careless Talk Costs Lives*. There are no glamorous spies involved, no dark hooded figures, no strangers, just friends and neighbours. That's what makes it so difficult.'

'I never thought of that,' said Robert. 'I'd supposed it must be something carefully planned like these films ye see. Could you really get all the information you needed just by asking bits and pieces?'

'You could, I think, but that's not the point. Even if it's one person in the pay of some group or other, what your man has done is alert the whole mill to the wee things. Like your wee bit of paper, Robert. He told me afterwards that's what gave him the idea.'

Robert smiled sheepishly and then shook his head.

'That trick only works once. We might not be so lucky next time.'

'If there is a next time,' Alex said crisply. 'He ended up by pointing out that any one of them sitting listening to him in the Recreation Hall might be able to foil another attempt simply by keeping their eyes open for any tiny detail that might seem out of place.'

'So why are ye wonderin' if ye did right?' Robert asked, his face creased with puzzlement. 'It sounds to me he's got the whole place payin' attention and ready to report anythin' out o' the ordinary.'

'But Robert, just think . . . if there *is* some person out there in the mill who *deliberately* collected and passed information, think of the mischief they can now do by spreading rumours and dropping hints. Its not just bombs that can blow things to bits. What about suspicion and bad feeling? That's my worry.'

'Aye, well . . . I see yer point. That hadn't occurred to me.'

Robert laughed suddenly as he stood up and stretched his shoulders.

'What's the joke?'

'I was just thinkin' that's why your sittin' behind that desk and I'm away back to make sure all's well with Number 3.'

Alex laughed, a great beaming smile breaking on his face and lighting up his eyes.

'I'll swop you,' he said promptly.

'You *will* not. Emily'd have m'life if I let you anywhere near an engine in that outfit. Tell her I missed her today with no picnic. I'll see her next week, maybe,' he added over his shoulder as he strode out, pulling the door behind him.

Alex was grateful for the mug of tea one of the office staff brought for him at half past three and the unexpected piece of cake that went with it. He'd made further inroads on the piles of paper, but he'd also come to the conclusion that there was no hope whatever of getting the quantity of materials they'd need to repair or refurbish so many worn out machines. He sat drinking his tea and staring into space, wondering what he could possibly do to fill the gap.

He couldn't believe his eyes when his door was pushed opened and what looked like a flowering bush moved briskly towards him. Only when it stopped barely a foot from his nose and a small, square figure emerged from behind it did he realise that a huge floral arrangement now sat on his desk. Before he could offer any greeting, or ask for any explanation, he was overcome by a huge sneeze.

'Bless you, sir. It's the daffodils, they do that to me sometimes as well,' she said sympathetically. 'I'm sorry for landin' them on your desk, but me arms was about to give out and I coulden see roun' them. I knowed there was a desk here, so I jus' headed up the bit of carpet,' she explained, stepping back from her burden and brushing some specks of pollen and a few fragments of green leaf from her clean white overall.

Alex recognised her immediately, one of their long serving and most experienced workers. Now a spinning mistress, Daisy Elliot had been at Millbrook since she'd left school and started as a doffer. For a moment, Alex hadn't the slightest idea what to say to her, but he need not have troubled himself.

'Now, Sir, if you don't mind, I need to have a word with you that nobody knows about,' she began, lifting the heavy visitor's chair with the greatest of ease. She carried it round to his own side of the desk and pulled it up close to his own.

He rather wondered if the floral arrangement was intended to hide them from any remote possibility of being seen by a curious passerby. Next she went and shut the door tightly, then she came back and sat down directly in front of him not more than two feet away.

'Now, Sir,' she repeated firmly. 'We did the flowers for the hall before the children's picnic had to be cancelled and I've said that I would bring this one for you to take home to Mrs Hamilton. So, if you don't mind Sir, lettin' everyone see you puttin' it in your car.'

She paused, took a deep breath and launched again.

'I think I know who gave away all the details Sir John was talkin' about, but the poor lad knows no better. He's not the full shillin,' if you know what I mean and he's easy started,' she said with a sigh. 'He likes to think he can mind things, and indeed he can *remember* as I should say, but he has no wit. So you've only to say *now I'm sure you don't know such an such* and he's just delighted to put

189

you straight and tell you all he knows. Now if I tell you who it is you won't sack him, will you, for his Ma has no one else. She lost one son at Dunkirk and the other is missing in North Africa,' she ended hurriedly as she ran out of breath.

'No, I won't sack him,' Alex promised, 'But we will have to do something,' he added, as he began to grasp what might have happened.

'Indeed, I'm sure you'll think of something, for you're very like Mr Sinton, God rest him, an' he forgave a young man who was the means of a big fire at this mill. An' I wouldn't be here talkin' to you if it hadn't been for his wife, though Miss Sarah she was then, that carried me out on her back when I took fright and hadn't the wit to get away when I saw the smoke. Though mind you, with the bad leg I had then, I mightn't have got far anyhow.'

'So, Mrs Elliot, can you tell me who would have questioned our young friend?' he asked quietly, as he saw her mind move far off into the past.

'I can, but that might be no good to you, for they're all decent men, apart from carrying on a bit and foolin' Jim . . .'

She clapped a hand to her mouth and looked horrified.

'It's all right, Mrs Elliot, I'd worked out it must be Jimmy. Now go on with what you were saying. Jimmy'll come to no harm.'

She looked him full in the face and went on immediately.

'I've heard some of our ones talking to Jimmy an' I never though a bit of it till today, but these same ones go for a drink on a Saturday night to the pub where my Mary helps out at the weekend when Bert is at home to mind the childer. An' she told me there was strangers there, Trade Unionists she said, interested in working conditions in the mills. Well, I know all about Trade Unionists, for we all went on courses to Belfast to find out about such things years ago before the four mills was a cooperative. But when I asked Mary what they asked about she niver mentioned pay, only working conditions. Sure, that can't be right for a real Trade Unionist, can it?'

'No, it can't,' he said firmly, looking at the worn face leaning forward so close to his own.

It was his turn now to remember the tale Rose had told him about the stoppage at Millbrook which Sarah had resolved with the aid of a young doffer she'd once saved from a fire.

'Do you think Mary could describe these men?' he asked, drawing his mind away from that past time and focusing on the woman who now sat watching him.

'Oh dear aye. They weren't from these parts at all. She's a great mimic, our Mary, and she had the accent of them. But I couldn't place it,' she went on shaking her head and looking severe. 'Not the

North, that's for sure. An' not Dublin, for I've a neighbour was brought up there and still talks that way.'

She broke off and stood up.

'I must go, sir, in case anyone saw me come in and knows how long I've been in here. It only takes a minute or two to bring in flowers.'

'Quite right, Mrs Elliot. I'm very grateful and I'll see what we can do. Can I let you know what's happening via my wife?'

'Ach, the very thing,' she said, clicking her fingers. 'No one'll pay a bit of attention to two women having a gossip, as they *always* think,' she said, shaking her head crossly.

'Would ye mind takin' the flowers out to yer car now, sir, in case anyone's lukin'. I know she has plenty of her own, but she'll understan'. An' I'll see her in the lunch hour before the next picnic . . . or whenever it is the new boys'll come.'

She led the way to the door while Alex struggled to get a hold of the container without immersing his head in either the green foliage with sharp points, or the fully-flowered daffodils. He followed her out, along the corridor and through the main door, which she opened for him.

He had just negotiated the short distance across the forecourt and managed to rest the container on the sloping bonnet of the Austin when he sneezed again.

'Bless you, sir,' said a voice from near at hand, a

warm and friendly voice with a marked Canadian accent. 'Can I give you a hand with that?'

Alex sneezed twice more before he was able to greet the young man who then helped him get the large, spiky arrangement into the back seat.

'Glad to help, sir. Wish I could do more to thank you for all you've done for us,' he added, as they both brushed off fragments of green leaf.

'I think we're *much* in your debt, Hank,' Alex said shaking the young man's hand firmly. 'We'll miss you and your colleagues. Is Major Hicks going?'

'No, sir. Our loss, your gain. He's doing such a good job with the youngsters, they'll not let him go. I guess there'll be a lot more of them coming through, but our group has been posted and the five of us are off with them. I came ahead of the column to deliver a present,' he said, reaching over into the back of the jeep and re-emerging with a well-filled cardboard box.

'Easier to handle than the flowers,' he laughed, as he passed it over. 'Mrs Hamilton once confessed that she loved coffee, so the boys and ourselves have been saving up for her from our parcels from home. It's from all of us to you both with thanks. She made us feel so welcome. And so did you, sir. We appreciated that,' he said, lifting his head as both of them caught the sound of heavy lorries moving towards them.

'Best of luck, Hank,' said Alex, holding out his hand again. 'We'd like nothing better than to see you back here again after the war. Don't forget that.'

'Not likely.'

He seemed about to say something more, but changed his mind and put his hand into his uniform pocket.

'For Mrs Hamilton, sir. Didn't want to have to send it through the censor or risk the post. Just a few thoughts . . . Must go . . .'

He hopped up into the jeep, roared off up the slope, paused on the verge and slipped neatly into a small gap between two Army lorries moving at the head of the long column bound for the docks in Belfast and an unknown destination beyond.

By the time Alex had cleared his desk and written a report to be delivered by messenger to Sir John, it was after seven and the main street of Banbridge was almost empty as he drove through it somewhat faster than usual, spurred on by a more than normal desire to be sitting by his own fireside.

It had been a long day and a tiring one, though he had to admit it was not without its moments of humour. He was looking forward to telling Emily about the flowering tree that had invaded his office and set him sneezing.

The sky was darkening as he came to the foot of the hill, a huge black cloud piled up behind

Cook's farm. The pleasant afternoon had turned progressively grey, but now a chill and boisterous wind was whipping the branches of the trees overhanging the road. He reckoned that any minute now there would be a heavy shower.

As he changed gear and turned up the hill, he was amazed to see a small figure away up ahead on the empty road, a hand clutched to a bright red headscarf that threatened to blow away, a waterproof coat inflating with the gusts of wind and trousers blown flat against her legs. As the figure was carrying neither bag, nor basket, nor wheeling a bicycle, it was a couple of minutes before he realised it was Emily herself.

He pulled up a little way ahead of her, leant over and pressed the door handle at the very moment the clouds opened and threw a rattle of sleet against the windscreen.

'That was good timing,' she said, breathlessly, as she pulled the door behind her and swept fragments of sleet from her waterproof.

'What happened to your driver?' he asked, as he peered through the windscreen, the wiper blades struggling to move the accumulating fragments of ice.

'No driver today, love,' she said, smiling and rubbing her cold cheeks. 'Have you forgotten? They've gone. All except Chris. But he won't have any transport till tomorrow, so we were out delivering the cakes and biscuits to the sick and the elderly. Don't you remember he sent Hank the Tank to warn me last week?' she prompted, as they turned into the avenue, which was already beginning to look like a Christmas card.

'So how did you deliver all that stuff?' he asked, puzzled.

'Bicycles. What else?,' she said promptly. 'No one has any petrol. But some of the older girls from the Academy came to help us. You can't carry all that much in a bicycle basket, but there were fifteen of us at one point. After all that cycling around, I couldn't face pushing my bicycle up the hill, so I left it with Mary,' she explained, as they came round into the yard.

'And you had it all planned?'

'Well, of course. That was why Chris let me know. We couldn't *not* bake in case the picnic went ahead. But if it didn't, what did we do with all that lovely food? It's not just cake for teatime. The children get a little bag to take home for their family. So, it does add up, sixty or seventy for tea, then at least thirty take-away bags and a little something for the office staff and the flower ladies who help us to set things up in the lunch-hour.'

'Like doing the flowers?'

'Yes, of course. Can't have a picnic without flowers,' she said lightly, as they stopped opposite the back door, now obscured by a further squall.

'Have you seen what's in the back?' he asked, as they continued to sit, the sudden, angry fusillade bouncing noisily off the roof of the car.

She turned awkwardly in her seat, her waterproof catching on the Rexine covered seat.

'Where did you get that?'

'Long story. But I'll tell all when we're sitting in front of a good fire. Shall we make a dash for it?'

Emily laughed.

'I'm so tired, I couldn't dash to save my life. The hill finished me off. But I'm game to get battered or soaked. We've plenty of dry clothes indoors and I would just so love to be home.'

The house was so cold that Alex plugged in two convectors, one upstairs and one in the hall, and brought the paraffin heater into the sitting room until the freshly-lit fire started to produce some heat. To his great surprise both convectors began to whir and produce the stream of warm air he'd not dared to expect.

Power cuts could occur at any time, but on a Friday night it was almost predictable. As he hung his suit on a hangar and found a warm sweater to pull over his shirt and warm trousers, he wondered what was so special about Friday night. Was it an extra demand that put up consumption or did output drop? He certainly wasn't aware that any of the power stations worked other than a seven day week.

Emily had made Irish stew in the morning and the large saucepan only needed careful reheating. After one of the afternoon gatherings which were now a regular feature of life, it had become a regular thing that they had a supper that could be reheated and eaten by the fire in the sitting room.

Tonight they ate in silence, tasty, hot food and the fire burning up brightly creating a smell that Emily loved, easing away the cold, hunger and weariness of the day. She blessed Sam Hamilton. On his last visit, he'd brought them bags of turf he'd managed to buy in Portadown from a man who had a strip of bog at Annaghmore.

'That was great, Emily. I didn't realise how cold I was till the food began to warm me up.'

'There's no warmth in a suit, Alex. At least dungarees give you a double layer,' she added, as she finished off the last of her meal. 'Aren't we so very lucky to have food and fire?'

He looked at her sharply, disturbed by something in her tone.

'What is it, love? Something's on your mind.'

She nodded, leant forward in her armchair and held out her hands to the blaze.

'Alex, I know about poverty and I know about old age, but what I saw today really got me down,' she said honestly. 'Some of those wee mill cottages have two or even three families in them, maybe seven or eight children and an old granny bed-ridden in the same room. There's people that were bombed out in Belfast two years ago still staying with the family that took them in after the Blitz. They've nowhere else to go. There's no new houses going up, only more of the old ones falling down. I've seen better old cottages being used to shelter cattle.'

Alex nodded and said nothing. Sometimes he didn't notice things and then when he did, he was ashamed he'd not paid more attention. But there wasn't much time for thinking these days, not beyond the problems in front of him, and there were plenty of those.

'Have they enough to eat?' he asked abruptly.

'Just about,' she replied. 'The WVS are very good. But you should have seen the eyes of those children when the Granny opened her packet of cake and biscuits.'

Without the slightest warning, he saw himself looking at a table covered with food. He almost imagined he could smell it. It must be Thanksgiving. Turkey on a great decorated platter. Roast potatoes piled high. Small dishes with sauces and little spoons in saucers for putting it on the slices of meat. It was snowing outside and he'd been sent for more logs for the fire. As he went to put them down on the hearth, he caught sight of a great pyramid of fruit on the sideboard, oranges and bananas and something else he'd never seen before, a large fruit with scales on its skin and sharp leaves sticking out at the top.

Then a hand fell roughly on his shoulder and someone said, 'Leave them down there and get out,' and shoved him towards the door.

'Alex?'

'Sorry, something just came into my head.'

'Tell me,' she said, as she saw the hard lines of concentration ease.

'Nothing very interesting, love, but I will if you want me to. How about a cup of coffee?' he asked, standing up.

'We haven't very much left.'

'You haven't seen the box your friends sent you. It's in the back seat of the car,' he replied, beaming at her. 'Not surprised you missed it with the size of that thing full of daffodils. But if we haven't enough in the cupboard for two cups, I'll go out and bring it in, sleet or no sleet.'

It was as they finished their coffee that Alex suddenly remembered Hank's letter in the pocket of his suit. He fetched it from upstairs and handed it to her.

'But when did you see him?' she asked in surprise.

'He came ahead of the column and dropped back in as they passed Millbrook. He's very nippy in that jeep of his.'

'We met them further out when we were coming back from our deliveries,' she replied. 'He spotted me and waved and tooted his horn and of course the whole column saw us then. At least we were able to wave them goodbye, though what the passers by thought of the racket they made shouting and waving at us, I'd rather not know.'

Alex saw her glance down suddenly at the crumpled envelope and wondered why she looked so uneasy.

'I wish we knew where they were going,' she said sadly. 'No, that's silly, I don't mean that,' she corrected herself. 'What does it matter where they are going. What matters is that they'll be safe. And no one is safe anymore, anywhere.

'Maybe we never were,' she went on, surprised at her own words and close to tears. 'We only thought we were, but now we know for sure. Death is round every corner. I can manage death, I think, but I can't manage loss. I can't bear the thought of Hank, or any of those boys, never coming back, or never going home.'

'It's hard, love. And its harder for you than for others. You give so much. It's the way you are, but it costs. That's why those boys cheered when they saw you. You need to remember that.'

Emily wiped her eyes quickly with her hanky.

'I'm sorry. I'm probably just tired.'

'I'm sure you're tired after all you've done today, but that's not what's making you weep.'

'What is then?'

'Fear of loss.'

To his great surprise she smiled. A bleak little smile. After which, she seemed steadier.

'The worst thing about you, Alex Hamilton, is that you have a habit of being right,' she began. 'I can't complain that you don't understand me. Do you realise how irritating that is?' she asked, her face softening, as she pushed back her hair from her forehead and looked across at him.

'Sorry about that,' he said, trying to look repentant.

She looked again at the envelope lying in her lap, took it up, tore it open and pulled out the small, neatly written sheets.

'It's to both of us,' she said coolly, 'Shall I read it to you?'

'Yes, please,' he said, leaning comfortably back in his chair.

Dear Aunt Emily and Uncle Alex,

She paused for a moment only and then went on, her voice steady, her tone clear.

I hope you will not be upset or disturbed that I should address you thus, but I should regret it so if I were never to have that opportunity again.

I am neither optimistic or pessimistic about what lies ahead of any of us, I simply accept that now is the only time we can be sure of, so I take my chance.

I cannot help wishing that the conversation I had last Friday amid the geraniums could have taken place when first we met. But that is a useless regret. Better to say that I have had a whole week in which the picture of my world has changed and a quite unlooked for happiness has come to me.

I have written to my mother and told her that I think I have found her lost brother, or rather, that her lost brother and his wife have found me.

This is not a fond hope. I have gone over and over in my mind the fragments that would give weight to my argument and I have listed them on a separate piece of paper for you to check out for yourselves. But I have to confess that the piece of evidence that weighs heaviest in the scales of logic came to me in an extraordinary way.

When I searched the house for Aunt Emily, finding the door open and believing she would have locked it if she'd been out, I went quickly into every room. Later, when I apologised for what then might have seemed an intrusion, you said . . . you didn't intend to steal the family silver or check that I had dusted under the bed.

Going over and over the evidence in my mind as I have, of course, been trained to do, those words came back to me and suddenly I remembered that I had 'stolen' something. I had 'stolen a glance' at a picture of a young woman who was so like my mother that at the time I had to tell myself not to be silly. Homesickness can play strange tricks and I thought I had imagined a real likeness when I was simply looking at a picture of a pretty, blonde-haired girl.

Now, I feel sure the explanation is simple. This girl, whose name I do not know, is most certainly your daughter. She is also my cousin, for my mother was not romancing when she said she had a brother and that his name was Alexander. The mutual arrival date of May 1895 from Liverpool is too much of a coincidence to be other than a fact.

Time grows short and there is much to do before departure, but I shall find some means of delivering this letter in person to one of you.

The additional notes are for you both to pursue if you will. Fragments retrieved from my memory of my mother's stories stimulated by the happiest of thoughts that we may solve some old puzzles, while at the same time rejoicing in the good fortune which chance has brought us.

I am, happy to be,
Your nephew,
Alexander Lachlan Ross
alias, Hank the Tank.

CHAPTER ELEVEN

The sea was as calm as the proverbial millpond, a grey sheet spreading as far as the eye could see, the pale gleams of the setting sun catching the wash of the ship, tipping the white foam with gold. The hills of Antrim were a misty outline, those of Down had already disappeared beyond a light evening mist rising from the cool water after the first warm day of the year.

A strange journey it had been from the quiet of his own home in the early morning with Emily trying hard not to bother him with questions or reminders. First, to the mill, full of the throb of machinery and the stuffiness that the warmth of summer always brought. Then, to Belfast, through the burgeoning countryside, the May blossom already heavy on the boughs though it was still only the fourth of the month. On through the familiar towns and villages of the Bann valley, till suddenly the city lay before him, a haze of smoke hanging on the air from mills and factories as hard-working as the four he had left behind him.

Above the city to the north, the hard edge of the hills stood out against a brilliant blue sky, gorse blazing flame-yellow set against the rich green of new grass and the snowy mass of the hawthorn bushes. So, on through the city, its streets full of movement and clatter, Army lorries, and cars mixed up with wagons, drays and horse-drawn bread carts brought out of retirement to help save petrol.

The office in Linen Hall Street for which he was bound before his night crossing had not changed since before the first war. Some of its staff he had known for twenty-five years or more, since he had come there with the company's accountant to make arrangements for the payment of sums of money for materials or machinery so enormous he had difficulty then in grasping them.

Not any longer. He could now speak the language of finance as fluently as he spoke French or German. It was only a matter of familiarity. He sat at the well-polished mahogany table and studied the handsome, gold-framed portrait of the *Titanic* on the wall opposite while a white-haired man in a dark suit went through the sums requested on the Letters of Credit he'd brought with him and handed him discreetly a neat packet of papery notes for his hotel bill and personal expenses.

This was something to which he had never

grown accustomed, the obligation to stay at a particular hotel, to use taxis, to entertain lavishly, or as lavishly as the circumstances of war now permitted. But, however he might feel about such expense, even that had grown familiar.

He was glad to be free of the confining atmosphere of Head Office and to sit back in the obligatory taxi, his car now secured in their own small parking space. He felt even better as he strode up the gangplank to board the Liverpool boat, the prospect of the open sea bringing an unexpected delight.

Clear of the lough, the marked channel far behind, the ship was correcting its course to run east of the Copeland Islands and north of the Isle of Man, its destination Liverpool in the early morning.

Liverpool. He found himself repeating the name to himself like a new word in a foreign language. It felt as if the name meant something quite different from what it had meant back in March, before Hank had written to his mother. He'd known that the boat which took him to Canada had sailed from Liverpool, but any recollection of it was remote and unreal. In her first letter to them his new-found sister Jane had told them she and Alex had come to Liverpool from Manchester where they had lived near a big school.

'But Emily,' he'd protested, 'why didn't *I* remember that? I must be at least a year older than

Jane, but she says here she remembers Manchester. She even remembers things about the street where we lived.'

'Alex dear, Jane was a little girl,' she said patiently. 'Don't you remember how worried we were about Johnny, because he seemed so slow compared to the girls, slower to talk, slower to walk, certainly slower when he went to school, until one of his teachers told us it was perfectly normal. Girls move faster at times. They seem to be more aware of what's going on around them. It's later on they go dreamy. She said sometimes boys don't fully catch up till the very late teens.'

'So you think it's a genuine memory?'

'Yes, I do,' she said, nodding vigorously. 'And don't forget,' she went on, 'the Ross's never stopped Jane talking about what she remembered. They only thought she was romancing about her brother, because she'd invented a couple of brothers to replace the one she'd lost. But *they* didn't know much about little girls, they only had boys. While you, my dear love, were not encouraged to talk about anything, never mind your past. The things we remember best are the things we talk about, the stories we tell most often. You didn't have that possibility, so the things you might have remembered just slipped away.'

He looked down at the sparkling wash and saw it slip away, rippling outwards until it was finally absorbed into the undisturbed water beyond. Surely he must have looked at the sea on that long voyage. Prompted by the image before him, he did his best, but nothing came to him.

And then, quite suddenly, there was something, a smell and the sound of fabric flapping in the wind, the deck wet and slippery. Of course, he'd stood on tiptoe, but he still couldn't see over the tarpaulins that covered the inside of the ship's rails.

Startled, he stepped back from where he'd been leaning comfortably above the after deck and sat down on one of the wooden benches attached to the superstructure. He had just calculated that the top of the rail was over four feet above the deck when a woman with two children strolled past in front of him. The children paused, their shoes scuffing against the lowest section of the rails, which were covered with fine metal mesh. They poked their heads through to point to something in the water below. Then they ran on to catch her up.

He sat for a long time watching the light fade and listening to the muted throb of the engines. Perhaps there might be something to be retrieved from the dark corridors of memory. At least now, with Emily beside him and his sister returned to him, he had no fear of what might be revealed.

Despite a beautifully-served, if somewhat meagre dinner and the quietest of night crossings, Alex slept badly. He was haunted by bizarre dreams in which

German spies asked him questions he couldn't answer. It was not that he was being brave and withholding information, as happened in most of the war films he and Emily had seen, it was that he didn't know the answers. There was just a blank.

He was aware as he woke in the night that he'd had the same dream more than once, but what that dream was he couldn't recall.

'Cheat 'em. Cheat 'em,' the voice insisted, getting more and more irritated with him.

He woke, perspiring and confused, to find the steward standing by his bed saying 'Tea, sir.'

The tea was good and breakfast much more generous than dinner. Revived and steadied, he made his way around the decks of the ship studying the vessels docked alongside or lying at anchor beyond the harbour entrance, pale fingers of light playing on the grey camouflage of corvettes and cruisers, merchant ships unloading, the quays piled high with timber and sacks of grain, barrels and containers of all kinds.

From the stern of his own ship, the gangplanks had already been run out and soldiers were disembarking, heavily laden with equipment. He watched as an Army vehicle arrived with a senior officer, saw the soldiers form fours on the dock and march off in good order. He thought of Chris Hicks, taking delivery of yet one more bunch of young lads straight from camps in Louisiana or Texas, coming to train for what had to happen if the war was to be won.

As he descended the gangplank and reached the quay, he was greeted by a former employee of Bann Valley Mills. Roy Ainsworth, who would be his companion throughout his visit had once worked at Ballievy. Sent by his uncle in Manchester, the director of Bollin Valley Mill, he'd wanted Roy to broaden his experience and to work away from home. His nephew had done well and been recalled to a much more senior position.

The morning was fine, the light clear and he studied the very different countryside beyond Liverpool as Roy drove him to the mill on the outskirts of Manchester. He hadn't made this journey since early in the war and he noted the tangled barbed wire surrounding the featureless, prefabricated munitions factories, dropped down in the flat, green landscape, so different from the little hills of County Down that had long been his home.

An hour later he was standing in the weaving shed of a mill. The only sound the intermittent flicker of a faulty fluorescent strip light and the occasional helpful comment provided by his companion.

He cast his eye over the silent machines, taking in the fine layer of dust that had settled since they last ran, the small personal tokens one always found attached to uprights or a nearby wall. Vera Lynn. Glenn Miller. Tommy Handley. People who sang or made your feet tap or gave you a laugh.

As he decided that he really must say something to Roy, having been silent for so long, he thought that one of the saddest things he knew was a derelict mill, the motes dancing in the bright light, its life at an end, the sound of voices and laughter faded away.

'When did you close?' he asked politely.

Roy seemed relieved and Alex remembered what Emily had said to him so often in the past. 'Alex, dear, you look so cross when you are thinking, you'd frighten anyone who didn't know you.'

She was right, of course. Robert Anderson had told him the same thing years later. 'Yer a different man when you smile, Alex.'

Alex smiled now and listened as the young man gave him an account of the last months of the mill's functioning and the progressive run down as the orders for rationed goods, like household linens and clothing fabric, diminished week by week.

'Yes, we'd have had something of the same problem in Bann Valley Mills, but we moved over to war production early on,' Alex replied. 'I know its none of my business,' he went on, with an apologetic smile, 'but what about your workforce?'

Emily was right. So was Robert. Roy had never known Alex personally during his time at Ballievy. Now, he positively beamed at him and responded vigorously.

'That *is* good news, Mr Hamilton. You may have seen all the new factories on your way here. They need enormous numbers of workers. Munitions,' he added, with a quick nod, 'I don't think anyone will be short of a job. Not with what will have to happen next in Europe.'

They exchanged knowing glances and began to walk round the machines together in comfortable silence.

The day went swiftly by and at the end of it, when Roy Ainsworth drove Alex to his hotel in central Manchester, he was well pleased with what he'd found. Much of what he'd seen for both spinning and weaving were machines even older than what at present provided the backbone of Bann Valley Mills, though here and there were one or two obvious replacements that were much younger.

Far more important for his purposes than the actual age of the machines was the degree of wear they showed and that was what he'd spent his day examining. Wear was caused by continuous running and poor maintenance, but this machinery had been well looked after and due to the nature of what was being produced, there'd been periods of both short-time working and even full shut down. The progressive fall in demand over the war years had been fatal for the mill itself, but it had left the machinery in much better condition than the more recent models of the same equipment that Alex and the team of engine-men and mechanics were trying to keep going, especially at Millbrook.

Between the end of the working day and his meeting over dinner with the former directors of Bollin Valley Mill, Alex was preoccupied by the idea of removing the parts he needed on the spot. It would save the cost of transporting bulky equipment. Besides, there were bound to be delays in finding cargo space and he needed the parts urgently. It would be to the sellers advantage to receive payment as soon as possible, so speeding up the process should suit them well enough.

It was only as they sat over coffee, that evening, the negotiations amicable but somewhat slow, that a further inducement occurred to him.

'If it were possible to do the extraction work over here, you would be left with quite a valuable collection of scrap metal. Enough for a couple of tanks at least,' he said, smiling.

'Well now, I hadn't thought of that,' said the Chairman. 'And you'd not be asking for a reduction in the agreed price?'

'Most certainly not,' he replied firmly. 'We will have the benefit of reduced shipping costs, you'd benefit by the sale of the scrap.'

'And what about the extraction process? Is it a difficult job?'

'Quite a long one, but not difficult. I could mark

up everything we need in a morning. I could then send a couple of our men over to do the work, or employ some of yours. I noticed your repair equipment was still intact. That's all that would be needed, though some heavier duty cutting equipment would make the job quicker.'

Alex noted that the second pot of coffee summoned to aid the negotiations was even weaker than the first and not a patch on what they had at home, but the atmosphere grew steadily more agreeable as they consumed it and by the end of the evening there was goodwill all round.

The Chairman of the group to which Bollin Valley Mill belonged, had offered to arrange transport via a subsidiary company of his that had formerly delivered for the mill, but had since diversified and was still operating. He also suggested using labour from two mills now producing army uniforms on whose Board he also sat.

All that remained was for Alex to return to Bollin Valley the next morning and mark up what he wanted removed from the machines.

The sunshine was becoming hazy as Alex said goodbye to Roy outside the hotel. They had got on well together and today over lunch, they'd talked about the young man's new job in a sister company, about life in Manchester and the changes already planned for after the war.

It seemed the City fathers had given much thought to the redevelopment of the older parts of the city and particularly to the areas which had suffered during the bombing raids. As Alex listened to the enthusiasm of the younger man, he couldn't help but consider the contrast with the plans for Belfast. Or more precisely, the complete lack of them.

'You're sure you wouldn't like a tour of the city?' Roy asked, as they parted on the steps of the hotel. 'Or a short drive out into the countryside?'

Alex did wonder how the Chairman of Bollin Valley had managed to supply petrol for the car Roy had used. One of the perks of running your own transport company, perhaps. He thought then what a pity it was Cathy and Brian were no longer living just south of Alderley Edge. It would have been such a pleasant end to a successful trip to spend a few hours with his daughter before he was driven to the boat.

'No, thank you,' he said warmly. 'That's very kind, but I have some work to do and I may do just a little shopping for my wife. I don't often have such a good opportunity.'

'Well, then, if you are quite sure, I'll come back at six and drive you to Liverpool. Enjoy your afternoon.'

Alex turned back into the hotel and went up to reception.

'I wonder if you could help me,' he began, remembering to smile.

'Well, I'll certainly try,' said the smartly-dressed older woman behind the desk, her smile in return totally devoid of warmth.

'I've been wondering if there is somewhere nearby called Cheatam . . . or something like that,' he said tentatively.

'Well, yes, of course. There's Cheetham Hill and Chetham's School. Do you know the city at all?'

'I don't think so,' he said, wondering what fragment of memory might float back next.

'I have a map here,' she offered, producing one from below the desk. 'I'm afraid it's rather out of date and not the one we used to provide for guests, but it *does* show you how to get there,' she continued, turning it round towards him and pencilling a path from the door of the hotel to a large building at the end of a street called Long Millgate.

'Well, thank you very much,' he said promptly, making up his mind that perhaps shopping could wait. 'That's just what I want.'

The streets were crowded with men and women from all three services, their smart uniforms in marked contrast with the shabbiness of the other pedestrians. When the sun came out again, he took off his jacket, carried it over his shoulder and felt less uncomfortable and less conspicuous than before.

The bright light showed up the peeling

paintwork and soot-stained facades of the buildings, but here at least there was no bomb damage and he studied the tall, red-brick buildings carefully, remembering the comments he'd heard about the similarities between Manchester and Belfast. He noted the Corn Exchange and smiled as he turned into Long Millgate itself. One didn't have to guess what activity had gone on beyond the high walls.

To his great delight, he found the cathedral on his left appeared to be completely undamaged. In the small area of green in front of it a number of old men and old women were sitting on seats enjoying the sunshine. They looked as if they had always been there and that neither bombs, nor inclement weather would prevent them from sitting outdoors at all seasons.

He decided to walk all the way round the cathedral and thus found himself standing on Hanging Bridge.

'Why's it called Hanging Bridge?'

'Because that's where bad people were hanged.'

This time he was not startled. He just knew that once, long ago, he'd asked the same question and received the same answer, but he didn't know who had answered him.

He continued his walk and came back round to the point in Fennel Street from which he'd set out. There, across the road was Chetham's School of Music. If this was by any chance the school Jane had remembered, then somewhere nearby there would be a row of houses, probably ordinary little mill houses. Had they lived in anything grander, the two of them might have fared better than being sent to the Workhouse. Always assuming that it was the Workhouse they'd been sent to.

He consulted his map and decided to walk towards Cheetham Hill Road. Chetham and Cheetham. Was it the same word differently spelt, or two different words? He smiled to himself and thought that he should have Emily here. While he felt frustrated that he appeared to be doing a crossword puzzle without clues, she would actually enjoy the challenge. Besides, she had far more imagination than he had.

He found several small rows of houses, but all of them had suffered in the bombing. Here and there, a house was boarded up because the roof had fallen in and the whole structure was dangerous. In some places, a house was missing, like a tooth extracted from an otherwise perfectly functional set. In one place, two rows of houses set at an angle to each other had lost their join. Where one street should have changed its name to another, there was nothing but a heap of rubble, already crossed by well-tramped paths and colonised by grass and weeds.

He stood staring at the place, wondering how such prolific growth could possibly spring from such apparent barrenness, so engrossed that he did not notice the slow and painful approach of an elderly woman with a stick.

'Did you have family here?' she asked, without any preamble as she turned aside to stare at the rubble in front of him.

'I might have done, but it was a long time ago. Maybe fifty years or more,' he replied.

She laughed shortly.

'I was thinkin' maybe you knew the Cunninghams or the O'Sheas or the Grimleys,' she said sharply.

She waved her stick to one side of the heap of rubble where a small bush poked out between the edge of the rubble and the wall of the surviving house beside it.

'That was my mine there. Next that buddleia.'

Her tone softened a little, as she walked over to a piece of remaining wall and slowly lowered herself down, her legs splayed awkwardly, her stick clutched in both hands before she continued. 'I was visitin' m' daughter five doors up, or I'd not be talkin' to you now. Where're ye from?'

Alex laughed.

'Depends what you mean,' he said cheerfully. 'I could say, Banbridge, County Down. Or I could say Canada. But I might even be from here. *Somewhere* around here,' he ended, waving a hand around.

'What makes you think that?'

'Well, something lovely happened a few weeks back,' he began, deciding she must be tired and needed an excuse to go on sitting down. 'We discovered that I have a sister in Canada. We were sent out as orphans and separated. I didn't remember her, but she remembered me and by pure chance her son came to our part of the world with an American regiment of engineers and we found out who he was. Lovely young man. They called him Hank the Tank.'

To his amazement, her wrinkled face creased with laughter.

'I was in America once,' she admitted, still grinning. 'Not for long, for I didn't like it an' came home. And I knew a man was called Hank the Tank, but he was a drinker. You couldn't fill him. An' he never got drunk. Was your fella like that?' she asked, with a sideways look at him.

'No, he was just a good engineer, great with tanks.'

'Aye, I thought that was more like it,' she nodded. 'Could you drink a cup o' tea?'

For a moment, Alex was so taken back by the abrupt tone, more of a challenge than an invitation, that he didn't reply.

'It'll only be tea, most likely, but my Jeannie is only five doors up an' she's expecting me. Sure there's always another cup in the pot.'

'Thank you, that's most kind of you. Can I give you a hand up?'

Without waiting for an answer, he bent down and lifted her gently to her feet.

* * *

222

The house was small, even smaller than some of the old mill cottages he'd known round Ballievey, Tullyconnaught and Ballydown and seen demolished back in the late twenties. Jeannie, an untidy-looking woman with straggly hair, made him welcome without the slightest introduction having been made. She simply took another mug from the cupboard, said she was sorry there was no sugar, and offered him milk.

'So, Missus Campbell, where did you find this young man?' she said, laughing, as her mother sat herself down and hooked her stick over the back of her chair.

'He was standin' lookin' at the rubble as if he'd lost all belongin' to him. But he hasn't. He's found a sister in Canada an' he thinks he might even have been reared roun' here. Isn't that right?'

'Right indeed,' he agreed as he sipped his tea and glanced surreptitiously round the dim, stuffy room.

He noted the small coal-burning stove, alight even today which must mean it was the only source of heat for cooking. The armchairs had worn woollen rugs thrown over the original upholstery, there was broken linoleum on the floor and flaking brown paint on the wooden staircase to the upper floor.

'I seem to have no memory worth talking about, but my sister mentioned Manchester and living near a school. And then I had a funny dream about 'cheating 'em.' It kept going on in my head all day when I was working, so I finally thought, I'd ask someone.'

'An' did ye not know about Chethams or Cheetham Hill?' demanded Jeannie.

'No, any time I've been in Manchester it's been to visit mills. That's my job,' he added easily. 'I've never been in this part of the city before.'

'So what's your name then?' asked Mrs Campbell, leaning towards him.

'Hamilton,' he said. 'Alex Hamilton.'

Mother and daughter looked at each other and shook their heads.

'No, there's been no Hamiltons here that we know off and we've been here nearly sixty year now. An' Ma knew everyone, didn't you Ma?'

'Aye, when you're a midwife, you know people right from the start,' she said with her usual short laugh. 'An' I'll tell ye somethin' else. If I'd knowed your father or mother, I could see them in your face.'

Alex nodded and tried to think of something to say. He was quite shocked by his unreasonable sense of disappointment.

'Does your sister look like you, Alex? asked the younger woman, as she refilled the teapot from the kettle on the stove.

Alex smiled.

'No, she's better looking,' he said, with a brave attempt at a joke. 'She's blonde with blue eyes and looks just like my own youngest daughter.'

'An' what did you say her name was?' demanded the older woman sharply.

'My sister? She's called Jane.'

'An' what age would she be, younger than you?'

'A year or two. We don't really know. Neither of us ever had birth certificates. Or if we had, they didn't go with us.'

'He means to Canada,' said Mrs Campbell as Jeannie refilled her cup. 'The pair of them went to Canada, as *orphans*.'

'God forgive them,' said Jeannie, sitting down abruptly, her face pale.

'Alex Hamilton, I don't know who your father was,' began the older woman, 'but your mother was the sweetest woman I ever knew. She lived at the far end of this terrace and her name was Mary Jane. She musta been a widow, because she had a wee boy only just walkin' when she came here newly-married to Charley Williams. An' a year or so later, she had Jane. And I know it was Jane because I was with Mary Jane the night she was born and that child was lovely even then. Can you remember her at all, Jeannie, for you'd a been near ten when Mary Jane took ill?'

'Aye, I remember her,' Jeannie said firmly. 'Sure, she came running down to our house to tell us her mother wasn't well and she and Lekky didn't know what to do. She couldn't say your name when she was small, so you never got anything but Lekky,' she added, turning towards him.

'They took your mother to hospital and we were told the two of you would be looked after at the orphanage until she was well again. But she was ill for a couple o' months and when she came back home, the pair o' you were gone.'

They both looked at him, their faces blank, their eyes wide. He saw now the resemblance between mother and daughter. It was there in the face, particularly in the eyes. The same wide grey eyes.

'And then . . .'

He could not bring himself to ask, but he knew that the end of this tale was a sad one. He waited as patiently as he could till the older woman took up the story.

'Yer mother was out of her mind with worry. She couldn't find out at first what had happened, then when she did find out, they said there was nothin' she could do about it. It seemed that no one could help her though she wrote a letter to someone in Parliament and went to see a whole lot of people.

'She was a clever girl, she'd been a teacher, but no matter what she did, they said they didn't know where the children had been placed or that they didn't know where they now were. There was letters back and forth to Canada and when Charley came home he was for goin' out there to look for them. He was a merchant seaman and away on

226

the Australia run, so he didn't know what he was comin' home to. He gave up the sea to stay with her, for he was as bad as she was about the pair of them. He was on the dole a long time before he got a job and things were very hard for them. Then she took ill again. An' she died.

Charley sold up their few bits and pieces and went away. He talked about going to Australia, but the poor man didn't know what end of him was up. He might have gone there and he might not. He went away and he never came back.'

'And we never knew till today what happened to Jane and Lekky,' Jeannie added, as her mother stopped speaking and leant back wearily in her chair.

CHAPTER TWELVE

Emily was up even earlier than usual on Friday morning. After a calm crossing from Liverpool, the ship sometimes docked as early as six o'clock and Alex would ring her as soon as he arrived back at Millbrook. He had offered to drive home for breakfast, but she knew there would be a pile up of work waiting for him and after three days away goodness knows what emergency into the bargain. When he'd phoned briefly from Manchester after lunch on Thursday, she'd told him she'd rather he had breakfast on the boat and arrived home at a respectable hour on Friday evening, so his dinner wouldn't be spoilt.

There had been rain in the night, but as Emily filled the kettle and began to make her solitary breakfast, she saw the clouds roll back and patches of blue appear. By the time she'd eaten her toast, sunlight was falling on the kitchen floor and the drips hanging from the crossbar of the window were making tiny rainbows before they shimmered and fell.

She was feeling remarkably happy. Quite why she was so happy after a busy week with more than its quota of problems and no Alex to share them with, she didn't know, but as she moved around the kitchen tidying up and wiping crumbs from the breakfast table, she felt something was different, some anxiety had moved away, though she could put no name to it.

In the past, when Alex had to go to Manchester she'd worried about U-boats or bombing raids, but this time she was less anxious. Fairly, there was much less chance of a raid and everyone knew that the U-boats no longer risked operating in the Irish Sea, but she wondered if there was some change in herself that had made this absence easier to bear than she had expected.

Of course, it was possible that her good spirits were nothing more than the fact it was a lovely morning and Alex was coming home. He'd probably arrived in Belfast by now and would already be out of the city and driving the familiar roads in the freshness of a lovely May morning.

She was sure he'd be pleased that the much talked of change of government had finally come about while he was away. Basil Brooke, who'd been so successful with the farmers and then in reinvigorating war production, a practical man with

229

a gift for getting on with people, was now the new prime minister. If he were to address the problems of keeping up the morale of a workforce stretched to the limits, it would certainly improve life for Alex and his fellow directors.

Although Emily had read everything she could lay hands on about the new government and its ministers, she didn't think anything so public as government policy could have made her feel so sure things were really going to be better. No, it had to be much more personal than that.

She listened to the seven o'clock news as she washed her breakfast things and tidied the china cupboard while she had the time. There was no doubt that, despite the predictable grim news of battles fought and casualties sustained, there was now a rising tide of hope that the worst of the war might be over. The huge bombing attacks on German cities, including Berlin, and the landings in Italy had cost many allied lives, but each days brought news of German armies in retreat, U-boats being sunk and industrial areas devastated. Now everyone was talking about the Second Front, the battle to restore freedom to Europe and to rid Germany of the Nazis.

When the phone rang she dropped her damp dishcloth and ran into the hall.

'Alex?'

'Who were you expecting?'

She laughed, knowing from the tone of his voice that all was well.

'Did you have a good crossing?'

'Must have done. Don't remember a thing about it.'

'And you got what you wanted?'

'Oh yes, I got what I wanted,' he said quickly. 'But there's something I'd like tonight, if it's not too much trouble.'

'What's that?' she asked warily, as she picked up the tense edge in his voice.

'A bowl of champ.'

'Oh Alex,' she said laughing again, 'what *did* they give you in the restaurant?' she demanded, remembering his hotel had been famous for its French cuisine before the war.

'Carre d'angneau, beurre noisettes.'

'Alex,' she expostulated. 'What is that when it's at home?'

'Stringy lamb chops with the bones cut out, tied in a circle, in thin gravy. And new potatoes.'

'And were they?' she asked dubiously, thinking of the progress of her own crop.

'Well as they were all circular, exactly the same size and tasted of nothing very much, I rather doubt it.'

'But apart from being half-starved, you're all right?'

'I'm fine. I'm so glad to be home.'

* * *

The day seemed long to Emily, though she enjoyed the sunshine and having such an uninterrupted stretch of time to herself. There was always a great deal to do in the garden in May and there were jobs in the house that had been neglected so she could get on with the sowing and planting out. She made a list of the most urgent and tried not to exhaust herself.

'If they've waited this long they can wait a bit longer,' she said to herself, late in the afternoon, as she looked at what was left on her list, took off her apron and sat down with her book.

By the time she heard the car in the drive, however, she had reached the stage of walking round the house looking for something to do, a restless agitation threatening to take away the sense of ease and pleasure she'd had in the day.

'Hello, love,' she said, as he came through the back door clutching a small suitcase, his overcoat draped over his arm.

He dropped them both on the kitchen chair and hugged her.

'I was planning to bring you a present,' he began sheepishly, 'but I didn't get to the shops after all.'

'Don't worry about that, it's just lovely to have you home.'

'I have actually brought you a present, but its not the kind you put in a bag. I've found my mother.'

'Alex!'

Emily clapped a hand to her mouth, her eyes

wide, a sudden reassuring sense that this was it, this was the source of the happiness and the agitation that had come upon her at intervals through the day.

'She died many years ago,' he said steadily, 'but now I know who she was and something about her and I know what happened, I feel so different. It wasn't her fault.'

To her absolute amazement, he burst into tears and wept.

As she put her arms round him, she tried to remember the last time she'd seen him cry apart from that night when they had both wept for Ritchie. It was such a rare event, it came to her almost immediately. It was the night they'd had the news that John Hamilton had died. A warm August evening, the evening of the very day on which Alex had gone up to Rathdrum to tell him that little Johnny had arrived at last and mother and baby were doing well.

Later that evening, the sky cleared and the temperature dropped like a stone. Alex insisted there was even a hint of frost in the air as he lit the sitting room fire. As it crackled and sprang to life, casting reflections on well-polished furniture, she sat, neither knitting or sewing, simply listening as he told his story.

For a man who was normally so sparing with words, she was surprised at how detailed an account he gave her. How carefully he must have observed Mrs Campbell and her daughter and what a clear picture he'd been able to put together of their small corner of the city as it had been some fifty years ago.

'And Mrs Campbell just asked you in for a cup of tea?' she asked, when he paused to drink his coffee.

Alex smiled and shook his head.

'I didn't spot the accent at first,' he confessed, 'but when she told her daughter that *I was standin' there as if all belongin' to me were dead* I realised she was an Ulsterwoman and *you* know very well that your countrywomen can be very direct along with their being very kind.'

'Yes, that's true. If I saw a stranger looking a bit lost I'd speak,' she replied, nodding thoughtfully.

'She said her family were from Portadown, but she met Campbell at a dance in Belfast. He was on the cargo boats so he had a girl on both sides. So she said,' he added, raising his eyebrows. 'When they married, he got a job on the railway down at Victoria Station and he walked back and forth to work for over thirty years. But he had a weak heart and died in his sixties.'

It was clear to Emily that Mrs Campbell had taken a liking to Alex and that she'd appreciated the way he listened to her story rather than question her about his own. She waited now as patiently as she could while he told her about Maggie Campbell's life as a midwife and her daughter Jeannie's unhappy marriage to a man who drank and abused her before finally going off with another woman.

'She only realised who I was when I described my sister Jane,' he began again, after a pause. 'She was the midwife who delivered her and she lived nearby, but she said at first she didn't remember me at all. Then she said that when our mother became ill, Jane ran down to her and said that she and Lekky didn't know what to do. Jane called me Lekky, because she couldn't say Alex. And once the name Lekky was mentioned she began to remember a whole lot of other things.'

'She'd said she thought my mother was a widow, newly remarried when she came to the street, because she had a wee boy barely walking. My mother was Mary Jane Williams, she'd been a teacher and she taught us both to write before we were old enough to go to school. My step-father, Charley, was a merchant seaman, so he was away for long periods of time which is probably why neither Jane nor I remember him. But, then suddenly, when she was talking about Charley, she said that he'd been Lofty's best friend.'

'Lofty? So who was Lofty?'

'Lofty was my father,' he said simply. 'He died in an accident at sea and his best mate Charley came to tell my mother. What Mrs Campbell actually said was, *'In those days a woman was in a bad way if she was a widow. Charley might well have fallen for her, but even if he hadn't and was a good man, he might have married her, so she'd get the separation allowance.'*

'Apparently,' Alex went on, 'the merchant service sends a monthly allowance direct to the wives,' he added, 'so she'd have had something to live on. I doubt if there was even such a thing as a widow's pension in those days.'

By the time Alex had told her how Mary and Charley had searched for their lost children the fire was burning low and the room had grown dark. Emily sat looking thoughtfully into the last embers of the fire while he stood up and turned on the smallest of the table lamps in the large room.

'So you've found your father too,' she said, now able to see his face again in the pale glow.

'Well, you could say that,' he agreed, 'At least I know I had one, if you see what I mean.'

'Yes, I do see what you mean,' she replied. 'You were no unwanted child from a passing fancy. You had a mother who loved you and a step-father who treated you as his own. You even know a little now about your own father.'

'That he was tall and a sailor. That's about the height of it.'

'Height indeed,' she said, laughing. 'But he must have given you your broad shoulders. Your mother didn't, did she?'

'I never thought of that,' he said, his face lighting up with the smile that always delighted her. 'You're a very clever girl,' he said, putting his arms round her.

Emily took one look at her youngest daughter as she stepped into the kitchen, reached out her hand for her overnight bag and pulled a chair from under the kitchen table.

'Oh Jane dear, you look exhausted. Did you have to walk from the station?'

'No, I'm fine, Ma. Been on nights and need to sleep a bit, but I got a lift with the bread man. He'd have brought me up the hill, but he's short of petrol and hills eat it up, so he says,' she reported, with a big smile, as she collapsed gratefully onto the chair and leant her elbows on the table.

'What's happened to his horse?'

'Cast a shoe and needs to go to the forge tonight, so he had to use the van and the emergency can of petrol,' she explained, yawning. 'Any chance of a piece of toast, Ma?' she went on, as she watched her mother fill the kettle.

'Yes, of course. Are you just hungry or did you skip breakfast?' she asked cautiously.

'Both,' Jane replied laughing. 'I got a lift to the Great Northern, but it meant going straight from the ward. Gave me an extra two hours at home though.'

'You *could* have scrambled eggs with a small piece of bacon on top,' Emily offered, with a twinkle in her eye.

'Oh Ma, and real eggs too I'll bet.'

'Of course, nothing but the best in this restaurant,' Emily replied. 'Even your father came home from a top hotel and asked for champ.'

'He sounded so happy when I phoned,' Jane said, as she watched Emily move around the kitchen preparing to make breakfast for her. 'And excited,' she went on, 'as if something wonderful had happened.'

'I think it has,' agreed Emily. 'He's different and it's lovely. I've never known him in such good spirits.'

'What about you, Ma?'

'Better than I've been for a long time,' she said honestly. 'I hadn't realised just how much I worried about everything, especially my family. I still do it, probably always will, but it's seemed easier since the Manchester trip. I know there's no point in worrying about things, but do you have anything in *your* textbooks that tells you how to stop someone worrying?'

'No. There's plenty of stuff about the importance of reassurance,' she said, yawning again, 'That works quite well in the short term, but tell someone with a brand new leg, just out of the sterile wrapping, that it's all going to be fine, just fine, and you're simply

238

being silly. Sometimes it's far better to make a joke and that reminds them they're still here and not in bits somewhere . . . I'm sorry, I can't stop yawning. I'm not *that* tired.'

'Maybe it's the fresh air. When did you last see any?'

'Last week. I had a walk on The Mall in Armagh with my fiancé.'

Emily laughed as she set Jane's scrambled eggs in front of her, dropped two extra slices of bread in the toaster and poured tea for them both.

'You're teasing me,' she said with a smile.

'No, I'm not,' Jane replied, as she munched happily. 'Look!'

She put down her fork and waved her left hand just long enough for Emily to see a small gold signet ring on her engagement finger.

'Weren't we lucky? It's the only thing Johann possesses and he had to ask the Camp Commandant if he could please have it back. I'm sure it's against the regulations, but they do bend them quite a lot up in Dungannon. Which reminds me, I have a present for you,' she went on quickly. 'Bottom of suitcase. Don't let me forget. Yes, please, I'd love another cup, I'm so thirsty. Aren't you going to have a piece of toast with me?'

'No thanks, love. I had a proper breakfast. Do eat that other piece if you can, the birds have plenty of food in this weather.'

'I'd forgotten how good food can taste,' Jane said, sitting back in her chair, her teacup to her lips. 'They do try hard at the hospital, but mass cooking can be grim. Usually when one comes off night duty things are either hot and dried out or cold. That was lovely.'

Emily laughed and refilled the teapot. If the kitchen got any hotter as the June sun rose higher in the morning sky, they'd have to move into the sitting room or find a shady spot in the garden, but she was reluctant to move just now until she'd found out rather more about what had been happening just recently.

Despite the dark circles and the rather too pale skin, Jane was full of liveliness. Very much Jane's own particular brand of liveliness, but one that hadn't been around for quite some time. Not surprising in one way, given how hard she and all her colleagues worked and the very badly damaged people they worked with. Jane seldom mentioned the bodies being patched together, the men who would never walk unaided again, whose job was now to learn to use a stick, a walking frame or a wheelchair.

'So what about this walk in Armagh? You can't mean it, can you?'

'Yes, I can, but you mustn't mention it to anyone.'

'Mum's the word.'

'The guards are all pretty decent. They know

240

perfectly well that most of the boys in the camp were forced into action and want nothing more than to go home. Except Johann, who wants to stay with me. They all know me pretty well now. They even try to get me the odd extra pass. Well, a couple of weeks back, one of the guards told me that he was taking Johann to see Armagh. He told me the day and the time, and where the bus stops on The Mall.

'I knew he wasn't pulling my leg, because some of the other boys told me they'd been billeted at the Gough Barracks last autumn and had been set to work sweeping leaves. So I went to Armagh on the day, got out of the bus on The Mall and sure enough there they all were, weeding the paths and cutting the edges and pruning the side shoots on the trees.'

'But they must have been in POW gear?'

'Yes, of course they were. But by good luck it was a cloudy day, threatening rain, so when I appeared, one of the guards just handed Johann a cape and an umbrella and said: 'Off you go. Show him the sights, Jane, but don't go outside the wall. Anyone comes too close, put your arms round him an' they'll look the other way.'

'And did they?'

'I didn't actually notice,' she said honestly. 'We just walked round and round all afternoon and talked and I pointed out the two cathedrals and all the churches and the courthouse and the jail. And when the rain came on, we stood under a tree with

241

the umbrella up as well and Johann asked me to marry him. Then we went and told everyone and they all shook our hands, guards as well. Then he had to march back to the Barracks and I caught the bus back to Belfast.'

'That's one to tell to your grandchildren, Jane,' said Emily, who was blinking vigorously, determined not to cry.

'Yes, we thought of that and we made a note of the tree. It's a fairly young one, so we reckoned it would be there for a long time for us to go back and visit.'

'It is quite the loveliest little bird I have ever seen,' said Emily, as she turned the small gift in her hand, studying the details of beak and feathers. 'How kind of him, Jane, when he doesn't even know me. Has he always made things?'

'No, never. It's the South Germans who do the woodcarving and Johann's home is in the north, just outside Hamlin, the Pied Piper's town,' she explained. 'But he wanted to learn and they were happy to teach him. They make lots of little things to give to the locals and to the guards. Sometimes they get a packet of cigarettes in return, but more often they just give them away. I think they're lovely too.'

'Have you had any news of his mother?' Emily asked, sitting down on the bedroom chair while Jane folded up her nighty and repacked her small case.

'Nothing yet. The Red Cross are very good at finding people, but things in Germany are very bad . . .'

She broke off and sat down on the edge of the bed.

'The worst thing, Ma, is listening to the news and hearing about the raids. So many tons of bombs on Dortmund or Hamburg and how many were drowned when the Mohne and Eder Dams were blown up. Everyone round me being so pleased, because that's how we'll win the war, but those poor people didn't want the war any more than we did,' she said sadly. 'Da can't bear to talk about that night he was in Belfast, but it must have been a hundred times worse in the German cities . . . Do you think about it, Ma, or is it only me because of Johann?'

'No love, it's not just you. I've always thought about it. Even more in the last week since your Uncle Sam came over to see us. What he told us reminded me that you probably have cousins in the Wehrmacht and the Luftwaffe and perhaps even the S.S.'

'Ma, how come?' Jane demanded, her eyes wide with amazement.

'Well, if you remember, Granny Rose had a brother called Sam. He'd be your Great-Uncle Sam. He went to America and married a German woman called Eva. They had four sons and two daughters and rather a lot of grandchildren. One of the grandchildren, Lieutenant Sean McGinley turned up at Liskeyborough a few weeks ago asking for Sam Hamilton.

'He had a letter with him that your Granny Rose had written to his grandfather, Sam McGinley, back before the First World War. Quite how he came to have it, Sam didn't tell us, but the young man had carefully brought it with him. In that letter, Rose mentions all the family by name and refers to Ballydown and Liskeyborough, which was how Lieutenant McGinley knew where to go. But one of the things she asks your Great Uncle Sam in her letter is whether Patrick is still determined to go to Germany and whether it really is a visit to his mother's people or whether it is to carry letters and requests for weapons. We know Eva had a large family back in Germany and it looks as if some of the McGinleys were in touch with them, though I really don't know anything about the gun business. Either ways, we have a German connection through them.'

Jane shook her head and smiled.

'My goodness, Ma, we don't know the half of it, as Granny Rose used to say when we were small. There's always more to know and things aren't always as clear-cut as one might think.'

'That's what makes life difficult at times,' said Emily thoughtfully. 'I do try to think round things and see if I can find another way of looking at them, but sometimes that only makes it worse.'

'What is it you've been trying to think round, Ma?'

'Lizzie,' she replied honestly.

'Have you had anything from her since I was last home?'

'No.'

'Oh, I am sorry. I'm sure it was me and Johann upset her. I did try to explain,' Jane said, looking at her sadly. 'I wrote and told her how things had happened between us, but she didn't reply. I wrote to Cathy as well,' she went on quickly. 'She was fine and wrote back straight away. She understood, but she didn't know what to make of Lizzie. She said she was sorry she couldn't think of anything to help. The only thing she said in the letter that really struck me was that Lizzie says she wants to go to university when the war's over. That seemed like something quite new. I never thought she'd want to go on studying, she was so glad to leave school.'

'Maybe going to university is the opposite of getting married. What do you think?'

'I think something made Lizzie very unhappy and she's not telling any of us. But she's got a plan of some sort. There's something she wants to do, or something she wants to be, and she probably thinks we wouldn't understand.'

'But we'd never stop her doing what she wanted to do, you know that, don't you?'

'Yes, I *do* know that,' she replied reassuringly. 'You said it when I wanted to be a nurse and I believed you. But Lizzie doesn't believe things, unless they are all cut and dried.'

'The last time she came home she'd just got a stripe,' Emily began, trying to remember as exactly as she could. 'It was as a result of a course she'd been on and she seemed very pleased about it. She was very tired and when I mentioned her being tired, she said *endurance was part of it.*'

Emily stopped and looked at Jane, hoping she might see something she herself had missed.

'Cathy did say she'd got another stripe, but that was recently, so that must be another one, mustn't it?'

'Yes, it must be,' Emily agreed, thinking once again of that last unhappy visit before her posting and wondering if there was anything else she could tell Jane about it.

'Do you think it's ambition, Ma? Does she want to get to the top of whatever it is she does that we know she can't talk about to any of us?'

'That would fit with wanting to go to university after the war wouldn't it? She did mention she might be moved to London. I think she said something about the Air Ministry . . .'

'Ma, you're worrying again.'

246

'Oh dear, and I was trying to give it up, wasn't I?'

Jane beamed at her, that warm smile which had never changed since childhood. She wondered if that was the way she encouraged her patients. Jane's smiles had always been hard to resist.

She smiled herself and suddenly felt lighter. Talking to Jane always helped. There was something about the way she listened that made things smoother and calmer.

'Have you and Johann decided what you'll do when he's free to go home?' she asked, knowing they had only a little time left before Alex arrived to take her to the station.

'Yes, we have. If we know where his mother is, we'll go and see her, but we'll be married here. Johann thinks he might be able to work as a gardener until he can train for some skilled work. We'd have to save up for that and I'd go on working till he was qualified. So you won't be a granny for ages.'

'Thank goodness for that,' Emily said, laughing. 'I'm feeling my age enough these days after I've been in the garden without someone around to call me Granny!'

CHAPTER THIRTEEN

As Emily stepped out of the back door and felt the sun warm on her shoulders, she decided what she was going to do. She made her way to the far end of her vegetable garden, sized up the ripening rows of peas and beans and came to the conclusion it would have to be the Women's Institute market on Saturday mornings. Probably every Saturday morning the way things were shaping.

Last autumn, when she'd been so surprised at just how welcome her produce had been, she'd thought ahead and ordered more seed and more bundles of young plants for the Spring. Helped by the dry weather in March and long hours of sunshine in April and May, she'd opened up some new drills and everything she'd planted was doing even better than she'd expected. Already, at only the beginning of June, she was producing far more than last year.

The problem was getting it to market.

At the peak of last summer, she'd used the WI

market to sell what she couldn't give away, but it meant asking Alex to get up even earlier than usual on a Saturday morning and then being left standing outside the Church Hall surrounded by her sacks and boxes till the caretaker came and let her in. That wouldn't do if she were going every week. Besides, it wasn't fair to Alex.

Alex had laughed when she'd raised so much money from the unused strip of land adjoining their garden and she would willingly work for the Red Cross again, but now she knew someone who needed money very badly indeed, a young man who didn't have a penny to his name, though he did have a girl who loved him, a girl who would work hard to support him.

As she stood fingering the ripening pods of peas, she cast her eye down the long rows and laughed suddenly. The front basket and the back carrier of her bicycle wouldn't go far to accommodate this lot going down to market in Banbridge.

She was still standing in the sunshine, looking out over the vigorous growth, hoping for sudden inspiration, when she heard a vehicle in the drive. Definitely not Alex. She came hurrying down the path to the yard just in time to see a jeep swing round the house and park opposite the back door.

A jeep arriving to deliver supplies or to collect cakes was no longer an unusual event, but it was unexpected to find Chris Hicks himself driving it.

He was in uniform but he'd shed his jacket and rolled up his sleeves. Without his cap and military markings, she had never seen him look less like the commander of a large and active camp full of young engineers.

'Chris, how lovely. What a surprise! How did you escape?' she asked, as he jumped down and came towards her.

'Been asked to vamoose,' he said lightly. 'Couldn't think where I might be welcome, except here.'

'Oh Chris, you'd be welcome anywhere you went,' she replied easily, though she'd noticed a heaviness about his face when he wasn't actually smiling. '*Could you use a cup of coffee?*' she added in her best Vermont accent.

'And how, Emily, and how.'

She sat him down at the kitchen table while she moved round making the coffee and cutting cake in a practiced routine, for she regularly entertained the young men who delivered her baking materials and collected up the results of her efforts.

'Come into the conservatory, Chris, it's not too hot in there yet and there's a nice smell of geraniums and lemon balm,' she said, as she completed the tray, carried it through and set it down between the two comfortable chairs.

'Now tell me about you having to vamoose.'

'Oh it's just a routine inspection,' he said off-handedly. 'Top brass give the place the once over.

Should have happened a couple of times already since we've been here, but staff are short.'

'And they send you away?'

'That's right,' he nodded, taking his coffee from her. 'It's a kind of tradition in the engineers that anyone can say anything during an inspection. Don't know when I last got a couple of hours away.'

'You look tired, Chris,' she said, passing him the cake.

'All God's children are tired,' he replied, a weariness in his tone she had never heard before.

'Something's wrong,' she said gently, looking him full in the face. 'Look, if its top secret I can certify this conservatory is bug free and I have security clearance. Tell me what it is and it will be forgotten as soon as you get back in the jeep.'

What he said next took her completely by surprise.

'It's my little girl. She's forgotten me.'

He looked so utterly dejected, she wished she could put her arms round him and comfort him, but she wasn't sure how he'd feel about that and didn't want to embarrass him.

'Oh Chris, what makes you think that?'

'Carrie says so. She's tried, I know she has, but little Tilly is four now and she was only just two when I went away.'

'Can you send her presents?'

'Shure. Carrie buys them and wraps them and

251

says: *Look what your Daddy sent you,* and she just doesn't connect. All she has is photographs. And she notices the funny stamps on the letters.'

'Has she started school?'

'Not till the Fall. September, I mean,' he corrected himself, with a ghost of a smile.

Emily paused and looked around her. Her eye caught Johann's little bird which she'd put under a miniature rosebush on the shelf next to where Chris was sitting. She reckoned she'd see it oftener there than if it were in the sitting room or the bedroom.

'Come on, Chris, have some more cake,' she said, encouragingly. 'I've got the answer, I know I have. I'm just waiting for it to be sent up from wherever its lurking. Don't you ever have to wait for answers?'

'Shure. Sometimes you think they'll never come.'

'But if you've got the right problem, it helps, doesn't it? So often we just worry, we don't say '*This is the problem. Now how do we solve the problem*?'

'So what's my problem, Emily?' he said, looking a little more like himself, as he munched his cake.

'Well, apart from being homesick and missing your wife and family you have a little girl who has nothing to associate with you . . . except funny stamps . . .'

She broke off and beamed at him.

'I think it's just starting to come up. I have an idea. Now, how about another cup of coffee. These cups are a bit small for coffee American style.'

'Now, I know she can't read,' she went on, as she refilled his cup, 'but why don't you start writing her letters. Just short ones, in big letters. Can you draw?'

'Well, I suppose so . . .'

'Stick figures, faces, pussycats?'

He nodded.

'The important thing is that they are addressed to *her*. Miss Tilly Hicks. And she'll have to open them herself,' she explained. 'Carrie can read the words, but there must be something Tilly can grasp by herself. Have you ever pressed flowers?'

'No, Emily, I think I can assure you that is a skill I do not possess,' he said, with a small glint of laughter in his eye.

'Well, it's easy and I'll show you how,' she said quickly, 'But just imagine when she opens the letter from Daddy and some rose petals fall on the floor, or a spray of lemon balm that still smells of lemon, all the way across the Atlantic,' she went on, waving to the plants on the shelf beside him. 'I know the post is good, Chris. I have an old school friend lives in Texas and when she writes, it only takes four days, and she says mine are the same . . .'

She broke off, delighted to see a broad smile on his face. He looked a different person, younger, easier and happier.

'Emily Hamilton, you are one remarkable lady,'

he said slowly. 'You'd make a good general if you weren't a lady, but I'm glad you are and I'm grateful,' he continued soberly. 'Now, how do I press flowers? Between finger and thumb or with a mallet?'

Thursday 10th June, 1943

My dear Cathy,
I was so delighted to get your letter and I do apologise for not replying immediately.

I had a quiet morning in the conservatory last Friday, but first Chris Hicks arrived and we talked for a long time about his family and mine and then, just after he'd gone, Daisy, arrived gasping that Mary had fallen and couldn't get up. She'd been off school with a bad cold and had run up the hill to tell me.

I'm afraid she's sprained her ankle rather badly and is only just able to hobble around, so I've been going down the hill each morning to help with the jobs she simply can't manage. Typically, just when I'm busy there, the vegetables are shooting up, there are pounds of peas and beans to pick and because its bone dry and not a sign of rain, I'm having to water. I love watering, as you know, especially in the cool of the evening, but I seem to end every day ready to fall asleep in my chair, when yet once again I had thought I would spend the evening writing to you.

So, my dear, let me begin in case anything else should happen to prevent me getting this letter to you at your new address by the weekend.

What wonderful news! Da and I were so delighted and relieved to hear that you'd found a real flat with your own front door. There is no doubt having a room and sharing kitchen and bathroom is very problematic, though of course, you didn't have any choice whatever.

I was particularly delighted that it is an old house divided into floors and that you are at the very top. I know it's a nuisance when you've shopping to carry all the way up, or rubbish to bring down to the bins, but I got the feeling that you and Brian were glad to be private again and to have that view over those old gardens with real trees.

I know you'll want to go back to your work with the WVS, indeed, I know it is now required that you work, as you have no children, but do see if you can get some time in which to settle in. Even in a furnished flat, you can make things nicer, especially as you are so good with a needle, but it does take time.

I am enclosing a small gift which I hope will buy something to brighten or freshen the flat. Da says my garden is just growing money and I must admit it is nice to feel I can send you some. I'm sure you'll be pleased to know I'm opening an account for Jane and Johann. You and Brian had a whole year's separation before you decided you couldn't wait any longer, but Jane may have much longer to wait than that and, unlike you and Brian, she can save very little from a nurse's salary.

Yes, Johnny is well. His letters are very short, but mercifully they have been more frequent lately after some dreadfully long gaps. I now really understand that saying: NO NEWS IS GOOD NEWS. While there is no letter from his Commanding Officer or the MOD we must be grateful that he is alive and well, even if we don't hear from him.

The postmark on this recent one was obliterated, as one expects, but the fragment of stamp poking out from the Censors marks looked slightly exotic, certainly not Europe. Both Da and Chris Hicks say that somewhere in the Mediterranean is most likely. After the Allied successes in North Africa they both agree it is only a matter of time before there is a landing on the European coast, perhaps

Greece or Italy. So he may be moving again in the near future.

There has been nothing from Lizzie. Jane and I did talk about her when she was last home and she said she thought Lizzie had another stripe. I'm afraid I've got mixed up and can't work out how many that is now. Do please tell me in your next letter. I'm glad you are still in touch and hope to see her when she comes to London. It is sad that she hasn't written to us, but sometimes family can seem a burden, even when they don't mean to be. Give her our love.

Da is as busy as ever, but mercifully there are no 'extra' problems, if you know what I mean. A certain person we cannot name has escaped over the border, but has been interned by the Garda and we think the 'mole' is a young man you knew from school days. Very large and very strong, but not very bright.

Goodness, do you remember one of your girlfriends once wrote in your autograph book:

When you marry Jimmy and have twins
Don't come to me for safety pins!

I'm afraid he was a bit of a joke at school, but it was never unkind, at least to his face.

Now, my dear Cathy, this letter is getting

*out of hand. Looking at that last sentence
I think I am wandering, so I will stop and
either catch the bread man or walk down the
hill to post this myself.*

*Da sends his love with mine and we wish
you and Brian joy of your new home. Take
care of each other,*

Lots of love,

Ma.

Emily was watering in the vegetable garden
when Alex arrived home that evening a little earlier
than usual.

'Don't let me get in the way of the good work,'
he said smiling wearily.

'I'd nearly finished,' she said, placing the hose
carefully in the trench alongside the beans. 'If I leave
it on for another ten minutes or so it'll do the job
for me,' she explained, as she came up and gave him
a kiss.

'Wasting water?' he said sharply.

She burst out laughing.

'If there's one thing we don't have to worry
about on this island it's having enough water,' she
retorted, shaking her head. 'Have you forgotten
what last autumn was like? I'm surprised the Silent
Valley didn't overflow.'

'I like teasing you,' he said quietly, as they
stepped into the kitchen.

'What news from Bann Valley Mills,' she asked, as he flopped down on a kitchen chair while she lit the oven.

'Had a brief word with your friend Daisy Elliot,' he replied with a grin. 'Said to send you her best and hoped you were well.'

'Oh that's nice of her. How is she?' she asked, as she stepped into the larder, took up the casserole she'd made in the morning and put it in the oven.

'Pleased with the plan the pair of you hatched out between you,' he replied matter-of-factly.

'Hmmm,' she muttered, straightening up, 'But is it working?'

'*She* thinks so. Jimmy wasn't happy about giving up the sweeping and tidying, but then he discovered he could tidy the stores to his heart's content, as the saying is. He does have a remarkable memory, so it doesn't actually matter all that much that he can barely read. Head Storeman says he's getting on grand, can do the work of two men when it comes to lifting or carrying, and he remembers everything he's ever laid a hand upon.'

'And I presume you have no classified parts in the storerooms?'

'Not a thing. He could list every spare stenter hook or shuttle and no one would be a bit the wiser.'

'Oh Alex, that is good news. What about money? Does he earn a wee bit more?'

'No, not for that job. We couldn't bend the

rules on that, but we found a way round, or rather Daisy did. She suggested we give him a small weekly gratuity for being on twenty-four hour standby as a First Aider.'

'And how's he managing that?'

'Very well, I'm told. He's still very slow when he bandages, but he's good at it. And he's so pleased with himself. That's the nicest part.'

'Oh that's lovely, Alex. Isn't it nice to have good news? I told Cathy that your man Patrick Pearse Doherty had been interned, so that's the end of *his* bomb making career,' she said cheerfully. 'Oh Alex,' she went on instantly, 'don't look like that. I'm not *an idiot*. I didn't mention his name to her in a letter . . .'

She broke off, looked at him carefully.

'Are you teasing me again?'

'Yes,' he said, smiling. 'Shall I go and turn off the Silent Valley while you serve up?'

'And what news from the Home front?' he asked, as they finished their meal and took their coffee into the sitting room.

'I finally managed to write to Cathy and I had a visitor. He sends his greetings and says he thinks he'll see us for dinner every two months now and not every three.'

'Chris? How did he get away?'

'That's what I asked him too, given he can never come and have a meal with us. He says it's a kind of

260

inspection. He rather suspects that he's about to be asked to take more lads and train them faster.'

'Makes sense. But hard on Chris. It's fairly concentrated training as it is, but then there was a time when pilots were being turned out in two weeks.'

'Was there? But surely Johnny was nearly three months at Greencastle.'

'Possibly that was due to lack of staff and aircraft,' he responded. 'As far as I remember, they weren't building fighters over here at that time. Shorts were on Sunderlands and planes for Coastal Command, so they'd have to get planes for training from across the water. But over there during the Battle of Britain, training just got shorter and shorter.'

'And the losses in training got higher, like poor Ritchie.'

He nodded and said nothing.

'Chris had a problem with his little girl,' she began, when she had collected herself and could be sure her voice was steady.

She told him about their efforts on behalf of Tilly.

'He's gone off with some red rose petals and he's promised to show me his sketches when we go up to meet the next new team. And then he solved a problem for me,' she laughed, having just remembered.

'And what was your problem?'

'Surplus production and inadequate transport,' she replied crisply.

'And how did he solve that without misappropriating scarce resources?'

She laughed.

'The one thing I hadn't thought of was how much a camp eats,' she replied, shaking her head. 'They have stewards looking for fresh food all the time, so they can take everything I can grow. They'll come and collect it when it suits me and if I need pickers, he'll send the most homesick boys he has and expect me to cheer them up.'

'And he's going to pay . . . ?'

'Yes, of course. We did argue a bit, because he offered me far more than the WI but I said no, the WI was the going rate. So we agreed I was to have a small bonus in coffee. I think our supply is now guaranteed. Aren't we lucky?'

'We are indeed,' was Alex's heart-felt response. 'Long may it continue, as the saying is.'

Throughout the long weeks of June and into July, it seemed as if everything that could go well, did go well. To begin with, Alex had to work even longer hours while the machinery cannibalised from the mill in Manchester was re-installed in the most elderly and worn of the Bann Valley machines, but the results of his effort were instantaneous and tremendously encouraging. Production rose immediately, stoppages were much less frequent and everybody in the workforce seemed happier.

As Robert Anderson said to him one morning, 'Sure if ye go home worn out and frustrated, you don't get much value from a bit of leisure, but life's easier for everyone when we're not worryin' about breakdowns and failin' our quota all the time. An' this weather's great, whether you want to dig your allotment, or try for a fish down at Corbet Lough, or just sit doin' nothin'. It would lift your spirits.'

As the fine June weather continued, it did indeed lift spirits and pale, tired faces began to look less pale and strained. The open spaces round the mills, the lakeside and the river walks, were full of work people in the meal breaks, sitting in the sun or chatting to friends or feeding the swans. The dances laid on by local social committees were so crowded, and the summer evenings so fine, the dancers spilt out into the street pursued by the sound of Glenn Miller's big band from wireless or gramophone.

Emily didn't spend much time *doing nothing*, but she made sure she didn't overdo it in the garden and that she had sitting down time every day. She used the space to write letters to friends and family, who hadn't written to her for a while, and she read devotedly, sitting under a tree in the flower garden, or in the conservatory when the day clouded over.

The social events arranged for Chris's boys went

well, the picnics now moving to the beaches or the lakeside. Emily and her helpers were delighted when some of the young Americans, always so willing to help them fetch and carry, came and asked them soberly if their regulation-issue book of helpful information had misinformed them about the rainfall in Ireland. Where was all this rain they'd been warned about?'

One of the happiest outcomes of Emily's letter writing was a sudden and unexpected response from her elder sister, Catherine, in Enniskillen. Catherine had never been a great letter writer, but knowing of Emily and Alex's friendship with Hugh Sinton, now an aeronautical engineer who regularly visited Fermanagh to work at Castle Archdale, she'd kept in touch by sending Emily the local paper, the *Impartial Reporter* from time to time. Now, in response to Emily's missive, she actually took up her pen to comment on life in an Ulster county in which, according to the newspaper itself, every fifth person was American.

21st June 1943

My dear Emily,
I'm so glad you've enjoyed the newspapers I've sent. It was a miserable substitute for writing to you but I can now confess that, after the girls all got married and I retired

from teaching, I became very depressed. The war didn't help, until suddenly, quite recently, I shook myself up and volunteered to serve in a canteen.

Quite what our mother would have made of me doing such a menial task, I hate to think, but it opened my eyes to the well of need all around me and now, like everyone else, I have too much to do and too little time to do it.

I did appreciate your long letter. I won't attempt to 'reply' to it now, but I will share with you some of my observations. I've been feeling rather like an anthropologist stepping out into an unknown culture. In fact, dare I confess, I've been collecting up some material towards writing a book. I've always wanted to write and at least it's something you can do in your old age should your legs give up on you.

What inspired me to begin with was a young American quoting the old saying which he'd only just heard:

*'In summer, Lough Erne is in Fermanagh
In winter, Fermanagh is in Lough Erne.'*

That set me thinking about where in time Fermanagh was to be placed. What do you make of this?

'If I were given £500 I would not put my foot inside a picture house. I consider them filthy places.'

This was said by one of our local worthies addressing the Boys Brigade. He then went on and told the boys 'he got up at 5am every morning and spent two hours talking to God, and again ten minutes before his dinner.'

Do you realise, Emily, that in one local cinema only married couples are permitted to sit together. Otherwise, the boys have to sit on one side and girls on the other?

However, to set against this straight-laced view I must tell you that smuggling is a popular pastime. The lists of goods harboured (a new word for me) are quite fascinating. Recently at Lisnaskea it amounted to 5 dozen cycle freewheels, 25 dozen tubes rubber solution, 9 dozen brake blocks and 9 dozen cycle repair kits.

People harbour the most extraordinary things. One woman had hundredweights of turnip and mangold seed. When he fined her, the Resident Magistrate commented that she had enough to plant all of Fermanagh!

But last week produced an even more extraordinary haul: Sarah Ann Maguire has harboured 12 cwts 7 stone and 2lbs of rice, also 1,125 lbs of horse nails, 5cwt of boot *rivets and tingles and 210 lbs of toe plates.*

This time the prosecutor said there were enough nails to shoe 3,000 horses and there were only 200 in the sub-district!

Now that I've confessed to you what I've been up to, I promise I will send the newspaper every week, so that you can follow these activities for yourself and I will then try to write letters as thoughtful and interesting as yours.

Meantime, you will be pleased with the item on Page 4 about the greatest convoy battle of the war. Not only did 95% get through, but there is a new weapon being used against the U-boats. Of course, they don't give details, but I suspect this is another Ulster contribution to the war effort, and perhaps we shall hear further good news in due course.

Now it is time for me to don my green overall. Sometimes I feel like Mrs Mop, but that's better than feeling like Mona Lot.

Thank you again for writing,
My love to you and Alex,
Catherine.

Emily was delighted by her sister's letter and by the prospect of having the *Impartial Reporter* every week. She had always found local papers a fascinating source of information, often throwing quite new light on the important events reported by the BBC. What she was not expecting was such a rapid clarification of the hint Catherine had dropped regarding the biggest convoy battle of the war and the possibility that there was a local connection.

Letters from Sarah Hadleigh were rare. Either she was out of the country with her diplomat husband, Simon, or she was immersed in some project of her own, almost certainly connected with the well-being of working women.

Her letter was short and bore the signs of haste.

My dear Emily and Alex,

My abject apologies, as per usual! I do actually think of you often, but that is as far as it gets.

However, I have some wonderful news which I'm sure will delight you as much as it delights me. My dear son Hugh has been summoned to Buckingham Palace to receive an award for some important work he has done, of which I may not speak.

The silly boy hasn't even told me what honour it is to be. He merely said 'a gong', which may be modest, but is also infuriating. Simon suggests it is one of the civilian honours and almost certainly it was recommended by the Air Ministry.

*I am told I must wear a hat. Emily knows
how I feel about hats, but for Hugh's sake I
will sacrifice that much of my principles.*

My love and good wishes to you both,
Sarah

*PS: Emily, do you remember a young
man in Dublin in 1916 who lent Hugh all his
books about aircraft? His name was Nevil
Norway and his mother was very kind to
us when we were shut up in Dawson Street
during the Rising. Well, it seems that a book
you and I both read at the beginning of the
war What Happened to the Corbetts was his!*

*He writes as Neville Shute, something
I found out quite by accident when I was
choosing books at the library for women in
hospital.*

Isn't it amazing how people turn out?
S

CHAPTER FOURTEEN

Suddenly and without the slightest warning, large, sixpenny-sized drops of warm rain splashed on her hands as she gathered up the withered foliage of the oldest of the rows of peas now ready to go to the compost heap. Emily threw back her head and stared in amazement at the heavy clouds overhead, now the colour of a bad bruise. She simply hadn't noticed the light level dropping as she pulled out the pea sticks, disentangled the long strands of vegetation from their twiggy branches and bundled them in piles ready to carry to her store behind the garden shed for use again next year.

She dropped her pile of pea haulms and decided there was nothing for it but to dash under the chestnut. If she tried to get back to the kitchen, she'd be soaked to the skin long before she got there. Not that getting wet would do her one bit of harm. The August rain was warm and there were clean everyday clothes ready to pull on, but it was a nuisance.

As she sat down on the stone seat under the tree, she recognised the source of her irritation. She'd been deep in thought and didn't want to be interrupted, by the rain or by anything else. For the moment, however, she simply couldn't remember what she'd been thinking about.

The threshing of the rain in the canopy of the chestnut was fierce enough to send some tiny yellowed leaves flying down beyond the bone-dry circle of well-tramped earth where she sat. First to come, first to go, she reminded herself. Even in early August, a chestnut had a few yellow leaves in its crown, like a woman with grey hairs. There might not be many, but they certainly reminded you that time was passing and there would be more.

Was that what she'd been thinking about? Certainly, she'd been miles away and equally certainly she had not yet arrived back. She stared at the opaque, vertical curtain surrounding her on every side. It was so heavy it couldn't last, but it would leave the ground wet and muddy and the residues of the peas wet and slimy. She never minded the soil being damp or sticky when she planted, but she hated wet hands when she was weeding or doing other garden jobs.

After the dryness and long hours of sunshine in the spring and early summer, she wondered if August might be wet, as it often was in this part of the world. She was always amused when Cathy complained of the heat in London when she'd had to pull on an old sweater over her summer blouse, on that very same morning because of the brisk breeze and the threat of sudden showers like this one.

Life was so varied, so different for individuals, she often wondered how they managed to get on with each other at all. It was always a lovely joke between her and 'her boyfriends,' as Alex called them, when one of them used an American phrase and his friends promptly corrected him, because *she* might not understand.

After all these months, she knew most of the alternatives, but she was always touched by their concern, their awareness of the different ways of speaking they'd already met in their time here, and by their efforts to meet their hosts more than halfway.

Words were one thing, but what about ideas? Some of the boys had such a bitter hatred of the Germans, she wondered what their experiences had been before they came to County Down. It certainly wasn't Chris Hicks who had taught them to hate.

Chris accepted there was a job to do. Whether it was building bridges or fixing tanks, his boys would often be working under attack. They had to be able to defend themselves just as effectively as fighting troops. If they were responsible for clearing an obstacle or crossing a river, they would sometimes have to attack as well, so the art of killing was a normal part of their training.

She wondered if you could kill without hating and thought of the last newsreel she'd seen.

When they'd gone to see *Mrs Miniver*, the Newsreel had shown shots of a rain of bombs so dense it had filled the screen. How did pilots feel about dropping death from the clouds? She'd read later that the raid on Hamburg they'd watched from their comfortable seats in the cinema in Banbridge had been so heavy it had caused a firestorm. The estimated casualty figure was so large, she'd had to read it twice to grasp its magnitude.

Bombing the oilfields in Romania to deprive Hitler of petrol was one thing, but incinerating ordinary human beings, most of them civilians like themselves, seemed to her something very different. Or was it that, now, everyone was part of the war effort and became a legitimate target?

Just as suddenly as it had started, the rain stopped. The throbbing roar all around her was replaced by quiet, the curtain of rain by a shower of drips and the dimness, by brilliant shafts of light that caught the wet foliage and struck gleams of brightness from hanging drops of moisture.

At the edge of her circle of dry, tramped earth, the rain had left little pock marks like the trace of ricocheting bullets in a cowboy movie, or a spray of machine gun fire from advancing troops in a newsreel.

She remembered now what she'd been thinking

about while she was pulling out the pea sticks. Johnny, probably in the Mediterranean, flying Mosquitoes on his nineteenth birthday. She'd been remembering that day in 1924, when after the most awful time she'd ever had with a baby, he had finally emerged, red and cross, his tiny fists waving in the air as old Biddy McBride held him close to her, so she could see for herself that he really was all right.

What a different world that had been. Quiet and poor. No one had any spare money, even those in work. Without Alex's skilled job and the low rent for their home at Ballydown Rose had insisted on, they too would have had difficulty keeping four children fed and clothed.

In those days, every person you met was a friend, or an acquaintance. A stranger was such a rare occurrence that you could be sure he or she would be the topic of conversation until every fragment of available information about them had been chewed and digested. You could also rely on a certain degree of invention about the newcomer if facts were hard to come by.

It was not that no one died nineteen years ago, but mostly funerals were for old people who had lived 'to a right good age,' as the local saying was. Accidents happened and many people, particularly children, still got tuberculosis, even though much more was then known about the disease than when her own mother had succumbed to it in 1910.

The great loss in that quiet world was a remembered loss. No one would ever forget the First World War and the Battle of the Somme and those endless casualty lists in *The Leader* and every other local papers across the north.

Now it was all happening again and her daughters were just as much at risk as her son. Just like those young men who smiled from the old photographs, marching down the main street to the railway station waving their handkerchiefs to the cheering crowds. They were still smiling as the train got up steam and carried them away to the waiting troop ships to be transported overseas and mown down by the thousand.

Emily was right about August. It rained at some point almost every day. Fortunately, there was plenty of sun between the showers and a good drying breeze with it, so she was able to keep up her work on the garden. In the first two weeks, however, the drier days were at the end of the week and that was a problem as those were the ones she needed to prepare for a picnic or dance.

By the third week of the month, she'd found the best solution was to start her baking on Monday morning while the garden was still damp, stop as soon as it was dry enough to work outside. If it didn't rain as much as expected in the next three days, she'd simply catch up on her baking on

Thursday evening before one of Chris's young men arrived late on Friday morning to collect her and her cake tins for delivery to the day's event.

She had just put a couple of sponges to cool on a wire rack on the third Tuesday of the month when she remembered she wanted to look up Messina. When she'd heard on the BBC news at 8am that American troops had taken the town and the allies were now in control of Sicily, she'd not been able to remember where exactly it was.

With Johnny *somewhere* in the Mediterranean area, she felt she needed to know where he *might* be, so that she could think of him properly.

It was Lizzie's old school atlas that had remained on the bookshelf in the sitting room, Cathy having asked for both the others because of the shortage of books in her Cheshire school. Emily thought of Lizzie as she turned the pages, looking for the map of Italy. No under linings or notes in the margins. No scribbles or dog-eared pages, just Elizabeth Hamilton in a small, very legible hand on the flyleaf.

Standing at the sitting room table, her finger poised over the names of Italian cities now more familiar than they'd ever been when she was at school, she paused as she heard the rattle of the letter box and the plop of letters on the mat.

She smiled to herself. Tom must be behind schedule or have a delivery to the hut that served as an office at the quarry. Usually, he came to the back door, put her letters on the draining board, sat down for five minutes to recover from the hill, or even tramped into the garden to sit under the chestnut if she was outside.

She gathered up the letters shuffling them like a hand of cards. There were four of them. A fat one from her sister Catherine, full of newspaper cuttings no doubt, an Airmail from her new-found sister-in-law, Jane Ross in Boston, a note from Brendan McGinley and a Basildon Bond envelope postmarked Belfast from the boxed writing set which had been her own Christmas present to Jane.

Dear Ma,
I'm afraid I have some very unhappy news for you. I am perfectly well, so don't worry, but Johann is very upset indeed and is finding it hard to cope with his feelings.

You know that some months back the Red Cross agreed to search for his mother. It seemed to be taking such a long time, but six weeks ago he was told that she had left her home in Hamlin and gone to live with a friend nearby.

We know that houses have been requisitioned in Germany as they have been here, and Johann guessed that she might be very unhappy if her own house was full of strangers.

The Red Cross said they would continue trying to find her in the Hamlin area and they did indeed find her friend Anna. But Anna said she had gone to stay with her sister. The Red Cross have now confirmed that she was staying with her sister in Hamburg on July 24th last and that that particular area of the city was totally devastated.

What can I say to comfort him? His mother was his last link with his home and with his childhood. He is now an orphan, and there'll be no happy discoveries.

I simply haven't had the courage to ask if he hates the British for the way they destroyed the city.

I was hoping to come home again at the end of the month, but I know you'll understand if I try to get an extra pass to see Johann again. There is a kind lady works in the canteen at the camp who told me last time I was there that I can stay overnight with her anytime, if it would give me the opportunity to meet him 'by chance' out working the next day.

Sorry Ma, to make you sad, but I know you'd want to know.

Love and hugs and kisses to you both,
Jane

Emily sat down and wrote to Jane right away. She said she couldn't think of anything to say either, but sometimes, when someone was very unhappy all you could do was sit beside them, literally or metaphorically. It was knowing someone cared about them that sometimes helped in the first sharpness of grief. She sent Johann her love and said to remind him, when she felt the moment was right, that one day he would have a new family. She and Alex were looking forward to the day when they were free to welcome him to Rathdrum and take him to meet all their friends and cousins.

She put the note in an envelope and propped it up beside the breadbin, so she wouldn't forget to ask Danny to post it for her when he got back into Banbridge. It would get to Jane more quickly than if she posted it herself in the box near the foot of the hill.

Either the note from Dublin had taken a long time to come or had been mis-delivered somewhere on the way. It was a very lively missive from Brendan to say he'd be delivering books to a private collector in Belfast next Tuesday afternoon and then heading back south. He would like to call to see her. If he didn't hear from her in the meantime, he'd be like the beggar man and arrive when he knew the kettle was on and the household could not drink their tea without offering him a cup.

She smiled at the thought, then looked at the date

again. She registered with a shock that Tuesday the 17th was *today*. She didn't mind that the remains of her lunch were still on the kitchen table, but there were dead flowers in the sitting room and she hadn't combed her hair since breakfast. If it *was* going to rain again, which looked more likely with each passing moment, then a bit of a fire would be nice and the ash from the last one was still in the grate.

'My goodness Emily, that fire looks good. Apart from chopping up my bookshelves, I've no hope at all of a fire these days,' he said, settling himself comfortably in front of the blaze.

'I saw a cartoon in a magazine last week with a butler bringing in coal to Her Ladyship,' he began. 'He had it on a silver salver and the punch line was: 'One lump or two, my Lady?'

Emily laughed, partly at the joke, but even more at the way Brendan was eyeing the tea tray. Dublin was still a long way away, so she'd made him some egg sandwiches and there was even a choice of cake because she'd baked on both Monday and Tuesday mornings.

'We can't get much coal either,' she agreed, 'but it looks as if all the dead wood that lay around the local forests for years is now in great demand. Amazing the things that suddenly have currency. According to the *Impartial Reporter* there are firms down in Fermanagh advertising for rabbits in tens of thousands.'

'You're very well informed, Emily, and not just on matters literary, for which I have particular cause to be grateful. If it's not a rude question, how do you keep tabs on Fermanagh?'

'My elder sister,' she said promptly, as she poured tea and handed him his cup. 'We were never close and she seldom wrote to me until just recently, but since then she's really made up for it. She retired from teaching some years ago and now she has a plan to reveal the delights of country life,' she went on, as she passed over the plate of egg sandwiches.

'She sends me the most remarkable stuff. She can't make up her mind whether to devote the whole volume to smuggling back and forth across the Border, or to broaden it out to include the crimes, follies and misfortunes of the local worthies. They really are quite remarkable when they pontificate.'

'I don't think that gift for pontificating is confined to the North,' he said sharply, 'though there are those who might suggest it was. Did you read about a certain person who said that 'The Irish people would have to be made to understand that they should speak Irish?'

'I did, Brendan, I did, and I thought of you at the time,' she said grinning. 'And what about the happy maidens?'

'Ah, but you mustn't leave out the sturdy children and the athletic youths, and, of course, ourselves,' he replied, his tone ironic. 'Do you think we qualify for sitting beside 'those firesides which would be the forums for the wisdom of serene old age?' he asked, his eyebrows raised quizzically.

'Well, we have the fireside, but I do rather wonder if anybody will ever have a serene old age again.'

'Why so?' he asked, regarding her with piercing dark eyes.

'I think the world is changing,' she replied. 'It's as if the war has opened out our world. We know more about countries and people we'd never even heard of. There are new inventions, not all of them designed for killing. New ideas, new possibilities. If we could jump back fifty years, to when we were children and walk around in that world and then jump back to today and the invasion of an island we'd never even heard off, that would be a beginning. But even better if we could jump fifty years forward. What then? What sort of *Brave New World* might we perceive in 1993?'

Brendan nodded briefly.

'We'll be dead and gone, Emily, but I think we can be sure that the happy maidens won't be speaking Irish, even if they've found a way to stay in Ireland in the first place, or managed to find happiness if they have.'

The egg sandwiches disappeared rapidly once Emily had assured him that she would not share them. She explained that she and Alex were once again bidden to Major Chris Hicks well-supplied table, to meet his new Lieutenants prior to the arrival of his next consignment of young engineers.

'Do you ever hear what happens to these young men you feed and encourage, Emily?'

'Individually no,' she responded shaking her head sadly. 'The most we hear is when a group has been attached to some larger unit, American or Allied. For instance, there were some of Chris's lads attached to the Fifth Army in the 160,000 troops that landed in Sicily so we hear the good news from the BBC, like today. But we know the casualty figures get censored. I don't think Chris knows anything more than we do, certainly he hasn't up till the present. Though things change all the time, even for him,' she ended, thinking of the new, larger team they were to meet that evening.

'Now tell me about this good husband of yours. What news of Lofty?'

'None whatsoever, I'm sorry to say,' she replied with a wry smile. 'Unless Mrs Campbell is struck by memory, I think that's as far as we can go, but we *have* solved the puzzle of little Jane Ross being Mrs Jane Ross even though she married the son of a lawyer from Boston. Apparently she married a cousin of her adoptive family. A first cousin, rather older than herself, but of course not actually related to her at all.'

'Ah, I see. And that's why Hank the Tank was

studying to be a lawyer. Has Jane any other family?'

'Yes, she has two more sons, one older and one younger than Hank. The older one, Robert, joined a Canadian regiment, the Ottawa Cameron Highlanders, and the young one, Bruce, is in the American Air Force. He's only a month older than Johnny.'

'So *you* have three girls and *she* has three boys. I wonder if she wanted a girl as much as Alex wanted a boy.'

'I never thought of that, Brendan,' she said quickly. 'I'll ask her one of these days. Alex wrote to her after he'd been to Manchester, but since then he's left it to me and she doesn't seem to mind at all. I'm really rather delighted to have a sister-in-law.'

'Not surprised she doesn't mind,' he said crisply. 'I'd trade Alex's letters for yours any day, however much I like the good man.'

Brendan glanced at the clock and down at his empty cup and plate.

'Like the proverbial beggar, I eat and rise,' he said, moving slightly in his chair. 'Look, there's one thing I must say before I go. There's going to be massive security in the run up to the Second Front. They're talking about closing the border to prevent leakage of information. Not only will I not be able to come up, but they'll start censoring letters. Don't let it stop you, Emily. Even if we can only talk about literature, at least I'll know how you are. Promise me you'll go on writing?'

She nodded vigorously and thought of all she'd read about security.

'You're probably right about closing the Border,' she agreed. 'Some of what the newspapers are saying about spies able to move up and down quite freely does seem quite sensible. My friend Dolly says they never even look in her handbag when she goes to see her sister. She could have a sheaf of State Secrets in it, for all the attention they pay. In fact, in Dolly's handbag, you could probably conceal the parts for a new tank,' she said, smiling. 'But I promise I'll still write and so must you.'

'Oh yes, you won't stop me doing that,' he replied forcefully, as he pulled out a small packet from his jacket pocket. 'A little offering,' he said sheepishly. 'Food for the mind, but the sandwiches will be much more use to me on the way back to Dublin.'

She walked out to the car with him and observed the change in the colour and texture of the panelling where repairs had been done after his brush with an Army lorry back in April '42. What a long, long time ago it seemed, she thought, as she waved him off down the avenue.

'Do you really think they'll close the Border before the Second Front?' Emily asked, as they drove down Rathdrum Hill, turned left at the bottom and headed for the Castlewellan Camp on what had turned into a lovely, summer's evening.

'Can't see how they can myself,' Alex replied, relaxing at the wheel. 'There's thousands of Southern workers coming over the Border to work every week and going home at weekends and there's legitimate trade as well as smuggling. Think what problems stopping all that would be.'

'So if people have to be kept out, it means they'd lose their jobs. And if trade had to stop, that would be even more jobs. That would be dreadful. And we wouldn't know how long it was going on for, would we?'

'No, we wouldn't,' he agreed matter-of-factly. 'Sometimes the powers that be don't know themselves what's happening. Sometimes they have to put out false information as part of strategy. If you lose your job, it doesn't matter which it is. You still have no money for next week.'

'The border is amazingly long for such a small country,' she began, 'it's so full of twists and turns. And there's bog and mountain and lakes and forest along it, as well as towns and villages.'

She'd gone back to the atlas after Brendan had left to study the wiggly line that had caused so much heartache in the course of their lives. She been even more surprised than she'd expected at the length she traced with her finger.

'Think of trying to close off the border in Fermanagh when half of it is lake or islands,' she said, 'and then there's the Sperrins and the hill country of

South Armagh down to Slieve Gullion and . . .'

'And if you're determined to get through and have local knowledge, what chance do British or American troops have of stopping you?' Alex demanded, interrupting her. 'Smugglers seem to have no difficulty from what you read to me,' he said, his tone lightening.

'That's true.'

She smiled to herself and looked across at him, his face sombre, his eyes on the road.

'I haven't told you the latest from the *Impartial Reporter*.'

'Do proceed.'

'Well some of the practical problems will be quite insuperable,' she began. 'I am reliably informed that, in one dwelling, the bedroom is so aligned that whoever sleeps in the bed has their head in the North and their feet in the South.'

Emily watched Alex's face as it broke into a grin. However often it happened and despite the many years in which she had observed the sudden transformation, she could never quite believe the difference it made when Alex smiled. What a sombre little boy he must have been. Or could it be that it was the other way round. That the little boy who could smile so winningly had been turned into a frightened child and a sombre young man.

'Here we are then,' Alex said, as they stopped at the barrier.

The guard checked Alex's pass meticulously, leant over to look at Emily and then waved them on with a broad smile and a salute.

Camp security, stores, supplies and medical services were provided by personnel from other regiments and they had remained unchanged since Chris had first arrived. Emily knew them all and had ensured from the beginning that they too were included with the activities set up for the young engineers.

'Emily, Alex, it's good to see you,' Chris said, shaking hands and beaming at them. 'Come and meet my new team.'

Emily couldn't remember exactly how many times they had now met a new team. Five, perhaps six, since that evening at Millbrook when she herself had talked to Chris and introduced him to Alex.

Coming to the camp was now a familiar and most pleasurable routine, not least because she loved the handsome reception room where such care had been taken of the original furniture, the flock wallpaper and the heavy velvet curtains.

She shook hands and studied the young faces, tried hard to remember the new names and knew she wouldn't manage it. Faces she always remembered, but names had a bad habit of getting away from her. Places were rather better and she often found herself asking friendly questions about a young man's town, or city, or state, to give herself time to try and retrieve his name.

Tonight was going to be more difficult than usual, she reflected, not because her fellow guests were other than pleasant, but because there were more of them. She shook hands and smiled at nine of them and then realised that the tenth young man was not nearly as young as the others.

'Emily, this is Giovanni Hillman, *Captain* Giovanni Hillman, and my new Number 2. Thanks to him, I shall now be able to accept your kind invitations to come and have supper with you . . . if you haven't changed your mind, of course,' he said lightly, amid general laughter.

Captain Hillman was tall and dark-haired with rather splendid dark eyes that looked down at her attentively as he took her hand. This was one name she would certainly be able to remember though for the moment she would certainly make no comment.

The evening proceeded with much good humour assisted by excellent food and several bottles of wine. Chris made his usual speech of welcome. She was always impressed that even when what he had to say was the same each time, it never lost the freshness of a genuine welcome and he always managed to make little jokes that revealed how much of a relationship he'd made with his new lieutenants, just in the two days since they arrived.

As she listened to Chris, Emily thought of Hank the Tank and how he had introduced him formally as Lachlan Alexander Ross before referring to his more familiar name. Hank was the young man she had liked more than any of the others, so how happy a chance it was that he had turned out to be her nephew by marriage.

Chris's speech was as warmly received as ever. To her surprise, Giovanni Hillman got to his feet as Chris sat down. He smiled across at her and began to speak.

'Ma'am, Sir, Mr Hamilton, colleagues,' he addressed them, gazing round the candlelit table, 'it is my pleasant duty to respond to our welcome from Lieutenant Colonel Hicks and to have the honour of being the first Captain to address him by his new rank. In saying thank you for your kind welcome, Sir, may I commit us to doing our best for this training unit which has been so *very* successful under your guidance. Let us raise our glasses and drink to the health and continuing success of Lieutenant Colonel Christopher Hicks.'

Emily raised her glass, looked across at Alex and then at Chris, saw the broad smiles they exchanged with each other and felt sure this was a moment she herself would remember for many a long day.

CHAPTER FIFTEEN

September, always a favourite month of Emily's, began most happily indeed. The weather turned fine and sunny and although the nights were sometimes chilly, certainly cold enough to need the fire in the sitting room, the afternoons were very warm.

The new raspberry canes which weren't supposed to produce a crop in their first year, surprised her by doing exactly that. The fruit was tiny at the beginning of the month, but she decided to leave the berries as long as she could given the warm sunshine and see if they got any bigger and ripened. Not only did they get bigger, but flavour became richer as each week of good weather passed.

At the end of the month, when a few fat berries dropped to the ground she gathered them all within the day, claimed her jam sugar allowance from the grocer and produced eight jars of a rich, dark red preserve. With pretty gingham covers cut from a worn-out table cloth and a handmade label, she glowed with pride at having some Christmas presents ready to put in the cupboard.

There was good news too from Cathy. Shortly after they'd moved to the new flat, she'd put her name down at the local Education Office, hoping she might get a teaching job sometime in the future. She wrote and said they'd been pleasant and helpful and had commented on the value of her special additional qualifications, but to their own surprise, they seemed to have more teachers than jobs.

Then, suddenly, only two days before the beginning of term, a young man who'd had to be turned down by the Air Force because of his eyesight, was offered a job in the Air Ministry. The Education Office was happy to release him at such short notice, because they had Cathy on the books.

In turn, she'd had no difficulty with the WVS unit with whom she'd been working since the move. Her senior officer had simply said that getting the work done was what they were in business for. Children needed teachers. She could teach. Other women couldn't. Good Luck.

It was clear to Emily how delighted her daughter was to be back in the classroom, especially in a city school, which was large enough to have a proper staff and much better facilities than her single-teacher school in Cheshire. She wasn't entirely surprised when Cathy owned up to the fact that she'd become dispirited in her village school with no one to share the problems of a large class, mixed in age and ability.

The new flat was a source of great joy. The cleanest and tidiest of girls, she'd surprised her parents by searching out the street markets which sold carpets and curtains from bombed-out houses. Dirty and torn, they didn't look much, she told them, but they were cheap and did not require points, unlike fabric in short supply in the shops. Moreover, Brian had put his knowledge of solvents to good use in helping her make them useable. One particular square of carpet, a very soiled dark red when they bought it, had revealed a pattern of blue butterflies by the time they'd finished with it.

Thinking back to the letters she'd had from Cathy a year earlier, Emily could hardly believe the difference. Then, she'd found herself dreading having to respond to the newest problem, but now she looked forward to hearing from her.

Cathy's new-found happiness did something to offset the sad fact that there'd been no letters from Lizzie for over a year now. Emily had sent a letter and a birthday card via Cathy, so that she could deliver it when they met, but she and Alex had decided communicating with her that way was not fair to Cathy. The only thing to do now was let Lizzie make her own decision and wait and see what happened. Meantime, they had established that she was now working in London and had three stripes.

The last time Cathy had seen her she was smoking heavily, but seemed in very good spirits, but she could say nothing whatever about her work, not even in which part of London she was based.

October came with cold nights and sudden chilly squalls, but Emily was heartened by a visit from Jane. This time, she had not been on night duty. She looked fresh and very pretty, her blonde curls cut short for convenience, her blue eyes sparkling as she took in everything around her. One glance told Emily that the news from Johann must be good.

He had indeed had a difficult time over the summer. As he explained to Jane in his now fluent English, loss breeds loss. The loss of his mother in the Hamburg raids had animated all the other losses he'd suffered personally, starting with his father's death in a Labour Camp, followed by the insistence that he and his brothers join the fighting forces. He felt the sadness weighed upon him like a yoke across his shoulders. He told her that he couldn't put it down, yet he felt equally he couldn't carry it.

'As I told you, Ma, the prisoners at Dungannon are very varied,' she began, as they sat in the conservatory drinking coffee. 'Some are quite old, veterans from the first war, others are even younger than Johann. There are no Nazis or S.S. men, for they go to the high security camps in Scotland and the North of England, but there are some who are very pro-Hitler. Sometimes there are arguments that lead to blows.'

She paused, looked distressed and then took a deep breath.

'You know, Ma, sometimes the worst things can have a good side,' she said unexpectedly. 'I was so upset when I found out about the big fight. Johann had a cut on his cheek and a really bad bruise. It was still purple when I saw him two weeks after it happened.'

'One of the guards hit him with a rifle butt. Probably by accident, because Johann was actually trying to separate two men who were fighting. Typical Johann. He couldn't bear to see a man who was small and not very robust being set upon by this big chap, because he'd said Hitler was a tyrant.'

'Anyway, Ma, to cut a long story short, when it was sorted out, a young man whom Johann had never spoken to before, because he rather avoided contact with other prisoners, came to him and shook his hand and said how sorry he was he'd been hurt when he was trying to do what was right. His name was Matthew and his father was a Lutheran pastor, a lovely man by the sound of it. Matthew had been studying in Switzerland in 1938 with a man called Carl Jung when his father was interned for preaching against the state. Have you ever heard of Carl Jung, Ma?'

'Yes, I've *heard* of him, but I've only read a little bit about his work. I don't think any of his books have been translated into English yet. I'd have to ask Brendan about that.'

'Well, Johann and Matthew have become friends,' she continued. 'They talk and talk, and it's such a comfort to me to know that he has a real friend now, although he did always get on well with most of the others. Matthew wants to go to London after the war and finish his studies, but meantime, he's been helping Johann with his problem,' she explained with a smile.

'We did do some basic psychology in our nursing training, as you know, but Matthew is *very* clever,' she went on, shaking her head. 'He says no one can heal your mind for you, but you *can* be helped to heal it for yourself. If you have a hurt, you can't just fix it, but if you recognise it and become familiar with it, then you can move past it. He also said that when you suffer loss, grief is a necessary process. Denying your loss brings about a kind of stunting of one's emotional growth.'

'And Johann has been able to use what Matthew is offering?'

'Oh yes,' Jane said vigorously. 'That's why I'm so happy for him. He told me that once he'd let himself weep and stopped feeling he couldn't *do* anything, he began to feel better. Older, sadder and wiser, he said, but not so burdened and worn down.'

'Oh Jane, that *is* good news. There will be so many in need of people like Matthew when this war is finally over. What about Matthew's family? Does he know what's happened to them?'

'Oh yes. He knows alright,' Jane replied grimly. 'Matthew came back from Switzerland in 1938 when his father was interned. The family tried to have him released, but they failed. His father died in a labour camp in 1939, just like Johann's father and the authorities took Matthew's passport away. He couldn't go back to Switzerland and so he was conscripted. He tried to join a Medical Unit, but he wasn't allowed to, so he let himself be captured. It was the only way he could avoid having to kill.'

'But wasn't that very risky?' she protested. 'He might have got shot on the battlefield. The Geneva Convention doesn't always hold if someone sees a German and has a gun in his hand.'

Jane nodded.

'Matthew knew that. But he said it was a risk he had to take. There was no other way. Just like Johann that day he flew to Ireland and crashed on the edge of the lake at Millbrook. Is it any wonder they've become friends?'

Emily beamed at her and shook her head.

'You know, you've just reminded me of a story your father often tells about the First World War. He and your Uncle Sam sat in the workshop at Liskeyborough and the pair of them tried to decide what they'd do if there was conscription here. As Uncle Sam was a Quaker and your father has never had the slightest wish to harm anyone, they decided it would have to be the Ambulance Corp. Mercifully for me, and probably for you, Ireland was so unstable in 1914 that conscription was never brought in, so they weren't put to the test. But at least in this country it's possible to be a conchie.'

'Conchie?'

'Conscientious objector. People like Sam and Alex and Matthew's father. The worst that happens in this war is that our conchies are put in jail if they're not willing to accept the alternative to military service they're offered or someone manages to see them as a security risk. Hitler has no such scruples.'

'Such wickedness, Ma. Sometimes I just can't grasp the awfulness of everything that's happening round us.'

Emily smiled as she glanced at the clock. It was nearly lunchtime and she was due to leave for Lenaderg at 1.30 to prepare for an afternoon of games and music.

'Perhaps it's as well we can't grasp everything,' she said abruptly. 'Perhaps it's a necessary defence. Ask Johann to see what Matthew thinks of the idea next time you have the chance. And don't forget to tell me,' she said, standing up.

'Now, do you want to come and meet my new *boyfriends* as your father calls them or would you like an afternoon of peace and quiet?'

* * *

The sad thing was that Emily felt she'd only just got to know Chris's new young men when it was time for them to go. When they'd first started the various entertainments for these younger troops back in '42, they'd been staying for nearly four months. Now it was a bare two.

At times, Emily wondered if all the effort was justified for such a short period. The baking and packing that she and her four friends did almost every week, the transporting of the five of them, of the school children and of the young men themselves. Then there was the setting up of halls, community centres and church rooms. That meant more work for caretakers and church ladies and the office staff at the four mills. Not that any of these people ever grudged the time they spent, but one hoped that what they did was worthwhile.

She was ironing shirts and blouses in the kitchen one wet morning late in the month, when she heard a jeep come round the corner of the house and splash through the puddle that always gathered in front of the workshop after heavy rain.

Through the rain-spattered window, she saw a figure jump down and head briskly for the back door. She placed the iron carefully on its asbestos mat and got there in time to open it as he arrived on the doorstep, his jacket inflating as if he'd been blown in by a squall.

'Morning ma'am,' he said as he stepped inside,

the raindrops trickling down the black waterproof.

'Captain Hillman, how nice to see you. I wasn't expecting a visitor on such a morning. Is the hollow by Tullyconnaught flooded?'

'No, not yet, but I guess it soon will be. The dykes are full. Sheughs, I think you call them.'

'Do put your jacket over the chair,' she said, as she turned her iron off. 'I hope you've time for coffee.'

'I have, ma'am. In fact, I have a permit for coffee,' he said matter-of-factly. 'My superior officer says I need to talk to you about morale and he assured me I would be offered coffee and cake. He also sends his greetings and is looking forward to his next visit,' he went on, rather formally.

'Then do sit down while I make it and we'll go into the conservatory. It's pretty gloomy in there this morning, but the armchairs are more comfortable and it doesn't smell of starch,' she added, as she indicated a chair at the far side of the kitchen table.

With his long legs she needed to settle him as far away as possible from the sink and work surface while she put up a tray.

'Am I required to call you Captain Hillman or may I call you Giovanni?' she asked, glancing over her shoulder as she measured coffee.

'I answer to Chuck, ma'am.'

'Right, Chuck, then tell me about morale. Are you having problems at the camp?'

'No ma'am, not so far as I am aware, but it is my business to find out about such things. In fact, I have been giving a lot of thought to the social events laid on in the community for the boys,' he said flatly. 'You are aware I'm sure just how tight the training schedule now is,' he continued, in his usual matter-of-fact tone.

'Yes, indeed. It must put extra pressure on everyone,' she agreed, as she cut slices of cake and put the lid firmly back on the tin.

He stood up, opened the door to the conservatory, waited for her to go through and then sat down, the tray on a low table between them.

She looked across at him as she poured his coffee and wondered if he thought the time spent giving piggy-backs to school children would be better redeployed. He might be right.

Meantime, she passed him the cake and saw a slight softening of his rather sad face. She was beginning to think that Chuck was a rather unhappy young man.

'Did your grandparents emigrate to America?' she asked, before she had entirely thought about how he might respond.

The amazing change in his face took her aback.

'Who told you that? How can you *possibly* know that?' he demanded.

His reaction expressed fear rather than aggression and she felt sorry now she'd upset him.

She thought of Sam Hamilton who always claimed that sometimes one simply spoke when the Spirit moved. But he hadn't pointed out that, if you did, you had to take the consequences.

'Well, I'll explain if you want me to,' she said soothingly. 'No one told me. But there were three things that made it seem likely that your family had come from Germany some time back,' she offered, sipping her coffee and giving him time to recover himself.

'First, when we met and we talked about your home, you told me you were from Michigan,' she began. 'There is a very large German community there and many still speak German. Secondly, you said *sheugh*,' she added, smiling. 'I've never heard anyone *not* from Ulster pronounce that word correctly. My husband Alex can say it, but then he speaks German.'

'He speaks German?' he repeated blankly.

'Yes,' she explained. 'He was a farm labourer in the States at a place called German Township before he came to Ireland in the hope of finding his family. He'd been sent to Canada as an orphan, though in fact he wasn't.'

There was a moment's silence and Emily offered Chuck another piece of cake. He looked at it for a moment, then picked it up and said Thank You, as if he'd had to make a major decision in accepting it.

'You said there were three things, ma'am.'

'Yes, I did. Your name. Hillman. I know a very nice young German boy called Hillman who comes from Hamlin. We haven't met yet, but he is engaged to my daughter Jane.'

'But how can that be, ma'am? Is she abroad somewhere?'

'No, but Johann is a prisoner-of-war in Dungannon. They met when his aircraft crashed into the water supply at Millbrook on her birthday. She was here and went with her father to see what they could do to help him.'

'So you don't hate all Germans?'

Emily shook her head slowly.

'No. We fear for ourselves and our fighting forces,' she said honestly. 'Hate what Hitler has done and all the suffering he has caused. But Johann, or your grandparents, or my Pennsylvanian cousins' German cousins, why should anyone hate them?'

He nodded abruptly and looked at his watch.

'I'm most grateful to you ma'am.'

He moved forward in his armchair with all the signs of a man poised to leave.

'What about morale?' she reminded him. 'I think perhaps you were going to say that, with the reduced time available, perhaps social activities were not high priority.'

'No, ma'am, not so. I did think that when I first came to the camp. That was why I decided to produce a questionnaire and do a survey of the boys,' he said, reaching his hand back into his map pocket and bringing out a notebook.

'There were a number of questions about first impressions. I've copied up some of the replies for you. I think you'll find them interesting. They were all entirely positive. It was Lieutenant-Colonel Hicks who said I might benefit by discussing the question with you,' he added, as he handed over the black, waterproof notebook.

'Thank you,' she said, somewhat taken aback.

'He was quite right, of course, about talking to you,' he said, smiling at her for the first time, as he got to his feet and waited for her to lead the way back into the starch-smelling kitchen.

'No wonder he got promoted,' he added, as he pulled on his waterproof jacket and zipped it up.

He beamed at her as he raised a hand and stepped out into the pouring rain.

October ended in a blaze of autumn glory. Certainly not as dramatic as Vermont, but even Chris Hicks commented on the crisp mornings and the sunlight falling on the shoals of leaves brought down in their avenue by the first frosts. The hedgerows were bright with jewelled branches of hawthorn and the mountain ash on the eastern boundary of the flower garden was full of feasting birds.

'Grand mornin', Mrs Hamilton,' said Robert Cooper, as he met her coming up from the garden with a handful of dahlias and a few autumn-tinted ferns. 'I've left your letters on the drainin' board. A whole wee pile left waitin' for me at the office this mornin'. Someone loves you, as the sayin' is.'

'Thank you, Robert, that'll brighten up my tea-break,' she replied, smiling.

'Are you for the quarry?' she called after him, noting his purposeful stride as he humped his bag more comfortably on his shoulder.

'Aye, they're powerful busy these days, but I'll leave the bike in your gateway if that's all right. Wi' them big lorries yer safer on yer feet,' he said sharply.

'Of course it's all right. Any time. We don't get many bicycle thieves up here.'

She turned back towards the kitchen and eyed the little pile as she ran the tap and put the flowers and ferns she'd picked in a basin to drink before she arranged them in a vase. There were at least half a dozen items of varied sizes, secured with a rubber band.

Ten minutes later, she was sitting with a cup of tea in the conservatory, her family letters by her side, a seed catalogue, the electric bill and a circular abandoned on the kitchen table.

Dear Ma,
You know we always enjoy your letters but I had to write straight away and tell you how

much we laughed when we got your last one. We just could not believe that you had read about penicillin in the Impartial Reporter.

When Brian applied to join up and he was reserved, it was because he was working on penicillin, though they didn't call it that at the time. He had to sign the Official Secrets Act and he was warned of the dire consequences of what would happen if he told ANYONE what he was doing. At first he wouldn't even tell me!

In the end, I got very cross and asked him if he thought I was a SECURITY RISK!

And then, when he was moved to London, he had to go through the whole security thing again before he was allowed to carry on there. We know that the original idea was that it would not be released for civilian use. Looks like someone changed their mind. But nobody told Brian or any of his colleagues. While down in Fermanagh they know all about it. What it's called and which hospital has it in stock.

Don't ever let anyone tell you that rural areas are backward! We are amazed and highly delighted that Fermanagh is so well informed.

Please do go on reporting . . . the story of the fifty smuggled goats was wonderful, but the penicillin story beats all.

We're both fine and hope you are too . . . a
proper letter soon,
      Love from us both,
      Cathy

Emily smiled as she tucked the short letter back in its envelope. Such a cheering picture of Cathy and Brian and their life together had emerged in the last weeks. Cathy had never been very forthcoming as a girl and although Emily knew that she loved Brian very much and couldn't bear their being apart, she'd never before been allowed such an intimate glimpse into their life. The thought of them laughing over her letter was a real joy.

A further delight was a missive from Johnny. She opened it to find a single sheet with a mere two sentences in his generous hand, but inside the folded sheet were three photographs. With flare on the edges and burnt out sky and sea, they were not exactly works of art, but she was grateful to the owner of the Box Brownie who had taken Johnny with his arms round two other airmen, Johnny in uniform and Johnny in swimming trunks, looking brown and flourishing, his blonde hair so bleached by the sun so that it looked almost white.

Dear Ma,
Only a line I'm afraid. Just had some leave
and thought you'd like these. Some good

chaps in this lot and we have fun although
the nearest girl is miles away!

Good news from this part of the
world . . . we hope to make it even better. I'll
write again when we are settled.

Take care of yourselves,

Much love,

Johnny.

She studied the photographs carefully. Alex
and Chris were probably right that he was
somewhere in North Africa. Possibly in the
desert, as that comment about the girls would
suggest. But then, she argued with herself, it was
all guesswork. That he was well and happy was
the one thing she could be sure of from the note
and photos.

The third letter was an American Airmail, the
handwriting and the return address now familiar
and most welcome. Jane Ross wrote regularly and
she and Emily were busy sharing the detail of their
own lives as well as speculating about the remaining
puzzles over what had happened to Alex and Jane
as children.

As Emily opened her letter carefully so as not
to damage the stamps which she saved for young
Jimmy Cook, she noticed it was a good deal thinner
than usual. She pulled out the closely written airmail
sheet and began to read quickly.

My dear Emily,

I have had some dreadful news and there is no way to tell you other than to be direct. My dear, lovely Lachlan has been terribly injured. He and his troop were part of the landing in Sicily attached to one of the American regiments. They moved forward to bridge a small stream for infantry coming up behind and were mown down by an enemy machine gun position. Only a few of them survived and Lachlan would have died but for a colleague who half carried him back to safety.

He was flown out and was expected to die, but the field hospital patched him up. He is now in Egypt. They were going to amputate his leg, but held back because he had also got malaria and they couldn't get his temperature down for the op.

He is alive, but that is all I know. He will be flown home when the opportunity arises. What is clear is that he will never walk again unaided.

Though we have known each other for such a short time, more than any one I know, you will understand how I feel. I see him smile, I see him walk and run and dance and I think my heart will break.

But he is alive, Emily. As my dear husband says, we must hold on to that.

I'll write when I have any more news.
With loving thoughts to you both,
Jane.

Emily wiped her eyes and read the letter through
again in case she had missed anything, but she
hadn't. It was one of the commonest stories of the
war, the enemy position that no one had identified.
Hank and one of Chris's groups, boys who had
played games and given chewing gum to children
and smiled and carried her baskets and boxes.

She thought of the morning he had said goodbye
to her, when he told her his mother's name was Jane
and she had guessed that Alex had found his sister.
She had kissed him and said the kiss was from his
mother, to wish him luck.

He was probably lucky to be alive, but at this
moment all she could think of was what he had lost.
She went into the sitting room, took out her writing
materials and sat down where she was in the dim,
cold room and wrote to Jane.

It was only when she came back into the kitchen
and propped up the letter by the bread bin to give
to Danny, whose day it was to call, that she saw
the other items from the post, still lying where
she had left them. She picked them up, opened
the seed catalogue and leafed through it briefly,
glanced down and saw that it had covered a small,
dull orange envelope. In plain capitals above their

address it said POST OFFICE TELEGRAM. Down one side, in red lettering, block capitals spelt out the one word, PRIORITY.

Suddenly anxious and barely able to control the shake in her hands, she ripped open the envelope and drew out the single flimsy sheet. Under the time and place of dispatch and the address of the Air Ministry in Oxford Street, London W1, it deeply regretted to inform them that F/O John Hamilton was reported missing while on operations in the Mediterranean and that any further information would be *immediately communicated to you pending receipt of official notification.*

CHAPTER SIXTEEN

She rang Millbrook and Alex came at once. He strode into the kitchen and put his arms round her, then stared down in bleak incomprehension at the creased sheet of paper still lying on the kitchen table.

'Do *you* think he's dead, Emily? Do you?'

'No, I can't believe he's dead,' she replied, 'but isn't that how people always react when they hear this news? Isn't it just a defence?'

'No, not always. Some people have a sense of life going on. I have,' he said quietly.

'Have you really, Alex?' she asked, tears coming unbidden. 'I though it was just because I had seen the photos. Look, here they are. He is so very alive, isn't he?'

He picked up the photographs and studied them intently.

'Sometimes that matters,' he said, almost as if he were talking to himself.

It was then they telephoned Chris. He came immediately.

'That's not such bad news,' he said, reading and re-reading the short message. 'Missing *does* mean missing. Lots of men go missing. What it means is that they are not where someone expects them to be. Until you get this letter they've promised you, you're entitled to think the best.'

The days passed and still the promised letter failed to appear. The waiting was unbearable. Try as she would Emily could think of nothing else but Johnny though she forced herself to keep busy and do all the things she would normally do.

They told no one apart from Chris, not even Jane and Cathy. They agreed there was no point whatever in adding to their burdens until the question was resolved one way or another. Chris himself made some enquiries and when the waiting extended into the second week he rang and said he'd leave Hillman in charge and take an hour to come and see them.

His expression was set in a grim line as he came into the warm kitchen where they were still sitting over their coffee after supper.

'So you still haven't heard?' he asked, as he accepted a cup.

'Not a word,' Alex replied.

'Now this just won't do,' he began. 'I've asked around a bit and the word is that informing relatives

313

about a loss is top priority. You should have heard something by now, even if it's only that they haven't any more to tell you.'

'I've been thinking. Now I know how *we* proceed when something is not right, but your way is sure to be different. Have you any official contacts, Alex, like say, someone in Whitehall or the Air Ministry itself?'

There was a pause in which Emily thought painfully of Lizzie. She was most certainly in the Air Ministry, but where they did not know. Nor had they any means of contacting her. How official she was by now they had no means of knowing either.

She looked at Alex and saw his face brighten.

'There's Sarah,' said Alex abruptly.

Chris raised an eyebrow.

'Sarah's our cousin, she's married to a diplomat. He has contacts all over Whitehall,' he explained.

'Just what you need,' Chris exclaimed. 'The God damned English never tell you anything they can avoid telling you, but if you have an inside man, he'll know how to get to the right person. As far as I know Squadron Leaders are obliged to reveal their reports if they are requested by someone senior enough. But they don't tell anybody that.'

He had to leave them then for he had to be available in camp during the hours of darkness. He shook hands with Alex and hugged him. Then he hugged Emily and then kissed her on both cheeks.

'While there's life there's hope,' he said firmly. 'Dead is a four letter word, but Missing is different. Here's something to help you sleep,' he continued, putting a hand in his greatcoat pocket. 'I'm not a praying man but I'll get as near as I can. Keep me posted.'

He parked a bottle of Jack Daniels on the table and hurried back to his jeep.

Three long days later a telegram came from Simon Hadleigh's office in Whitehall. It had not been censored. It was so lengthy Emily could hardly believe it was actually a telegram.

The pilots of F/O John Hamilton's squadron had been sent to Tunisia in order to fly out to bases in recently liberated Sicily, the Mosquitos despatched in crates to North Africa and assembled there. The squadron had taken off in excellent weather conditions, but on arrival one of the pilots to the rear of the formation reported he had observed a plane lagging and then rapidly loosing height. He had logged its approximate position. This pilot had written himself to Flying Officer Hamilton's family, but the censor had impounded the letter, as it contained information valuable to the enemy. Efforts would now be made to trace the letter and to communicate the contents directly to them. A further communication would follow as soon as there was reliable information to report.

Chris was much cheered when he was shown the telegram, but Sarah was not pleased. It was one thing if Johnny or anybody else was shot down. War was war and it was tough. But he'd only been ferrying a plane from one base to another in an area where the Allies had complete air superiority. If he'd simply had engine trouble, why did no one circle back and see what was happening?

Three days later, the letter from Johnny's friend duly appeared, the Italian stamp almost obliterated, but the enclosed message bore no trace of the censor's blue pencil.

Dear Mr and Mrs Hamilton,
I promised John that if ever anything went wrong I would write to you. I have tried twice already, but my letters have been returned to me. In the circumstances it is so hard to say anything useful except that I think John may be all right. He is such a good pilot coming down in the drink would have been no problem to him. The problem is what happened then. As you know he swims like a fish and anyway he had a life jacket, but he could have had a bad bash on the head.

I don't want to raise your hopes or mine, but I think we have some hope, even if he's been picked up by an enemy ship or a sub.

John is a great pal. I am thinking about
him and you and crossing my fingers.
Yours sincerely,
Charlie Preston.

Emily and Alex agreed there was no point in upsetting everyone unless the worst had happened, so although they now wrote to Sam and told Cathy and Jane what they now knew, they did not tell their friends or neighbours. They both tried to get on with life as normally as possible. Emily even managed a Halloween party with witches on broomsticks and candles in turnip heads on a foggy Friday afternoon, though she did weaken and confess how hard it was to her old school friend Dolly, when they found themselves alone together in the cloakroom at Millbrook.

As no one beyond Chris, Dolly and her immediate family knew what had been going on, what happened next morning came as a complete surprise.

The phone rang a few minutes after nine o'clock and Emily hurried to pick it up, thinking perhaps it might be another call from Sarah or her sister Hannah, but the voice was male and sounded almost familiar.

'Mrs Hamilton, you don't know me, but I'm Robert Anderson's older brother,' it said, the tone warm and comforting. 'I'm Postmaster here in Banbridge and I know you've had a hard time over

317

your Johnny. He was at school with my son. Now, I think I have good news for you. There's a telegram here for you and your husband. It's from Johnny himself. Would you like me to read it to you?'

She had to get him to read it three times. Then, when he asked her if she'd like him to have it delivered to Rathdrum, or taken to whichever mill her husband was at that morning, she found her voice had gone, an ache at the back of her throat which completely prevented her from speaking.

But he was in no hurry. He waited till she'd coughed and blown her nose as if he had all the time in the world. Then he made a little joke about the way telegrams so often got garbled in transmission, particularly when they were from abroad.

She swallowed hard, found her voice again and thanked him. She told him she would probably remember this particular telegram to the end of her days.

It said:

Safe and well. Sorry if you have been married. Better fellows. Much love. Johnny.

If Emily and Alex thought they had kept their bad news to themselves, they were left in no doubt at all that their good news had spread like fire through corn stubble. It roared through the mills and from them raced on unchecked to all the surrounding villages.

Notes and letters arrived every day, some from people they hardly knew. Even more arrived after a paragraph in *The Leader* obviously written by someone who had known Johnny at Banbridge Academy.

Overwhelmed by relief and joy, Emily tried to keep a hold of her ordinary domestic routine and failed completely. She would find herself wandering round the kitchen trying to remember what she'd been doing before she'd answered the phone or the ring at the door.

Alex managed better, but most of his well-wishers were at work and could not linger as could many of Emily's visitors.

Four days later, Johnny's promised letter arrived. To their amazement, it had come from Norfolk and had not been censored.

Tuesday 2nd November, 1943

Dear Ma and Da,
I know you must have been worried and I'm so sorry. I'm now 'somewhere in England' and will be remaining here, having been promoted and become an instructor. My new boss has suggested that I tell you about my recent holiday and the delays I had in getting back home.

The problem was that our outgoing flight had engine trouble and this involved an unscheduled landing. There were further delays while alternative transport was being arranged. Fortunately the weather remained calm and the water relatively warm. When transport did appear there were some initial communication problems. The tour operators were committed to a scenic route which meant a considerable delay in landing me.

I am now permitted to telephone you, though I will be limited to six minutes. I shall try at seven o'clock, beginning tomorrow evening after you have received this. I shall try each evening till I get you.

I am so glad to be back
With love to you both,
John.

Emily made sure that Alex was home promptly and they waited together for the phone to ring. It was almost a year since they'd heard his voice, the last time being when he'd been allowed to phone home from Greencastle after Ritchie was killed.

'All's well that ends well,' said Emily, shivering, as Alex put the phone down at the end of their shared call.

'Come on, back in to the fire,' he said, putting an arm round her shoulders. 'This hall would freeze you tonight and there is just no paraffin to be had this week.'

'Do you think he's all right?' she asked, as they pulled their chairs up to the comforting flames, 'He did *sound* all right, but I thought his letter was rather strange.'

'Yes, he's all right,' Alex said reassuringly. 'He's grown up a lot. I think the style of the letter was a clever way to avoid the censor. But I think he was also trying to reassure us he wasn't unduly upset by what had happened, though he told me he was afloat on the plane for two days. Did he say that to you?'

'No, but he admitted he banged his head when he landed and came to thinking of the little red bits we'd put on the dessert for Jane's birthday last year.'

She paused, thinking through what they'd said before the pips went and she'd handed the phone to Alex.

'Surely landing like that and staying afloat must have been difficult?'

'Yes, it must have been,' he agreed. 'But his friend Charlie told us how good a pilot he was. Maybe it was all those nights he spent in the cockpit of that plane they were building down at Walkers,' he continued, putting another log on the fire. 'He knew how that plane was made and put together. The Mosquitos are made of light wood too, probably not all that different. That's why they can ship them out to North Africa in packing cases and put them together there. He knew if he got her down level, she'd float.'

'So why do you think he's been brought back? Was it because of what happened?'

Alex looked across at her pale face and saw she was rubbing her hands together. He paused, applied the poker to the fire and coaxed the log to burn up and produce flames. Probably the only way to warm her would be to make her a hot whiskey.

'Yes, I think perhaps what's happened has been hard enough on us but it has had a good side to it,' he said sitting back in his armchair, the flames lighting up his face. 'What does getting the plane down and staying afloat for two days say about a pilot? It shows skill *and* judgement. And nerve. Who better to instruct?'

Emily nodded and held out her hands to the leaping flames.

He was back in England. He was safe and well. Really that was all that mattered. So far, Johnny was one of the lucky ones, but she would never be able to forget the size, shape and colour of that envelope, or the words on the telegram it contained

The enormous relief over Johnny's safety came not a moment too soon for Alex. He'd been just on the point of confessing to Emily how difficult the situation was at three of the four mills when he'd had her phone call. Now, nearly a fortnight later, the problem was worse rather than better and he was no nearer to finding a solution.

'Thanks, Margaret,' he said, as one of the Millbrook office staff placed a time sheet on his desk.

He knew by the amount of blank paper at the bottom of the long scroll there were more absentees even before he studied the names.

November was always a bad time for illness, but this year it had started earlier and was more severe. James Wilson, their Health and Safety Director, had warned Alex back in early October that fatigue was now so high that people had less and less resistance to infection. Even with nourishing canteen food and the co-operative store where food prices were kept as low as possible, he said he was sure some women were not getting enough to eat.

James was almost certainly right. Alex knew perfectly well that, in a similar situation where the children might go short, Emily would have done just the same and passed over most of her own share. But there was a price to pay. These women were working all day, then trying to keep a home clean and bright with inadequate food and not enough fuel to warm it. It was one thing coping in summer with sunshine and fresh vegetables to help, but now the temperature was dropping fast and the influenza that usually struck in January was already active. As staff absences grew daily machines were having to be shut down to comply with safety regulations.

Alex sat at his desk, his head in his hands,

wondering what more he could do. He'd already rung James Wilson and asked if he thought a distribution of food and medicine would help. Money *could* be made available. He had no anxiety at all about persuading his fellow directors that it was the proper thing to do, whether they looked at it practically, or from a more humanitarian perspective.

But that wasn't going to solve the problem of silent machines, orders not complete and red notices from government departments who were as desperate for his materials as he was to fulfil their orders.

He was still sitting with the work sheet in his hand when Margaret returned with a mug of tea. As she bent down to put the mug close to his hand, he was suddenly aware of the gay yellows and greens of her pretty patterned blouse. He smiled to himself at the memory of the vast floral arrangement that had walked into his room way back in the spring.

The thought cheered him, he drank his tea yet more thoughtfully and then picked up the phone.

'Margaret, do you think you could find anyone to relieve Daisy Elliott for a few minutes? I need a wee word with her.'

Daisy and the knock on the door were indivisible. She stood in front of him before he'd even looked up from the note he was drafting.

'Ach, man dear, yer lookin' worried and *you* should be on top of the world,' she said briskly.

Alex beamed at her and waved her to the visitor's chair.

'I'm on top of the world in my spare time, Daisy. And so is Emily. But there are one or two problems I have that are a wee bit pressing.'

'Aye, I'm sure yer worried about all this absence. I was just saying to my Billy last night that we must be well down on production. You got us the machines fixed and now a third of them in my section are standin' idle. That can't be good.'

'What are we goin' to do, Daisy?' he asked quietly.

'I was wonderin' about that m'self,' she said promptly. 'Did you know that Hazelbrae has packed up?'

'No, I didn't,' he replied, somewhat surprised that she should mention a major shirt-making enterprise having to close its doors.

He tried to remember if they'd had any government contracts or whether they'd gone on producing solely for Saville Row. Certainly, he hadn't read anything about it in either the *Belfast Telegraph* or *The Leader*.

'Ach aye. It's partly the war and partly old man McFetridge. Sure the man's in his seventies an' he's worked all his life. Why wouldn't he retire? I think he only kep it up for the sake of the stitchers. There's

325

a queer lot of them will be hard up this Christmas,' she said shaking her head.

Alex reminded himself that it never did to assume that Daisy was not to the point, but he still failed to see how the unemployed stitchers could help him.

'What a pity they weren't spinners or weavers, Daisy. We could solve their Christmas present problem quite easily, couldn't we?'

'But sure that's exactly what most of them are. Did ye not know?' she demanded, her eyes wide with disbelief. 'When those women got married and had the first wee'un, if there was no granny handy or willin' they took up stitchin'. Hazelbrae has only a handful of women up there at the factory, packing and despatchin', all the work is done in the home and collected up. Imagine you not knowin' that?' she said, amazement written all over her face.

'Well I knew shirt-making is a home industry and that Hazelbrae collects all round this area. I even see the odd collection van round Ballievy or Tullyconnaught, but I'd no idea that stitchers were once mill workers.'

'Ach aye. I've a friend Lily McCready over in Tullyconnaught and she gave up when the first chile came. Sure her childer are all up and away now but she goes on stitchin' and glad of money. She might well be pleased to go back to the mill and she'd certainly be glad of work till this illness is over.'

'The mill is great company', she went on without

pausing for breath. 'I couldn't stan' sittin' at home stitchin', but then if that was all that was goin' I'd hafta, woulden I?' she demanded, laughing so loudly, that Margaret, in the office next door, wondered what there could possibly be to laugh at with the way things were.

'Forby that, there's women has lost husbands or sons,' she said dropping her voice. 'Charlotte Spratt over at Lenaderg lost her Joseph torpedoed off Tobruk. Ach, I could name a whole lot,' she said, suddenly stopping herself. 'Some needs money and some needs to get outa the house, but give me an hour or two and they'd be back on the machines. Sure it's like riding a bicycle, once you've done it, ye niver forget.'

'Could you give me a list of names, Daisy?'

'Aye surely. Have ye a pen?'

'I have indeed, Daisy, but I also have a meeting I mustn't be late for,' he said briskly. 'Would you go in to Margaret and give her names and addresses. I'll need a typed list.'

'Right ye are. How's Emily?' she demanded, pausing at the door.

'She's well and in good form,' he replied, smiling at her.

'Tell her I was askin' for her and that Jimmy is doing great. Dab hand with the bandages now. Cheerio,' she added, as she pulled the door behind her and left Alex to recover himself.

The woman was a gift, he thought to himself, as he collected up his papers, but he always felt after one of her visits as if he had been caressed by a gale force wind.

November produced more than its share of damp, foggy days. Emily hated fog. She could put up with rain and tolerate high winds, but the effect of the chill blanket of white moisture that muffled sound and vision was altogether too much for her. It was certainly her least favourite month, but this year, she was amazed to find how very depressed she still felt, despite the good news about Johnny.

It was not a new thing. More than once she had read the columns in the women's magazines that told you what to do. They always published advice in November, so perhaps she wasn't the only one to be affected by the dying flowers and rotting vegetation in the garden and the constant slow drip of moisture from the black twigs of the hedgerows and the sodden branches of the trees.

She had *not* survived the anxiety over Johnny, she decided, she had been *spared* from having to cope with his loss. The more she thought about it, the less she felt she'd have been able to carry on if he'd perished, as so many sons and husbands had.

She argued with herself as she caught up on the neglected chores, the sewing and mending she simply couldn't bend her mind to when every part of her was listening for the phone, the doorbell, or the letterbox.

What on earth would she do if Johnny had been killed or Alex had an accident, or any of her family or close friends were taken from her? It wasn't the first time she'd tried to make sense of her fears, but try as she would, she never got any further.

She knew she was a sensible, practical person, the kind others turned to in a crisis. That was all very well. She could deal with *their* crisis, but what about her own? She couldn't see how she could manage if something like the loss of Johnny were to come upon her.

There was no one she could talk to about it, except Alex. So one evening by the fire, she confessed. She told him as simply as she could that she just didn't know how she'd cope if something dreadful happened.

'Emily, do you think you ought to *know* how to cope?'

'Well, yes. I'm a grown up person with four children. I ought to be able to manage whatever comes my way.'

'And do you think other people manage?'

'Well, yes, I think so. Don't you?'

'I think we all manage, as you call it, in our own way,' he said thoughtfully. 'There isn't *a way of doing it*, like with a job. You have to invent your own way. And what you invent depends on who you are and what experience you've had. Not of loss itself, but of life, especially your own life. All that has happened to you.'

He paused, looked at her anxious face and wished he could put her at ease. She was listening so carefully, but he knew she didn't recognise her own strength. Everybody else saw it and he would be lost without it. But you can't tell a person such things. Or rather, you can't expect them to grasp what you're saying if you do. They need to *see* for themselves and however much you may want to make things clear for someone you love, you can't. Somehow, they have to find a way of doing it for themselves.

'Emily love, you don't know what's in the cupboard till you're hungry and have to go and look. You'll have to trust me that you've got plenty there to draw on, should you need it.'

However modest the gifts might be, Emily still thought it worth the effort to wrap and pack presents and send letters for Christmas. There were, of course, gifts for Cathy and Brian, Jane and Johnny, as well as a new sweater to finish for Alex, one she'd had to knit in her sitting down time after her lunch each day so that it could still be a surprise.

But as well as family and friends, Emily sent small offerings to anyone she knew who was ill and to those who had had a difficult or unhappy year like her sister-in-law, Jane Ross and her son Lachlan, now back in a military hospital in New England.

One of the boxes she carried in her bicycle basket to the Post Office in Banbridge contained a fruit cake and a pot of raspberry jam for Mrs Campbell, the old lady who had invited Alex to tea and helped him find his sister. Another was for Johann Hillman at Dungannon. She also sent a small embroidered handkerchief to Chris's wife and a card with pressed flowers to his youngest child.

Christmas she knew could be so happy if all was well with you, but it was a very different story if it was not. Christmas made the happy things even happier, but left the unhappy totally bereft. So she braced herself and set aside her own sober thoughts to give her mind to what she could do for those who had much less to celebrate than she had.

There was nothing like a little surprise, she thought, as she sat making her own greeting cards in late November. They would provide just that for some people who might be so in need of it.

But the greatest surprise in November came to Emily herself, in a letter from Johnny. To his own obvious amazement, he had been awarded a Distinguished Flying Cross. He would be going up to the Palace on a 48 hour pass next month which would allow him to visit Cathy and Brian in their new home, but when she read the final line, she just couldn't believe it. She hopped up and danced round the kitchen, then read it again.

*It appears to be a tradition in the squadron
that a seven-day pass is awarded to any officer
who is awarded a decoration that can be
listed on the honours board. Amazingly, one
is permitted to choose the seven days most
convenient. So with my customary modesty, I
have chosen December 23 to December 30th
so that I can be with you for Christmas.*

The news might not have resolved Emily's
questionings, but it certainly brought a lift in spirits
and gave her plenty to think about, for Jane would
be home as well and Chris had promised to look in
briefly on Christmas Day itself.

CHAPTER SEVENTEEN

As soon as Emily had tramped down the sodden garden path and put her small scraps of food on the bird-table, she made her way to Rose's viewpoint. From that point on the boundary fence the land fell sharply away into one of Cook's fields and a gap had been left in the planting of trees and shrubs so that the view of the distant mountains should never be masked.

She stood gazing out across the green countryside, the Bann flooded into the adjoining meadows, the Mournes outlined against a sombre sky. They'd had a covering of snow on their tops for days now.

'*The North wind doth blow and we shall have snow,*' she said aloud, rhyming to herself in the sing-song voice they'd all used in the small schoolroom in a remote Galway village. She looked up into the heavy grey sky and smiled. It was a familiar rhyme, but hardly ever true for this part of the country and certainly not today. There was no wind at all, just a heavy pall of cloud, sitting over the countryside, waiting. Waiting for some change of temperature, or pressure, not perceptible to human eye. Nevertheless, she'd be very surprised if a change didn't come before the end of the day.

Meantime, there was work to do. She turned her back on the mountains, set off briskly for her own kitchen and decided that if she baked first, the heat from the oven would help to keep the room warm enough for her to sit and write some letters at the table. After that, she'd think again.

She took out her cake tins and began the practiced routine. Soon her mind was far away, moving freely from time long past when she had lived as a child in one Coastguard house after another, to the recent Christmas, now receding fast as January dropped one grey day after another, a barrier behind which lay one of the happiest times she had known since the beginning of the war.

After their solitary Christmas the previous year, when they had read together and listened to the radio, venturing out only to go to the Carol Service on Christmas Eve and to call on the Cook's with presents for the children, this year had been an amazing contrast.

She would never forget the sight of Johnny grinning at her through the glass panel of the kitchen door as he pushed it open and dropped his suitcase on the floor. He'd arrived in uniform, looking smart and distinctly handsome, still sun-tanned, his hair fairer than it had been even in childhood. He looked both alive, in some vivid way she had never seen before, and at the same time, more mature.

For two days before Jane arrived, he'd helped her with her preparations. He'd cut holly from the garden. Dug up the little Christmas tree they'd used for years. Patiently decorated it with all the tiny toys and precious baubles they'd had since childhood, while she'd placed gold and white chrysanthemums in jugs and vases in the sitting room.

They'd drunk coffee in the warm kitchen and he'd talked about planes and sorties and comrades and the night sky. As the hours passed and they spent yet more time at the table, she thought it almost felt as if he were tape-recording all his experiences, so they could never be forgotten. He was quite right, of course. He knew how she'd always listened to his stories, right from when he could only just speak, and he knew the story of the months that followed his eighteenth birthday and brought him to this present moment was one she would never forget.

He opened for her a whole new world, answering her questions, describing the everyday detail as well as what was totally unfamiliar. All she could bring to the telling were the war films she and Alex had seen in the local cinema, images of crews sitting waiting, playing chess. Scrambling when the siren went, then the formations ripping across the screen.

She offered what she could and went on asking questions, sensing how much he needed to go on talking.

'Not many manage to play chess, I suspect,' he said, smiling. 'I've never seen anyone do it. Chaps are far too keyed up. More likely to knock the whole lot flying with the shake in their hands. That stops once you're up. It's a really strange feeling as you take off. A kind of sickening fear and then a wonderful sense of freedom. I expect it's adrenaline, but it's a wonderful moment as you soar off and see your pals up there beside you. Great solidarity, Ma. Whatever doubts and fears you have on the ground, there's no fear up there. Just focus. Skill. Cunning,' he said, choosing each word with care.

'But we don't use formation flying like you see in the cinema,' he continued. 'They did to begin with, but it had something of the same effect as the Charge of the Light Brigade,' he added sharply. 'There were high ups who thought it was a good idea and the first squadrons who broke it up and refused to fly formation ran into bad trouble. There were actually court-marshals.'

'But why, Johnny? Why was there trouble?'

'It was new, different, not in the book,' he replied flatly. 'But tight formation flying cost lives. It was predictable and made you easy targets for enemy gunners. Besides, you're so busy keeping formation, you're likely to get caught out by Messerschmitts coming in on your tail. You have simply got to keep them guessing, even when you're guessing yourself.'

It was after breakfast on the morning of Christmas Eve that Johnny suddenly spoke of his own ill-fated flight from Tunisia. Emily was preparing a goose from Cook's, making breadcrumbs for stuffing and preparing sauces she could re-heat next day.

'I might not have made it, Ma, if it hadn't been for Ritchie,' he said suddenly. 'And for you.'

She paused, startled, aware that for the first time, he was not taking his previous relaxed view of his ditching and the two nights he'd spent afloat. She knew well enough that the light-hearted letter he'd sent following his telegram was a clever way of being able to tell them quite a lot about what had happened and still get past the censor. But nothing he'd said since then had been other than equally light.

'How so, Johnny?' she said, not looking at him, though she noted the way he was twisting his almost empty coffee cup between his hands.

'Walker's Mill,' he said abruptly. 'If he hadn't got us the job there in the hols I'd not have seen how they shaped those fuselages and cemented them together. I mightn't even have known they'd float, with a bit of help,' he added shortly. 'I had to keep bailing, of course, but it gave me something to do while I was waiting to be picked up,' he went on, a look on his face that she couldn't read.

'The danger was not exposure, though it did get cold at night, nor enemy subs, because they'd all left the Med by then, nor even sharks,' he said, grinning briefly. 'I did remember you once told me there aren't any sharks in the Med.'

To her surprise, he stopped, put his coffee cup down on the table and gathered himself up from the familiar comfortable slouch he'd clearly not forgotten from schooldays. But he remained silent and thoughtful and a long way away.

'So what was the danger, Johnny?'

'What?'

'The danger, Johnny,' she repeated patiently. 'What was the danger?'

'Oh, giving up, of course. You've banged your head and it hurts like hell. You're sitting in a kite with no food and the only water is sea water round your ankles. The kite is about as protective as an eggshell if a ship comes your way or one of our own chaps can't read the markings and thinks you might be a enemy spy. Not a good situation,' he finished, with a great intake of breath.

'So why didn't you?' she asked lightly, hoping he wouldn't notice that she'd shaken far too much salt into the stuffing and was now removing it with a teaspoon.

'Didn't I tell you? Thought I had. I came to, seeing those little red bits you put on the pudding for Jane's birthday and I decided that it was a message from home. So I started thinking about everything I'd ever seen or done. Everywhere I'd ever been. All the things we'd talked about. And every time I bailed out water, I thought of that thimble of yours, for the cream. Do you remember? And I thought, if Ma can do it, I can do it.'

'Do what?' she asked, thoroughly confused.

'Oh Ma, all the things you do. Like saving up the coupons so we could have beef for Jane's party and growing veg to give to the Hospital and the Red Cross. Picking apart sweaters to knit something new. It is the way all the little things add up. Sitting there, I decided that *multiplication* is the most important thing anyone ever teaches you, the tiny things added and added to each other. Each minute. Each bakelite mug of sea water. Each walk up the hill to Rathdrum. That's how I did it, Ma. It's you that should have had the medal,' he ended, as he stood up, took his cup to the sink and washed it under the tap.

She saw the first flakes fall as she washed the cake tins. Soft, curved flakes, like feathers from a plucked goose, caught by the wind before you've managed to gather them up. She stood watching them float down, thinking how slippery the hill would be for the postman, and how much worse it would be by tonight if the temperature dropped and it froze before Alex got home.

But there was a kind of relief in the falling flakes. The waiting was over, the snow had begun and already with the thinnest skim across the yard, the roof of the workshop, and the hedge beyond, it was brighter. The gloom of the laden sky was offset by the blanketing sheet of whiteness that covered every surface, smoothed out the irregularities and reflected what light remained in the short, winter day.

Jane had been glowing with fresh air and effort when she arrived. She'd seen no one she knew on the road from Banbridge and she'd got as far as Cook's just as the parcel-post van had set off up the hill to deliver a gift from Cathy and Brian.

'Good exercise,' she said, as she dropped her suitcase and hugged her. 'Where's Johnny?'

'Right here,' he said, having run downstairs, shaving soap still decorating one ear.

Emily had turned away to put the kettle on as they threw their arms round each other. They had always been close and Jane had been distraught when they had to tell her he was missing.

'Didn't you wind your elastic up enough?' Jane said, disentangling herself, and staring at him.

'I wound it up all right, but it broke,' he came back at her, looking her up and down as if he'd never laid eyes on her before.

'When's the Big Day?' he asked, taking her coat and pausing by the door into the hall until he had her answer.

'Not just immediately. I have one or two operational difficulties, as a friend of mine used to say. Come and sit down and I'll tell you exactly what I need you to do,' she replied, though Emily could see she was teasing.

'Well, brother dear, there is this man Hitler,' Jane began. 'You haven't seen him off yet, and until you do my poor Johann is stuck in Dungannon,' she went on sadly. 'Now he does have a friend and the locals are kind,' she admitted, 'but he is *bored*. Wouldn't you be bored shut up in a camp? It will be two years on my birthday, more or less.'

'I'll have to see what I can do for you,' he said adopting the same sober tone his sister had used. 'Perhaps you'd like me to go ahead with the Second Front single-handed. Anything to oblige,' he added, as he looked hopefully at the rapidly emptying tray of cookies on the kitchen table.

'Help yourselves,' Emily said, pouring more tea for everyone. 'I refuse to ration out cookies at Christmas. When they're gone, they're gone, but we'll have enjoyed them.'

There was a sudden unexpected moment of stillness, as if she had said something significant and important. She looked from one to the other but for a moment they continued to remain silent.

'It's just something I wrote in a letter to Jane back last month,' Johnny began. 'I'm as safe as it gets in Norfolk, unless a kite blows up, or I have an encounter with a tree, or the North Sea in winter, all of which I shall endeavour to avoid. But I might buy it next time. I told Jane that if I'm gone, I'm gone, but we'll have enjoyed so much that we had'

'Good for you, Johnny,' Emily said reassuringly. 'And we're *all* going to enjoy this Christmas. Live every day as if it were your last, as they all say,' she went on, 'but just don't go getting indigestion and spoiling it if you can avoid it.'

No one did get indigestion, she reflected, as she cleared the cooling racks from the kitchen table and sat down to write. The only opportunity for excess was the huge pile of roast potatoes from her own plot and the carefully stored carrots and sprouts. The goose would serve eight with care, but it had to last for a meal on Boxing Day as well.

It was fortunate that none of her children had ever liked plum pudding, for she herself had always found it much too heavy. In the past, at Christmas, she'd made trifle or fruit pudding or even golden syrup pudding by special request, though she hadn't seen Golden Syrup in the shops for a long time now. This time there was only one possible pudding she could offer them

'Worth banging your head for, Johnny?' Jane said.

'Absolutely,' he replied.

He picked up his spoon, gathered up a collection

of the jewel like fragments of well-set red jelly and allowed them to fall, one by one, back down to the swirl of cream that sat atop the sherry trifle in the best sundae glasses.

'I've waited a long time to do that,' he said, lifting his spoon in salute to his mother.

'A good thing is worth waiting for, so they say in these parts,' said Alex, with a sideways look at both his son and daughter.

Her first letter that afternoon was to her 'other Jane', her new-found sister-in-law.

Tuesday 18th January, 1944

My dear Jane,
Christmas is now fast becoming a happy memory. We loved your card and had it in pride of place beside the clock where it marked your place given we couldn't have you yourself with us.

You were very much in our thoughts. Every time I caught sight of Johnny laughing and teasing his sister, or talking 'war talk' with his father, I thought how nearly we might have lost him. And how much nearer you came to loosing your dear Lachlan. It is such a lovely Scots name you'll have to forgive me if you find the beginning of Hank, scratched out, when I remember that this dear man has different names in different places.

I'm so grateful that he was flown back to America. I know the hospital is a long way away and visits must be tiring, but at least you feel you can get there if he needs you and I'm sure the telephone is a comfort. I'm very impressed with him having a telephone in his room. Here, I fear, telephones often don't work even if you have one, or you get cut off in mid-sentence without even the warning of the pips. Do the doctors really feel that he would be better off with an amputation and an artificial limb? It is such a big decision.

And how are your other two sons? I have found out that the Ottawa Cameron Highlanders have an association with the Winnipeg Rifles and we have a battalion of them only a few miles away. The Canadian Air Force is based mostly in England, but there are certainly many Canadian troops here in Ulster apart from our friends at the Castlewellan Camp that I've told you about. My sister down in Fermanagh says every second person she hears in the street is Canadian or American.

Our friend, Chris Hicks, did manage a visit on Christmas Day. We knew he wanted to meet Jane and Johnny and it was a rare *opportunity with their leave coinciding. He asked most kindly about Hank (Lachlan) and said how much he had valued him. He asks me to send you both his regards and to say to you: 'That's one fine young man, ma'am.'*

Your dear brother Alex is hard at work, but somewhat less pressed than he was before Christmas. He'd had a bad time, which he didn't tell me about, due to high levels of illness which lowered production. But he solved the problem by adopting the wise strategy of one of his senior spinners. She told him where he could find women to step into the breach now and also provide him with a part-time reserve for the coming year.

I confess I do worry about the long hours he works, but I also have the comfort of knowing he is well and eats properly. How many women have that comfort in these difficult times?

Now, I must see about an evening meal. The snow began a couple of hours ago and is beginning to be quite serious about laying a thick carpet over everything. Not like your snow in Canada which I know you measure in feet. Or even in Boston which I'm told is kindlier. But snow still makes life more difficult and for most people here it brings a sudden desperate longing for the spring.

Do you suffer from that longing as well? There seem to be so many things we share, weaknesses as well as strengths. It is a great joy.

I do hope your John is feeling better after his flu and that the news continues good from both Chester and Andrew. I shall be writing to Lachlan later this week, but will send it care of you as I forgot to ask you for the address of the hospital.

With love from us both to all of you,
Emily.

The snow continued intermittently through Wednesday and Thursday, but when Emily drew back the curtains on Friday morning she found a thin, mizzling rain already pitting the smooth contours that covered hedge and bush. She could hear the drip of water from overflowing gutters. Later, when she tramped through the slush to the bird table she found the air had lost its icy chill.

She could now breathe more freely in both senses of the word, for a winter picnic had been planned at the community hall in Seapatrick and at this rate by late morning the roads would all be clear. Even if the footpaths were wet and muddy, it would make life easier for everyone if they didn't have to carry bags and boxes over slippery pavements.

The picnic itself went well, the practiced routine never failed to create a lively good feeling, but she felt tired afterwards as she packed up plates and dishes, loaded her shopping bag and basket and gave them to the pale young man who stood to attention when she spoke to him, but had been a great success all afternoon with his impersonations of Superman.

It was so good to be home with no more to do than put a match to the fire and listen for Alex before she lit the gas under their champ. It was Alex's idea that they have a picnic themselves in the evening if she was busy with a picnic in the afternoon.

He was a little earlier than usual and in good spirits.

'Here you are, read that,' he said, taking an envelope from his pocket and dropping a large brown paper bag on the table.

Dear Mr Hamilton,
On behalf of all the women from Hazelbrae, and some others as well who have all signed below, we would like to thank you for making us so welcome at your mills. It was very good of you to insist that we bring our children and grandchildren to the Christmas party at Millbrook, even though we had only just joined your staff. And only temporary too.
Some of us would have been in difficulties

at Christmas with bills we could not pay, but
you have helped us out there.

We are most grateful to you and would
like you to accept this small gift which comes
from us all.

'Oh, how lovely,' she said warmly. 'What did they give you?'

By way of answer, he pushed the brown paper bag across the table.

She opened the bag and looked inside.

'Alex! Where *did* they get these?'

'I thought I'd better not ask, but the whisper was they all had odd bits of shirt in their work boxes and it took them till now to get the pieces they needed. You said the shirt situation was getting serious. Those will help, won't they?'

'My goodness,' she said happily. 'Saville Row label and all. These will last for years! Oh love, what a lovely surprise.'

'That and a bowl of champ and Sam's turf on the fire . . .'

He broke off in the middle of taking off his dungarees as he heard the phone ring.

'It's all right, I'll take it while you struggle,' she said, laughing as she went out into the hall.

She switched on the light and seeing how dim it was bent down and picked up the torch that sat on the floor beside the phone table in case the power should fail. The receiver was cold to the touch and there was a moment of complete silence as she put it to her ear.

'Hallo, Hallo, is that you, Ma?'

'Lizzie,' she replied, surprised and pleased, 'how lovely to hear you. Have you come over on leave?'

'No, Ma, I'm in London, but I'm in someone else's office and I may get cut off . . .

There was a loud noise in the background and a sudden crackle on the line. Emily knew she had missed some words, for Lizzie had gone on speaking unaware of the crackle on the line.

'What did you say, Lizzie?'

'I said I'm sorry it's such bad news.'

'What bad news?'

'About Cathy and Brian . . .'

'But what's happened?' she asked, anxiety stabbing her as she realised suddenly what the noise must have been.

'It was a direct hit, Ma. There's nothing left at all. They wouldn't have known a thing,' she said, her voice tight with anxiety. 'I'm afraid I have to go. This line is priority. I'll send you the notification, but I can't do anything more. Sorry and all that,' she added apologetically, as the line went dead.

Emily looked at the heavy black receiver as if there were more words in the earpiece could she only reach them. But she couldn't. There weren't any more words to be had. It had needed so few. And now a strange silence flowed all around her. Like the snow, it had come at last, the enormity of loss she had always feared.

She felt Alex's hand on her arm as he took the receiver and put it down.

'Who, Emily? Who is it this time?' he asked, his face featureless in the dim light.

'Cathy and Brian,' she said, the words coming out without the slightest difficulty.

'Dead?'

'Yes. I think it was an air-raid. There was an explosion, so I couldn't hear the first time,' she went on, wanting to share with him the smallest detail.

'Who rang?'

'Lizzie.'

'Lizzie,' he repeated, with a great sigh. 'I wonder how she came to be there.'

'I think they still see each other occasionally, but I don't ask. It's between her and Lizzie.'

She stopped and thought again. She couldn't say that any more.

'I mean it *was* between her and Lizzie.'

In the dim light, she couldn't see if Alex had tears in his eyes, but he looked pale and she felt herself shiver. The hall was stone cold. Once again there was no paraffin and the convector heater had cut out as the supply fell.

'Alex, we mustn't stand here. Let's sit by the fire,'

she said, putting her arm round him and urging him towards the sitting room door.

The fire had burnt up and the room was full of the faint aroma of turf. Its flickering flames reflected in the well-polished furniture and caught the gold and white blooms of the Christmas chrysanthemums lasting so well in the chilly room.

'What are we going to do, Emily?' he said bleakly as they stood warming themselves at the fire.

'I think we have to give thanks for all they had,' she said reaching for his hand, 'Like Johnny said at Christmas to Jane, *we'll have enjoyed so much.*' They did, Alex. They were happy. Happier in this last year than they'd ever been.'

'And that's been taken away,' he said bitterly.

'Yes, it has. But the loss is ours, not theirs. They had what they had and it was good. And they went together, Alex, as we would if we could choose. They were not parted.'

'No, they were not parted. That's some comfort. But not much. And it seems we've lost Lizzie as well. There didn't seem to be much in the way of a kind word for us.'

'No, there wasn't,' she agreed. 'I think Lizzie's given up kind words. But we haven't. We'll just have to be very kind to each other,' she said, putting her arms round him and holding him close.

CHAPTER EIGHTEEN

The hardest part on that Friday evening after the first overwhelming shock of Lizzie's phone call was trying to decide what to do for everyone else. Jane and Johnny to begin with, then friends and family. They wondered if Lizzie had also been in touch with Brian Heald's family, whom they'd never met. Emily wasn't even sure she had an address for them as they'd had to move twice in the last year, having been bombed out earlier in Manchester.

They forced themselves to listen to the Nine O'clock News so that they would at least know what was going on in London. It was no comfort at all to hear that the attacking force of over five hundred assorted German planes had been manned by such inexperienced pilots that only a small number of bombs had fallen on the city itself and that few of them had dropped in the areas outlined by flares. No casualty figures were quoted, but forty enemy planes had been shot down.

The wireless was in the kitchen and when they switched off, Emily moved to the stove.

'We must eat our supper, Alex,' she said firmly, lighting the gas.

'Like good children,' he said, unexpectedly.

'Like the way we did the night Ritchie died,' she replied, glancing up, as she stirred the champ, the most good-natured of meals they had ever neglected.

'Would you drink a hot whiskey?' he asked, remembering the bottle of Jack Daniels Chris had brought them when Johnny went missing.

'I'll drink a hot whiskey with you, if you'll eat your champ with me,' she replied, as she lifted the empty kettle from the stove and gave it to him to fill at the sink.

'I think we should do nothing tonight, Alex,' she said, as they put the bowls back on the tray. 'It will have to be one step at a time.'

'Will it be any better tomorrow?' he asked, his shoulders drooped, his head bent.

'Yes, it will. We'll have survived that much longer. We'll have kept afloat like Johnny did. Something may come to help us, and if it doesn't, then we'll just go on helping each other.

Sunday 23rd January, 2009

My dear Jane and Johnny,
This is a letter with bad news which will

make you both very sad. Cathy and Brian were killed on Friday evening during the raid on London which you'll have heard off by now. It was a direct hit on the house where they have the top flat.

It was Lizzie who rang us, but she had only a few minutes on the phone and even then there was an explosion in the background, so we were able to say very little to each other.

The only fact that is of any importance is that they are gone, together, as they would have wished. There is nothing whatever we can do to change that. We cannot even attend a service or send flowers. None of the customary rituals will be available, and they might not help us much anyway.

What might help us all is to remember what Johnny said to Jane before Christmas 'When I'm gone, I'm gone but we'll have enjoyed so much.'

You may wonder why your father and I did not contact you on Friday. We're not quite sure either. I think we just feel that the steadier we all keep the better and we were both exhausted that evening even before the news came.

Fatigue is a bitter enemy that gangs up with all that is unhappy, so perhaps we were trying to avoid that, for ourselves and for you.

I don't normally write joint letters as

you know, but it seemed so appropriate this once. We hope to hear from you by letter or phone when you've had a chance to collect up some of those precious things you shared with Cathy and Brian to help you stitch up the sudden tear in the fabric of your lives that this bitter news will have brought.

With love from both of us to both of you,

In the week that followed, Emily and Alex had to allow the community in which Cathy had grown up to speak about their grief. People long forgotten contacted them. Sunday School teachers and Brown Owls. Primary Teachers and Girl Guide leaders. Librarians and shopkeepers. They all looked at the obituary in *The Leader* and thought 'Ach, that's wee Cathy Hamilton, the parents will be in a bad way.'

With the kindness that is one of the most admirable qualities of Ulster people and the vigorous directness that often leads to their worst excesses, they took up their pens, got out their bicycles, harnessed the pony and trap, or took the bus to the foot of Rathdrum Hill and made their way up to knock at the front door, in a constant stream that led Emily to wonder why a kitchen door could not serve at such a time.

The minister of Holy Trinity suggested a memorial service which Alex courteously declined, pointing out that so many had died from the local villages that he felt it was not appropriate. But he did provide the material requested for the parish magazine, who were fulsome in their praise of a girl who had worked hard, had many friends and had become a very good teacher.

He could not afford to take time off work with bad weather at sea and urgent new orders together creating delays and pressure on the mills, but Emily was grateful when she saw that his work was a comfort to him. She wasn't entirely surprised, for she knew of old the solidarity men like Robert Anderson could offer without saying a word beyond the exchanges of everyday.

A week on from the evening of Lizzie's phone call, the first Friday in months she had not been driven to a winter picnic, she peeled potatoes in the dim and chilly kitchen and listened for the car in the drive hoping that he was still as steady as he had been when he left that morning.

He was coping well as far as she could see and she had not done so badly herself. The stream of visitors had been exhausting, but their memories of Cathy and their warmth towards herself had brought real comfort. But that would stop. Suddenly, without any warning, somewhere in the next few days the stream of well wishers would melt away, she would be left alone with the silence, the silence that had flowed in all around her when first she'd heard the news.

* * *

February was bitterly cold. Although there was more sunshine than in January, the strong light only served to sharpen the images of frosted leaves and twigs and trees. The countryside was thinly skimmed with white but it was frost, not snow, and the cold bit deeper, the house never warm, Emily feeling a chill she'd never felt before.

There were so many letters to write. She could not fail to reply to the kind thoughts directed towards her and her family but she found herself struggling, she who loved writing letters, discovered that words were deserting her. And all the while, there was a silence in her head.

She sat in the conservatory with a rug and a hot water bottle and stared at the light on the geranium leaves. Even in February, there was always a bloom or two, bright red, or pink, or even the unusual purple on the plant that Sarah had once brought from somewhere exotic. But it was the geranium leaves she was aware of, the minuteness of the tiny blonde hairs made visible by the angle of the light.

How could this fragment of life go on surviving in this world of noise and battle, of falling masonry and crushed bodies, of explosions and anti-aircraft fire, screaming fighter planes and chattering machine guns.

She scolded herself regularly when she found herself going over and over again what must have happened to the house near Waterloo Station. What did it matter how they died? All that mattered was that they were gone. And whether it was to the Heaven of the would-be comforters, who had arrived with gifts and offered their firm belief, fluent with quotations, or not, what did it matter? All that mattered was that they *were* gone.

Gone away. No longer resident at this address. Return to sender.

She seldom cried. When she did, it was usually set off by some small memory that crept upon her unbidden. She'd take up her knitting, force her mind to concentrate on the detail of a cable or the heel of a sock and it would remind her of teaching Cathy to knit. That small face, so given to sudden smiles, creased in a furious frown as she tried to master the largest and easiest needles Emily possessed.

She missed out on only one Friday afternoon commitment and when Chris asked if she could face a new instalment of lads arriving in the middle of the month she said, yes. Life had to go on, she insisted, and although Chris had come to see them as soon as he'd heard their news they had hardly seen him since Christmas. It would be good to see him as well.

'This could be the last batch, my friends,' Chris said soberly, in the few moments they always shared in his office before they went upstairs to the big dining room where five new lieutenants would wait with Captain Hillman and the five they already knew.

'How so, Chris, or should I just guess?' asked Alex, as they shook hands warmly.

'The whole world is guessing as far as I can see,' Chris replied. 'It has to be soon, but we have to be at full strength. Your man Montgomery showed how necessary that is as far back as Alamein. He was pushed to move sooner and he wouldn't. Got a lot of stick for it, but he made his point. This is the big one and we daren't screw up,' he said emphatically, glancing up at the maps on his wall. 'My bet is early summer, but that's hardly more than what the newspapers are saying. It's obvious in one way it has to be summer. What's important is the element of surprise. That's not my department, thank goodness. But we may not have time for much in the way of goodbyes,' he added, as he drew them towards the door and out into the grand hall with its elegant staircase.

Emily was happy to see Chris and Alex together. Alex had so little time for friendship beyond his work, while she had a web of friends at the end of her pen, in the shops she visited and the Women's Institute. She'd got to know so many new people since she'd first tried to do something about a bunch of homesick lads even younger than Johnny.

The evening went well as it always did. She enjoyed the food, the huge warm fire, the bright lights and the friendly faces, but she felt as she talked to the new Lieutenants that she was acting her part, speaking lines from a well-rehearsed script and seeing each face as one might through a light fog, the outlines clear enough, but the detail obscured.

Thinking about the evening as she stood over the ironing board next morning, she tried to remember something she'd read recently about fog or mist. Try as she would, it wouldn't come back.

It was later, when she sat down to write to Jane that it came to her and she went and found the letter she'd received from Johann some weeks earlier.

My dear Mrs Hamilton,
I hope that it is not incorrect that I should write to you at this time when we have not yet met each other.

Jane has told me about Cathy and Brian and although she says you are a very wise and sensible lady, I felt that I should write and tell you that I would have been even unhappier after the loss of my mother if it had not been for the assistance of my friend Matthew.

I had no knowledge at all of what happens to us when we are hurt by loss. I was so overwhelmed by the pain, I felt I could not go on living with it. Had it not been for my love for Jane and hers for me, it would not have seemed worthwhile to struggle on, in captivity, among strangers, with such a burden on my head.

You, I know, have a dear husband and a loving family, but even with this comfort you have, I now understand and have experienced other sufferings which may be common to all.

Tears and grief are often spoken about and are understood by many, but Matthew has also spoken about the mist that can enfold particular individuals so that they see things less sharply. It may be that this is a defence against the pain. This we do not know. But what we do know is that there is nothing of harm in this dimming of vision. It will pass, often quite suddenly, he says.

For me, it was a moment when I found a piece of wood in the fallen tree we were cutting into blocks for fuel. It was a piece of beech with dark markings, 'pleated,' a new word for me in English. I looked at it and saw something I could carve, a shape that would lend itself to a small figure.

I knew in that moment that something had been healed, and it was. After that it did become easier.

I write because I should like to offer some help or perhaps comfort in return for all your kindness to me, your acceptance, your concern, your kind gifts.

*Please do not trouble to write in reply.
There are many letters for you to write at such
a time. You can be sure that I shall request
a full account of your well-being from Jane
when next she is able to visit me.
Yours sincerely,
Johann Hillman.*

March roared in like the proverbial lion but it did
bring a rise in temperature, at least by day, the
evenings lengthened and there were grey shoots of
daffodils even if there were still no blooms by the
third week of the month.

Emily registered all the customary signs of the
coming spring, but she knew she was simply doing
what she always did when she ordered seeds and
planted her crops. There was no pleasure in the
work any more than in the everyday tasks which
she performed meticulously as if something of great
importance depended upon them.

Sometimes, as she prepared potatoes for
planting, cutting them one by one in the correct
manner, she thought of Johnny on his floating
plane, baling out with a small bakelite mug. She
comforted herself with the knowledge that the
bank account she had opened for Jane and Johann
was looking distinctly healthy from last year's
efforts and that this year's surplus potatoes and the

vegetable crop would add yet further deposits.

She had written to Johann and thanked him for his letter. She had, at last, written to the teachers who had been Cathy's colleagues and the young men who had written so formally from the laboratory where Brian had been admired and well-liked.

By the end of the month, when suddenly the wind dropped and the weather settled, as it sometimes did in March, after St Patrick had 'turned up the sunny side of the stone', she had written all the letters she needed to write telling more distant friends of their loss, or thanking all those who had written to them both. Now, when she sat in the conservatory in the warm sun, she could write letters again without having to refer to what had happened. It felt rather strange at first, as if it were not quite proper to talk about books to Brendan, or share her sister's treasures from County Fermanagh with her other correspondents and her new contacts like Carrie Hicks in Vermont and the Campbells in Manchester.

If Matthew's mist was lifting, she certainly didn't feel it, but then she wasn't even thinking about it when something happened that did take it away.

'Thanks, Alan,' she said, as she took her baskets and bag from the young man who had just held open the door of the jeep. 'Did you enjoy yourself?' she asked, as he hopped up into the driving seat.

He beamed at her.

'Yeah, great ma'am, great. It was fun,' he added, as he bent forward to the ignition.

'Hold on, Alan, what about Mrs Cook?'

'Sorry, I forgot. She said to tell you she was getting a lift with Ross to see her sister. She said she'd get the bus back home tonight.'

'Oh, of course. She told me she could always get a lift after a picnic because Ross has to take my friend Dolly to Dromore and that's where her sister lives,' she explained, settling back in her seat, as he set off up the steep slope at Millbrook, somewhat later than the other vehicles who were distributing children and colleagues after a 'March hare' picnic.

'How are you settling in Alan? Are you *very* homesick?' she asked after they'd turned onto the Banbridge Road.

'Well ma'am, it was bad at first,' he confessed. 'I'd never been away from home till I went to College last Fall. But there are some great guys here. And we have to *win* this war. We just *have* to,' he declared, with a firmness that surprised her in one so young.

'Yes, we do and the big push is getting nearer, don't you think?'

'Oh yes. It has to be this year. Hitler's on the run, but he's not finished yet. We've got to finish him off before he does even more harm,' he announced, so vigorously that the jeep wobbled on the bumpy road.

'How *are* all your family? Your brother joined up, didn't he?'

He glanced at her very briefly, a smile on his face. He was about to reply when a tractor came racing towards them, an elderly farmer looking wide-eyed, his hair flying, his mouth working.

Emily grabbed the door frame to steady herself as the jeep wobbled precariously. They slithered round a sharp corner and with a squeal of brakes just managed to stop behind an Army lorry which had swerved and skidded. It now lay on its side, on their side of the road, straddled across a low wall, its engine running, its wheels spinning in the air, a smell of petrol growing stronger by the moment.

'Oh my Gawd,' exclaimed Alan. 'Are you all right, ma'am?'

'Yes, I'm fine, but we've got to turn that engine off if no one else does,' she replied, as she kicked off her only remaining pair of high heels and reached into her bag for the flat leather shoes she wore with trousers for playing games.

They ran round to the front of the lorry and looked up at the driver's door. It was out of reach, even for a tall young man.

'Alan, bring the jeep round. Park it as close as you can and we'll try climbing up from the seat,' she said quickly, measuring the distance.

She heard a movement from the back of the lorry and hoped that some of the party were jumping down unhurt, but before she could look, she saw the jeep approach and stepped aside, so that Alan could swing it into place.

'Can you do it?' she asked.

'I'll try.'

He stepping up into the open window frame of the jeep and struggling with the heavy door above him.

She stood on the seat behind him and held on to his belt to steady him as he opened the door enough to get his hand in and turn off.

She breathed a sigh of relief as the throbbing stopped, but the smell of petrol remained.

'Will the door stay open?'

'No, it's too heavy.'

'Can you wind down the window before you close it again?'

'Shure.'

He wound down the window and lowered the door back into place. She released her grip on his waist and he stepped back down into the jeep beside her.

'Could you see if the two in the cab were hurt?'

'No. They're right against the far door on top of each other. One might be Hillmann, but I can't tell.'

'Right,' she began, taking a deep breath. 'Listen hard. Go back to Millbrook. Ask for two First Aiders and the big box and Jimmy Elliot. Bring them back *instantly*. Tell the Mill Manager, or either of the two grey-haired ladies in the office, that we

366

need the Fire Brigade with indoor extinguishers and a full team. And a carload of First Aiders as well. Ask them to ring the camp, the hospital and the police. Don't *you* do it, I need you here. Can you remember all that?'

'Yes, ma'am,' he said, as she stepped down from the jeep. 'But what about you?'

'I'll do what I can here. Hurry, but be careful,' she warned. 'A lot depends on you.'

He crashed his gears as he reversed, but as she glanced down the empty road after him, she saw he was picking up speed. She turned her attention to the drip of petrol. She'd hoped it would ease when the engine was turned off, but it hadn't.

It took her a few moments to rub away the mud and see exactly where it was coming from, the junction of a pipe with the petrol tank itself. She had a sudden vision of the young Dutch boy who had put his finger in the dyke to stop the leak. That wouldn't be much good with a leaking pipe.

She took off her pretty floral scarf, wound it as tightly as she could round the source of the drip, tied the ends and moved out from under the vehicle into the hot and dazzling sunshine which had made the day feel like summer.

She found herself face to face with a bemused young man.

'Gee ma'am, what happened?' he asked, looking all around him.

'Don't know yet, Don, but I need help,' she said briskly. 'Can you walk fifty yards or so?'

She wasn't entirely sure he wasn't concussed, but she'd have to risk it.

'Go that way,' she said pointing towards the town. 'Stop all traffic. Let nothing come this way unless it's the police, or ambulances, and keep *them* well back from the truck. If it's locals, tell them they know the diversions. If it's not, send them back into Banbridge and tell them to ask anyone.'

He nodded and looked easier.

'Don, are there boxes of ammunition in there?'

'No, ma'am, we send it separately. We just have standard issue,' he said, indicating the belt he wore.

'Great,' she said. 'That's good news.'

She walked with him to the back of the truck and found three more young men helping a fourth to struggle down.

The rifles were the biggest problem. And that's what had caused the injuries. All four of them had cuts on their faces where the collision with the wall and the sudden rotation had thrown them against each other.

'You three, go and sit back there under that tree,' she said quietly, as she saw blood trickle down their cheeks.

She pointed to a tree some twenty yards away and was grateful to catch a glimpse of Don firmly established in the middle of the road some distance further on.

'Drink lots of water, but *no* smoking,' she went on. 'Help is on the way. Ross, give Lance your rifle to look after and help me climb up into the truck,'

'Ma'am, you can't go in there,' he protested.

'I can if you give me a hand up.'

But when she managed to use the wall and Ross's hand to get high enough to see properly, she realised there was nowhere she could stand. Her way was blocked with tangled bodies trying to free themselves from the arms and legs of colleagues and the bench seating from the right-hand side of the vehicle which had sheared away with the force of the impact.

The wall was only about six feet high, but just as it was an obstacle for her to climb up, so it was a hazard for injured young men to get down, burdened as they were with rifle and ammunition belt.

She was just about to ask Ross if he had any ideas, when Alan drew up right beside them. To her delight, Jimmy Elliott sat in the front seat and both the senior First Aiders were in the back, the big box between them.

'Wonderful,' she said beaming at them all. 'Perfect timing, Alan. We can use the jeep like we did round the front. I've sent three young men to sit under a tree,' she explained to the First Aiders. 'Head injuries,' she added briefly, exchanging glances with both women as they got out and humped the heavy box between them.

'Jimmy,' she said smiling at him, 'Poor boys, very hurt. Can you carry them down to Mrs McMurray and Mrs Donnelly to make them better.'

'And bandage them?' he asked eagerly, smiling down at her.

'Yes, bandage them,' she said encouragingly. 'But we must get them all safe first, mustn't we?'

He nodded vigorously as Alan nudged the jeep right up against the wall and bridged the gap between the lorry and the ground.

Jimmy was now able to reach over and lift anyone close by. Emily had to smile at the look on Alan's face as he watched Jimmy carefully step back into the jeep, steady himself and then carry a shaken figure to the ladies who worked under the tree as easily as if it were a young child.

When space permitted, Emily was able to go in. The least injured, now able to move more freely, she asked to stay and shift to the right so as to keep the vehicle in balance.

They lay there willingly enough as she, Don and Alan helped move the more seriously injured to where Jimmy could lift them and carry them away.

It was only when Emily smelt a new and unfamiliar smell that she stepped back down into the jeep and went to see what was happening. To her delight, she saw Robert Anderson emerging from under the lorry. She was about to go and speak to him when she found her way was blocked by a large and familiar figure. It was the officer who had once interviewed her at Rathdrum after the theft of dynamite from the quarry.

'Mrs Hamilton?' he asked, his face grim as he recognised her.

'Yes.'

'I am told that you are in charge of this operation. By what right have you closed the Public Highway?'

Emily took a deep breath, thought of the young men still trapped in the truck, probably the most seriously injured of all. She looked him straight in the eye.

'Section 372 of the Highways Act. Hazardous substances. Protection of the Public. I'm sure you're familiar with it, but you might like to move back in case this lorry explodes. Now, if you don't mind you are in my way.'

With that, she stepped past him and ran over to Robert Anderson, who stood watching her, an inscrutable look on his face.

'What about the petrol, Robert?'

'You're safe enough now. One of those young men must have had a wee scarf in their pocket. Did the trick for just long enough.'

'Must go, Robert,' she said with a quick smile. 'This is the hard part.'

Three young men still lay against the left-hand wall of the truck, badly injured, one was having difficulty breathing, the other two almost certainly had broken ribs. In the driving compartment, Captain Hillman had hit the windscreen and was still unconscious but had been rescued by the Fire Engine team as soon as his driver had come round, stuck his head through the open window and called for help.

No sooner had Jimmy carried out the three most seriously injured soldiers than two ambulances arrived from Banbridge and two doctors, one from Dromore and one from Seapatrick along with them.

Emily watched as Jimmy carried each of the young men into the ambulance and laid him down gently on a stretchers. She turned away and went back to the jeep still standing by the empty truck to ask Don and Alan if either of them had any water left.

She was leaning against the side of the jeep drinking water from Don's water bottle when Chris himself came striding toward her.

'Emily, you're hurt,' he said anxiously.

'No, I'm fine, just a bit exhausted,' she replied, as Don and Alan slipped away and left them together.

'There's blood all over your hands and face.'

'Not mine, Chris,' she said shaking her head, 'Someone I held perhaps.'

He shook his head as if words failed him completely and took from his pocket a muddy, smelly, but recognisably once-pretty, floral scarf.

'How the hell did you know about the fire risk?'

'I read about it somewhere,' she replied, smiling up at him.

She looked at him and thought what a dear friend he was and how familiar his face had become. It seemed so particularly clear in the sunlight, a large, square face, the eyes a deep, dark brown, full of compassion and resolution.

How fortunate they were to have such a good friend.

CHAPTER NINETEEN

To Emily's delight and Chris Hick's great surprise, the departure date for his regiment was set for mid-April, just at the point when a new group of young men would have been arriving. So, unlike many of his brother officers, awaiting their instructions on a daily basis for the movement of the 300,000 troops now present in Ulster, Chris had some three weeks notice. It meant that the current group could complete their training, that almost all of those injured in the accident at the end of March would be fully recovered and that there could be one more dinner together at the Castlewellan Road Camp.

It was an evening none of the three would ever forget. Sad, because as friends they were to be parted, anxious, because the possibility of meeting again was so uncertain, and yet at the same time, joyful. The waiting time was over, the hour had come. The huge number of troops in Northern Ireland was but a small part of the three million men now assembled ready for the invasion of Europe and the camp was buzzing with a barely concealed excitement as Emily went down to the mess to say goodbye to the last group of young men for whom she had baked cookies and talked of home.

Chris had warned her that someone would be sure to make a speech, but nothing prepared her for the generous words, the deafening cheers, or the stack of boxes, gifts for herself and her four helpers. Most of all she was touched by the presentation of a silk scarf, more beautiful than anything she had ever possessed, and a small gold brooch with the insignia of the regiment entwined with flowers.

Back upstairs, in Chris's office, he produced a velvet-lined box with a more masculine version of her brooch. The same insignia, but larger and bolder, it was inscribed with the words, *James Elliott, for services to the wounded, 31 March, 1944.*

'Oh Chris,' she said, tears springing to her eyes, 'this will make him so happy. He's been a different man since it happened, hasn't he Alex?'

'We all need to be valued, don't we?' Alex replied, with a small smile, as he watched Chris move to open a drawer in his desk.

To Alex's surprise, he saw Chris pick out a familiar, worn, but very clean, floral scarf which he let fall on the desk in the small space between the well-anchored stacks of papers.

'Cleaned up well, Emily, didn't it?' Chris asked.

She stretched out her hand to pick it up, amazed that a scarf, already years old, could look so presentable after what she'd done to it. But Chris closed his large hand over it before she could pick it up.

'If you don't mind, Emily, I might just need this again,' he said, putting it back in the drawer.

Upstairs, in the room Emily had come to love so much, they were greeted by the ten lieutenants. Tonight, for the first and only time, there was no need to try to remember the new names or to ask where their home was.

Since that evening back in June 1942 when they had first stood in front of the impressive marble fireplace, Emily and Alex had met young men from almost every American state and she no longer had to refer to the atlas in the sitting room to make sure she was not confusing Michigan with Minnesota, nor Memphis with Minneapolis. The map of North America had become as familiar as the layout of her own garden, for there had been Canadians too originating from almost every province, including the young man from Saskatchewan, who had come via Boston and who'd proved to be her own nephew.

'Chuck, how are you?' she asked, as she found Captain Hillman smiling down at her. 'Is it healing well?' she asked, glancing up at the neat bandage on his left temple.

'Doing just grand, but it still looks a bit like raw

meat,' he said laughing. 'I thought a decent bandage would be easier on the eyes.'

There was a lightness about him tonight she was sure she'd not seen before, though since the morning he'd sat at her kitchen table, she'd found him easier to talk to and more forthcoming.

'Ma'am, I owe you,' he said soberly.

'You do?' she asked, not quite sure what the phrase might mean when said by an American.

'Yep. When I came here I was as touchy as bedammed,' he began. 'I was shit scared anyone would find out my grandfather was German and my mother Italian. But you sorted that out,' he went on. 'You showed me, ma'am, that it doesn't matter who your parents were, or where you came from, or what you had to do to stay alive, or earn a living. It's what you are *now*. And that's something you can do *something* about. Not very easily perhaps in time of war, but even then you can try.'

Emily beamed at him.

'I'm so glad I helped a bit, Chuck. Sometimes, I get frustrated that there's so little I can do when there's so much needs doing.'

He shook his head slowly.

'Never think that, ma'am. You've been one of the best things this side of the Atlantic,' he said glancing round the well-lit room, full of talk and gentle laughter. 'And not just for me.'

* * *

Everyone felt it when the last regiments left and the roads were suddenly empty and the airbases silent. For Emily and her friends, there were no more picnics, specially arranged dances or social events. The children stopped chewing gum and no longer talked with North American accents.

The quarry closed, the need for building material to repair runways now ended. The rain washed away the dust on the adjoining hawthorn hedges and with the sunshine and warmth of May wildflowers began to colonise the abandoned spoil heaps.

Emily missed her young men and was glad to have plenty to do in the garden. With no weekly baking for the picnics, Mary Cook now had extra butter and bread to sell, so she and Emily found a neighbour with a pony and trap and drove each Saturday to the WI market in Banbridge.

If life was quiet and less busy in the town itself, it was not the case elsewhere. In the absence of news, the newspapers speculated wildly, ran stories about spies, and left their readers only too well aware that the last thing they wanted was for *anyone* to know what was going to happen, when it would happen, and where.

The tension grew week by week and day by day until finally, switching on the wireless on a lovely, fresh June morning, after a night of rain and wind, Emily heard the news the whole world had been waiting to hear. Allied troops had begun landing in Northern France at 6.30am that very morning. *Operation Overlord* was a secret no longer. The invasion had begun.

Throughout June, wetter and far more unsettled in Ulster than May had been, there was but one topic of conversation. The coast of France became as well known as the country roads from Banbridge to Castlewellan or Dromore and French beaches, now renamed Utah and Omaha, Gold, Juno and Sword, as familiar as Tyrella, or Newcastle, or Dundrum.

Emily thought of her *boyfriends* when she and Alex went to the cinema, saw landing craft pour out of ships and young men wade chest deep in the sea, their rifles held above their heads. She gazed in amazement as she watched a Canadian regiment going ashore in similar fashion but carrying bicycles. Later, when the Mulberry harbour was put in place, they watched the trucks, dozens and dozens of them, the same trucks once so familiar on their own country roads, drive off bringing more troops and more supplies to support the bridgeheads.

The cost was inevitably high, but the landings had gone well, better than could have been hoped, except on Omaha. The bridgeheads had been taken and in the weeks following the battle of Caen, she added new words to her vocabulary like salient and bulge and pincer movement, as the armies began to sweep northwards following the line of the coast.

There were those who said it would all be over by Christmas, but Alex shook his head and said no.

As the summer turned to autumn, day after day there was good news, the newsreels now showing lively pictures of one city after another being liberated. Cheering crowds waved. Pretty girls kissed the welcome arrivals, or the new arrivals kissed the pretty girls. Yet more groups of German soldiers marched across the screen, hands on head, weaponless.

But the news was not all good. Casualty figures were high and from June onwards, V1 rockets fell on London by the dozen, all around the clock, creating devastation and anxiety. Each mention of a V1 made Emily think, with a bitter jolt, of the top floor flat near Waterloo Station. Cathy and Brian would never be forgotten, but such a sharp reminder of the manner of their death would always cause a stab of pain.

As the autumn deepened and the warmth of summer finally disappeared, Emily accepted that one more year was dipping down into winter and yet one more struggle against cold and shortages of all kinds.

If anything, the winter of 1945 was colder and more dispiriting than the preceding ones. As Emily sat reading her Sunday paper in a chill and dank

February, she noted the now familiar warning to cut down consumption of gas and electricity.

'Alex, listen to this,' she said, doubling the paper over to read the bottom half more easily.

'*Ice-bound coal trains and road transport, and unprecedented strain on gas works and power stations – those were the consequences of the recent abnormal weather. It will take time for coal stocks to recover from the effects of these conditions* . . . Have you had a notice to cut down?' she demanded.

'Oh yes,' he said wearily, 'Read on down. We got that one in from the Ministry of Fuel and Power last week.'

'But we haven't had abnormal weather,' she protested. 'It's always as cold as this in February and we haven't had any snow yet.'

'But they have in Scotland and the North of England,' he explained. 'The snow has been very bad there and the Ministry announcements are sent out to the whole country.'

'*Only the most drastic economy will enable war production to be carried on at full pressure,*' she continued. 'Can *you* economise, Alex?'

'No,' he said matter-of-factly. 'Apart from the lights in the corridors and the main office, the machines either run or they don't. We can make our own power or we can use electricity, it's six of one and half a dozen of the other as far as scarce resources are concerned.'

'Oh Alex, how long. How long will it be?' she asked, her tone as weary as his had been.

He put his newspaper down and looked across at her. It was not like Emily to let it get on top of her.

'Have you seen the cartoon on Page 3?'

'Hadn't got that far.'

'Have a look,' he urged, with a small smile.

Emily studied the cartoon. *Welcome Adolf* was obvious enough, but it took her a few moments more to make sense of the open Visitor's Book, the two porters with horns and tails and the dark tunnel leading underground. There were some goose-stepping soldiers in the background and a notice at the entrance to the tunnel, '*Abandon Hope All Ye Who Enter Here.*'

She paused, looked at the caption and then read it aloud: '*He shouldn't be long now.*'

'Do you really think it won't be long now, Alex? I'm afraid I think I might give out.'

'No, you won't,' he said, reassuringly. 'Things *are* moving now, really moving. The Americans are heading for the Rhine and the Russians for Berlin. It *is* only a matter of time. Remember Carrie's letter.'

Emily smiled and put her paper down.

'Yes, love. I'm sorry I'm having a bad day. Would you like a cup of tea? And we do have some cake.'

'Cake? How did you manage that without your boyfriends?' he asked, a twinkle in his eyes.

'I've found a new one,' she said, teasing him,

before she closed the sitting room door firmly behind her to keep the heat in.

The gas pressure was so low it was going to take ages to boil the water. She set up the tray, cut them each a piece of cake and found the kettle still hadn't even started to sing.

She pulled out a drawer in the dresser and struggled with a large, awkward folder of letters. It was bulging and she knew it needed sorting, but she found it so hard to throw away letters from friends. She leafed through until she found the most recent one from Carrie Hicks.

29th January 1945

My dear Emily,
How good it always is to hear from you. I never was one for writing letters until Chris went overseas, but you do encourage me. Perhaps there's more to writing letters than I thought.

I'm so glad your parcel arrived safely and has been useful. After all you did for Chris and his boys, it's a little thing to do and no trouble whatever. Please tell me honestly what you most need for next time.

I've heard from Chris only today and I know you'll be happy to hear that he's still in France. Having survived Omaha, he and what's left of his last team have been attached to another regiment of engineers and they are engaged in rebuilding port facilities along the French coast. He says that even with Mulberry, with which he is very impressed, the volume of supplies needed in Europe now and when the war ends will be enormous.

I can say to you, Emily, if to no one else, that I'm so grateful he's in France. Like your dear Johnny in Norfolk, he's somewhat safer there than in other places he might be.

I was so delighted to hear the good news about Hank. My brother, who is an orthopaedic surgeon, says he's familiar with the process you mention. It is sad, he says, that it takes a war to improve our surgery by such leaps and bounds, but it will benefit Hank and be some recompense for all the pain he has suffered and for his tenacity in the face of amputation. Jane must be delighted to know he will walk properly again, given time.

My little daughter can now write DADDY in very wobbly letters, but she can hardly wait to write them on a proper envelope. I still remember when Chris started sending her pressed leaves and flowers and drawing her funny faces and pictures. Actually, he's rather

*good at drawing and I shall encourage him
when he comes home . . . oh, Emily . . . I'm
almost afraid to write those words. So many
young men will not come home, including
many of the ones you made so welcome.*

*But we must keep up hope. It does seem
that at last the time is near, certainly in
Europe, which must come first before we
turn to the Pacific.*

*Please write again when you can. I think of
you often in your very different environment
and love to hear about your garden, your
neighbours and your activities.*

*They help me to hold on to sanity in a
world gone mad.*

*With love and good wishes to you and Alex,
Your friend, Carrie.*

According to the newspaper, Hitler really was
dead, Berlin was in the hands of the Allies and the
German army was surrendering all over the place.
But according to the BBC there would not be an
announcement until tomorrow.

'But that's what they said yesterday,' Emily
complained, when Alex arrived home late and tired
and as cross as his equable nature ever allowed him
to be.

'I wish Mr Churchill would get on with it,' he

exclaimed, as he struggled out of his dungarees. 'He may not be quite aware of it, but you can't just press a switch and turn off four mills at one go. Not even one mill at one go,' he added as an after thought.

Emily laughed and gave him a hug.

'I think we're all like over-excited children who've stayed up too late,' she said. 'If something doesn't happen soon, we'll throw a tantrum,' she said, as she bent down and put the casserole in the oven.

'Come on, let's go and walk round the garden while it heats up. With all those meetings I wasn't sure what time you'd get back and I didn't want it overcooked.'

He grinned sheepishly and followed her through the open back door, across the yard and into the flower garden.

'Have you got your decorations up?' she asked.

'Oh yes, yards and yards of bunting. The women have been making it for weeks from spoilt cloth. There's a bonfire ready too, down by the lake at Millbrook. There's one at each mill, but Millbrook's is enormous. There's a huge effigy of Hitler on top, moustache and all. I've told Robert Anderson he'd better be on Fire Brigade duty whenever the announcement comes.'

'And what did he say to that?'

Alex laughed, his good spirits restored by the sunlight of a fine May evening and the happiness of being home in his own garden with his wife at his side.

'He just gave me a look.'

'Any news from Jane or Johnny?' he asked, as they made their way down the main path, the air full of the scent of hawthorn blossom mixed with the varied perfumes of garden flowers.

'Yes, Johnny is off duty for whatever day it turns out to be, but he's expected in Norwich. It's the same girl he's been talking about . . . it's getting to be a regular thing, I think,' she went on, laughing, 'and Jane says she drew the long straw, so she's off on *the day*, likewise, and she'll go up to Dungannon if there are any buses or she can get a lift.'

'Maybe Johnny will get some leave soon,' Alex said thoughtfully.

'That would be nice, but we mustn't depend on it. As Carrie reminded me, there's still the Japanese. He'll be training pilots to go out there.'

'No more rockets, Emily, no more bombs . . .'

'Goodness, what was that?' exclaimed Emily, as a series of very loud noises shattered the quiet of the evening.

Moments later they heard a bugle, then car horns and then drumming from a long way away. They ran down to Rose's viewpoint and looked out over the summer fields, the shadows just beginning to lengthen as the sun dipped in a blue sky.

Beyond the river flowing placidly between green

meadows, they could see a couple of cars stopped on the road. Beside them, tiny figures hopped up and down. They shouted and waved flags, banged a spanner on the spare wheel and sounded the horn alternately with blowing the bugle.

'I *think* I know what that is,' said Emily.

'I *think* you're right,' replied Alex. 'It's come. It's come at last.'

CHAPTER TWENTY

Alex had to be up even earlier next morning to get to work before the day shift arrived. *If* they arrived.

At least he could rely on Robert Anderson in the engine house at Millbrook, but he would need to visit all four mills in the course of the morning and see that shut-down procedures and safety measures were carried out correctly.

It was the loveliest of mornings and already, at this early hour, as they finished breakfast it promised to be a fine, warm, day.

'So, when will you get back, love?'

'Late morning, certainly by noon.'

There was a small silence as each was aware what the next question would be.

Emily poured more tea for both of them.

'There's going to be a Victory Parade this afternoon and bands in the park. I think we should go, don't you?' she said matter-of-factly.

There was no need whatever to refer to the

reasons why they might *not* go. Many families would be faced with the same decision this morning. Some would decide they could not celebrate when they had suffered such loss, others that life must go on, that today marked a new beginning of some kind and they must make the effort.

He nodded briefly and smiled.

'Leave out my red shirt and the blue tie . . .'

She laughed and shook her head, thinking of some of the outfits in preparation that Mary Cook had told her about.

'I'll see what I can find. It'll just be nice to see you out of dungarees!'

The afternoon got steadily warmer and the bandsmen leading the parade all had red faces as they tramped down the main street thronged with gaily-dressed people and children waving flags. There was a fancy-dress parade, a smart turn out by the British Legion, the Boys Brigade ear-splittingly enthusiastic on their cornets.

It seemed to Emily that every organisation she'd ever heard off was included in the Victory Parade. Daisy Cook waved vigorously as the Brownies marched past, one little girl swinging her arms, military style, as her grandfather had taught her. Jimmy Cook was in the Cubs and managed to preserve an appearance of dignity, having made quite sure they'd seen him.

Emily was glad they'd gone. She'd had her bad moments, but that was no more than she had expected. Cathy had been a Brownie and a Guide and so had Lizzie. Poor dear Lizzie, who was clearly so successful, but perhaps not exactly happy. She hoped that, wherever she was this afternoon, she had friends with whom she could celebrate. She might come home one day, or she might not.

It was so long since Emily and Alex had been anywhere together other than the local cinema, that neither of them was prepared for the number of people who came to shake their hands and say what a great day it was. Many people from all the mills had chosen to come to Banbridge to celebrate, among them Robert Anderson and his family, Daisy Elliot and her Billy, and dear Jimmy Elliot, her nephew, who wore a big grin as he looked down at her, his 'medal' firmly pinned to his clean white shirt.

But to her surprise there were many others as well, friends she'd made in the Women's Institute and the Red Cross. People who'd helped when she was running the picnics for Chris's lads. Even customers from the WI market, women who had come each week to buy vegetables in the Church Hall and add to the fund waiting in the Ulster Bank for Jane and Johann.

After the parade, they went into the park. Solitude

had always seemed to Emily an inappropriate name for a public park and today it was more laughable than usual. Boys perched precariously on railings and walls, because every corner was packed with people, willing to stand if they could find no room to sit on benches or on the grass.

The brass band had been rehearsing for months and revelled in their big day. They were good, a liveliness in their playing that went far beyond mere competence. They'd have set the whole place dancing had there been room to move. As it was, the crowd clapped and cheered and urged them on till it was the turn of a silver band and then the Salvation Army.

They were still playing as Emily and Alex squeezed their way out of the park and walked back down the empty main street under the bunting that had been draped from every lamppost and the flags hung from every window.

Carried on the still air, the sound followed them out of town as they walked together under the trees to Ballievy, where they'd left the car, the only one in the mill car park. The mill itself stood silent, the sunlight glancing from the rows of tall windows.

They drove home, made tea and took it out into the garden.

'Are you glad we went?' Emily asked quietly, as they sat on their summer seat looking at the rise and fall of midges in the deep shade under the trees and the fumblings of bees in the opening blooms nearer at hand.

'Yes, I am. You were right to take us,' he replied. 'I'd never realised just how many people we knew and how many friends we've made over the years. Even more, these last years, war or no war. That really was a surprise.'

'Yes, it surprised me too,' she agreed. 'I suppose we had to work so hard at the big things, we didn't always notice the things that came to help us. People did pull together. I can never remember asking anyone to do anything that they didn't do willingly.'

Alex smiled.

'That may not be so much to do with the war as to do with Emily.'

'I try, Alex, I try,' she said, suddenly sad. 'I see so much need all around me, not just people being poor, or ill, or over-worked. I see people loosing heart, feeling that life is too much for them. I feel that way myself sometimes,' she went on honestly, 'but then I have you and our family and our friends. I have so much.'

'But you share, Emily. You give and it comes back to you. I watch you and learn.'

'Oh Alex, what a lovely compliment,' she said beaming. 'I'll not forget that one.'

They sat in the garden for a long time, talking quietly about all that had happened to them in the last long years, speaking of their family, of their hopes for Jane and Johann, for Johnny and Lizzie. They spoke of their new family, Alex's sister, Jane and her husband, her three sons, but especially of Hank. They remembered good friends like Brendan and Sam, whom they'd not seen for a long time and Emily's sister, Catherine, more a part of their life now, though they hadn't seen her since before the war.

As the shadows lengthened and the temperature began to drop sharply, they moved back into the house, had supper and put a match to the sitting room fire, grateful for the continuing supply of logs and Michael Cook's source of turf which Emily so loved.

'What would we have done without this fire, Alex?' she said, as she brought in coffee, the last spoonfuls from the last packet from the box her boyfriends had left her, just over a year ago.

'It's been a great comfort,' he agreed, as the kindling crackled and flames rose and the turf began to smoke gently, sending its aroma out into the room.

'There's something I have to tell you, Alex,' she began, with a little smile. 'It's good news, so don't worry, but it didn't seem right to bother you these last few days when you've had such a lot on your mind and Mr Churchill wasn't being very helpful.'

She poured their coffee and put his cup on the low table beside him.

'I've had another letter from your Mrs Campbell, or rather from Jeannie,' she went on. 'But one's as bad as the other as far as handwriting goes. You can try to read it for yourself, or I'll tell you what it says,' she offered.

Alex looked across at her. If she said it was good news, then it was, but he wondered why he felt so apprehensive about what she might be about to say.

Mrs Campbell was the only person who could possibly know anything about him he had not found out already. She had been the means of clarifying his relationship with Jane and that had been a gift to them both. But what now?

'Just you tell me, Emily,' he said abruptly, as he reached for his coffee cup.

'Well, it's a bit of a story,' she began. 'Mrs Campbell wasn't well back in February, as you know, and she had to go into hospital. She was rather poorly for a time and when Jeannie went to see her she was a bit delirious. She was wandering and talking about people from long ago. There was a woman called Annie. Annie Gamp.

'When she got home, Jeannie asked her about this woman and was told off. Mrs Campbell was quite cross and said she was imagining things. She'd never known any woman called that. And that was that,' she said, pausing to drink her coffee.

'Then last week, they were sitting having a cup of tea when Mrs Campbell suddenly says: 'Ach, I've remembered. It wasn't Annie Gamp. I knew I'd never heard tell of a woman called Annie Gamp. Alex's father, Lofty had a brother, Tom, a blacksmith, somewhere in Ireland and it was a place called Annie Cramp.'

Alex's mouth dropped open and he stared at her wide-eyed.

'Annacramp,' he whispered, his mouth suddenly dry.

She nodded and watched his face change, anxiety and amazement moving away until finally he smiled.

'So I really did remember Annacramp. And I *am* a Hamilton.'

'Yes, love. Are you pleased?'

'Not yet, but I will be,' he said crisply. 'It's who I am now that matters, I know that, but suddenly it's like a weight off my mind. I know now I was right in what I had remembered, just as Jane was when she said she had a brother.'

She watched him as he stared into the fire his mind moving she knew not where.

'Emily, shall we go over to Liskeyborough tomorrow and tell Sam?' he said suddenly. 'Mr Churchill did us a favour. The Directors said we might as well have a second day while we were about it after all that waiting.'

'But what about petrol?' she asked automatically.

396

'Gallon can in the workshop,' he replied with a straight face.

'Oh Alex, what a lovely, lovely idea,' she said, delighted by the prospect. 'How long is it since we drove anywhere beyond Banbridge together? And I'd love to see Sam's face when you tell him you're a Hamilton from Annacramp.'

ACKNOWLEDGEMENTS

The resources for writing a novel set during the period of the Second World War are formidable and I am very grateful for books, archives, exhibitions and websites. I have used many sources, but the ones that have contributed most to this particular story are the *unconsidered trifles* which I have been offered by individuals.

It never ceases to amaze me how generous people are when I ask my questions, a fireman who contacts former colleagues about hose fittings, young County Council staff who ring grandparents to find out about the prisoner of war camp, now lost under a new housing estate, friends who produce wartime cookery books and old photographs, newspaper editors who offer me access to their wartime editions.

For the first time in the Hamilton sequence, I have memories of my own, my first experience of moonlight on the night of the Belfast Blitz when the siren sounded in peaceful Armagh. There are harsher memories for my husband, who spent the nights of the Blitz in a shelter at the bottom of a garden in South London and experienced the V2's at school in the City. I am grateful to him for the details of the machinery of war, the day by day preoccupation of every small boy at that time.

Ulster was the only part of the United Kingdom to be invaded. But it was a friendly invasion and the links made are still cherished by many, like the Hamiltons at Rathdrum, for whom the war brought joy as well as sadness, hope and possibility, as well as the weariness of a long hard time.